THE CRAP SHARE
A BURR LAFAYETTE MYSTERY

The Gray Drake

A Burr Lafayette Mystery

Charles Cutter

MISSION POINT PRESS

Published by Mission Point Press
2554 Chandler Rd.
Traverse City, MI 49686
(231) 421-9513
www.MissionPointPress.com

ISBN-13: 978-1-950659-14-2

Manufactured in the United States of America
First Edition/First Printing

Cover design: John Wickham
Interior design and layout: Bob Deck

For
Christi

The grave's a fine and private place, but none I think do there embrace.

Andrew Marvell
"To His Coy Mistress"

CHAPTER ONE

June 21, 1989, Grayling, Michigan.

Traveler slipped through the river, two miles downstream from Chase Bridge, almost halfway to the High Banks. Quinn kept the boat in the fastest part of the river and the current carried them through the night. He didn't have to paddle. All he really had to do was steer.

As soon as the auction ended, Quinn had ducked out of the lodge. By the time he'd changed out of his tuxedo and made it to the river, it was past midnight. He'd have made it sooner except for what happened with Lizzie. At least she'd calmed down enough to help him launch the boat.

"Cassie, where's the big browns tonight?" he said.

His dog, an English setter with a black patch on her right ear, looked back at him. She sat in the bow seat, where the sports fished, and sniffed the night air. She always seemed to know where the fish were. Quinn thought she could smell them in the river.

The moon lit up the night, and the South Branch of the Au Sable River unwound in front of them. The moonlight gave the river a black sheen as it cut through the forest. They coasted through a riffle, then slowed when they hit the runout. The river bent to the east, a sandbar on the inside of the curve and a forty-foot bank on the outside. The moon made silhouettes of the cedar and black spruce on top of the bank. Snags had fallen down the bank where the river had cut it away.

A fat hen brown trout lived under that bank. Quinn had caught her once, lost her more times than he could count, but he wasn't going to fish here tonight. Tonight he wanted to get downstream to the High Banks, for the Hex hatch, if there was one.

The river pushed them into the bank, and he smelled the river smells—the wet sand, the dead leaves, the cedars. Cassie looked back at him again.

Quinn stuck the paddle back in the river. The boat turned away from the bank and swept back into the current.

They floated through the Mason Tract, past Daisy Bend and Durant's Castle. Then the moon set, and the river lost its sheen and turned an inky black. Quinn looked up at the strip of sky framed by the trees. The creamy band of the Milky Way stretched above and showed him the river in front of them. "Black water on a black night," he said.

* * *

Quinn Shepherd sat in the sprawling dining room of The Gray Drake and looked out at the river. Sometimes he sat on the bank just downstream and watched the kingfishers dive for the minnows, chased to the surface by the trout.

Tonight, though, as on every summer solstice for the past twenty-five years, all eyes—except Quinn's—looked at the auctioneer. Men in tuxedos and women in cocktail dresses filled The Gray Drake to overflowing. Two hundred strong and a waiting list three hundred deep. They were all there for The Gray Drake's Friends of the Au Sable charity auction. All Quinn wanted tonight was for the auction to end so he could get out on the river.

"Surely you can do better than seven hundred," said Wes Goodspeed, the once-a-year auctioneer. He raised a brook trout carving over his head.

Quinn looked at the hands wrapped around the carving, gnarled and arthritic from a lifetime in cold river water. Wes could still tie flies but probably not for much longer. Wes, his father-in-law, knew how to run The Gray Drake, but making money wasn't his strong suit. He paid Quinn to guide, which he would have done for free. He thought Wes probably knew that.

Wes stood behind a podium and studied the crowd, searching for anyone who would look him in the eye. "This was carved by our own Billy McDonough. Stand up, Billy." The old guide stood and waved.

"Who says eight? Eight, eight, eight. Who says eight hundred for this one-of-a-kind brook trout carving?"

The state senator from Roscommon nodded.

"Thank you, Senator." Wes took a drink from the glass on the podium. It looked like water but it was filled with gin. "Now who says nine hundred?

Who will give nine hundred dollars for this brookie? It was carved from the white pine that went down at Lucy's Hole."

Joe Gleason, the oil and gas promoter from Grand Rapids, raised his hand.

"Thank you, Joe. Now, a thousand. One thousand dollars."

Wes carried the carving through the tables—birds-eye maple tops and matching chairs with spindly legs. The floor, worn-out oak tongue and groove, creaked underneath him. The floor ran downhill to the southeast corner where the foundation had settled. Christmas tree lights were strung all over the room. C-9s, the big old-fashioned kind that didn't blink. Red, orange, blue and green. Hot to the touch. An altogether old-fashioned dining room all done up.

"It's all for the Friends of the Au Sable." Well, almost. The food and booze cost a fortune, and it was Wes who counted the money.

"Who says a thousand?" The crowd was tired of the carving, and Wes had bid it way up. It wasn't worth more than two hundred. "Senator?" He shook his head no. "Any more bidders? Going once, twice. Sold to Joe Gleason for nine hundred dollars."

Wes walked back to the podium and set the carving down. "Let's take a short break." The tables emptied and the revelers made their way to the bar. He nodded at the string quartet. The cellist raised her bow and they started "Spring," the first movement of *The Four Seasons.*

Wes gave them fifteen minutes to refill their drinks, then stopped the quartet. He drank the rest of his gin then clinked the glass with the butter knife.

"We saved the best for last. Back by popular demand: a night on the South Branch with our own Quinn Shepherd during the Hex hatch." Wes pointed to Quinn. "Stand up, my boy."

Quinn turned back to the dining room but didn't stand. He had sandy hair, too long in the back, and his nose was peeling.

"Up, Quinn," Wes said. "Stand up."

Quinn waved but he didn't stand up.

"Lizzie, go get your husband to stand up," Wes said.

She wound her way through the tables to her husband and twirled in her little black dress. She pulled him to his feet and kissed him on the lips.

"Thank you, Lizzie," Wes said. He clinked his glass again. "Let's get started. Shall we say five thousand?"

Noah Osterman, the lawyer from Traverse City, raised his hand.

"Thank you, Noah."

Quinn looked over at Osterman. He knew that Osterman had no intention of buying the trip, but he knew Osterman wanted his name in front of the crowd.

"Now who says six?"

George Feeney, the heir to Gratiot Stamping in Detroit, nodded. Then Frank Baxter, the judge from Lansing. They were at seven thousand already.

"Who says eight?"

Silence.

Wes swept the room with his hand. "Eight. Eight. Eight. Who says eight thousand dollars?"

A man sitting in the corner raised his hand.

"Ladies and gentlemen, my accountant. Who says they're all cheap," Wes said, pointing at him. "Thank you, Charlie." They all clapped.

"Who says nine?"

Silence again.

"Noah?" The lawyer shook his head. "George?" Another shake of the head. "Judge Baxter?"

"Too rich for the blood of a public servant," the judge said.

The crowd roared. Quinn didn't think the bidding could go much higher.

"It's all for the river. Sand traps, bank control," Wes said. "And lawyers."

Another roar.

"I bid nine thousand," Osterman said.

Another hand went up. "Ten thousand," said Thompson Shepherd, Quinn's father.

"Who says eleven?" Wes said. "This trip is for the Hex hatch. Tomorrow night. And I do believe Quinn is going to scout it tonight." Wes looked over at his son-in-law. "Isn't that right, Quinn?"

Quinn nodded.

Harley Hawken, the oil man from Traverse City, raised his hand.

"Now who says twelve? Who says twelve thousand dollars?" There were no takers. "Eleven-five then. Who says eleven-five?" Nothing. Wes scanned the room. "Going once. Twice."

"I bid eleven-five."

"Thank you, Thompson."

Wes looked around the room. No one moved.

"Twelve thousand," Harley Hawken said.

"Who says twelve-five?" Wes looked around the room one last time. "All in? All done?" He pointed at Harley. "Sold to Harley Hawken for twelve thousand dollars."

The crowd applauded. Wes nodded at the cellist.

There were more trips to the bar. A woman snaked her way through the tables to Quinn. She whispered something in his ear, then left.

* * *

At 1:00 a.m., they coasted into the High Banks. Cassie started to whine just above Dead Man's Hole.

"Is this where the fish are, girl?"

Quinn dropped the anchor chain over the side. It dragged on the bottom, then held. He lit a cigar to keep the mosquitoes off. Cassie whined again.

"Easy, girl. There's no hatch yet."

From his shirt pocket Quinn fished out a half-smoked joint and used his cigar to light it. He sucked in the smoke, held his breath, and then exhaled. Cassie looked back at him. She didn't like the smell.

Twenty minutes later the first of the nymphs broke the surface. It struggled in the current, then flew up into the trees. Then another . . . and the Hex hatch was on.

The first trout rose. Quinn couldn't see it, but it sounded like a small fish. Then the duns swarmed above the river. The beating of their wings sounded like the hum of a high-tension line.

He pulled up the chain, and they drifted twenty yards downstream. He slipped the chain back in, and *Traveler* settled upstream of the feeding fish. The dead flies—the spinners— started falling like snowflakes. He heard a slurp about twenty-five yards in front of them. "That's the one we want." He couldn't see the fish rise. In the black of the night, he couldn't see much at all.

Quinn grabbed his fly rod. He raised his rod tip and stripped line from the reel. He made two false casts and then a drift. It floated past the slurp. Nothing. He cast again. Still nothing. There were spinners everywhere. Browns, giant browns, rose to the dead bugs. He cast above a slurp. The feeding trout stayed where it was, finning in the current, waiting for the spinners to float by. Quinn cast again and let out line on a dead drift. Another slurp, but not on his fly.

He cast again, a little further right. The fish slammed his fly. He held the line against the rod and set the hook. The fish ran downstream, the drag screaming as the line peeled off the reel. Cassie barked at the fish, still running line, down to the backing. If the fish ran much farther, there'd be no line left on the reel. Quinn touched the line with his finger, trying to slow the fish.

"Eight pounds, Cassie. Maybe more."

There was nothing to do but follow the fish. He held the rod in his left hand, twisted behind him and pulled up the chain. The boat started to drift. He knew it was reckless, especially in the dark, but he was damned if he was going to lose this fish. He kept the pole in his left hand and tried to steer one-handed with the paddle. They bounced off a rock in the middle of the river, then they hit a deadfall. The boat turned sideways in the current and broached. The river poured in. The boat took on more water. All he had to do to save them was to give up on the fish.

* * *

Quinn didn't make it home for breakfast. He didn't make it home at all. He spent the night at the lower end of Dead Man's Hole, resting peacefully in the silt, the anchor chain wrapped around his left ankle.

CHAPTER TWO

Harbor Springs, Michigan. One Year Later.

At one in the afternoon, Burr Lafayette slept in the cockpit of *Spindrift*, covered by a Hudson Bay blanket. His dog lay at his feet, snoring. Burr woke up when the wind shifted and his boat swung on her mooring.

He looked to starboard, and what had been a view of Little Traverse Bay was now the shoreline of downtown Harbor Springs, the ritziest old-money port of call on the Great Lakes.

"Zeke," he said to his aging yellow lab, "an east wind bodes ill, but it's not raining yet." The dog looked up and cocked his ears. Burr lay back down and fell asleep again.

Half an hour later, "Burr. Stop that infernal snoring and wake up. I'm about to drown."

Burr sat bolt upright. He looked all around but couldn't see where the noise was coming from. He looked down at Zeke, who was still snoring. He shook his head and lay back down.

"Burr," said the voice again. "Wake up. I know you're there."

"Am I finally losing my mind?" Burr said. Late forties, not quite six feet tall. Still lean. Hawk nose, now peeling. Sky blue eyes. His hair was still the color of an acorn. He had a few gray hairs, but he pulled out the ones he found.

There was a sharp rap on the hull, then another. "I'm down here," said the voice. "Help me before I drown."

Burr peered over the side. There was his law partner.

"Jacob, don't bump my boat with the dinghy."

"Get me out of this rowboat before I drown."

"It's not a rowboat, it's a dinghy. And you are perfectly safe. And dry."

"This infernal boat is about to capsize. Get me out," Jacob said. He started to stand in the dinghy, an eight-foot, flat-bottomed pram.

"Sit down. You'll tip over," Burr said.

The dinghy tipped to port. Little Traverse Bay poured in.

"Help me, I'm drowning," Jacob said.

"Your feet aren't even wet."

Burr reached down, grabbed Jacob by the wrist and hauled him onto the boat. Jacob lay face down on the deck like a dead man floating in water. Burr tied up the dinghy and climbed back into the cockpit. "How did you find me?"

"This is the only boat in the harbor." Jacob sat up. He was short and wiry and so was his hair. His olive skin had turned a pea-soup shade of green. "How can it still be winter here?"

"Wrap yourself up in this blanket."

Jacob pushed it away. "I'm sure it's full of dog hair."

Burr went down below and returned with a sandwich and a bottle of wine. "It's too late in the season for Zinfandel, but it is a bit chilly and I thought a chewy, raspberry, chocolaty Zinfandel would go nicely with my sandwich."

Jacob rethought the blanket and wrapped himself up in it. "There's a reason I risked my life paddling out to this awful boat." He made a show of picking a dog hair from his slacks. "This is what we must do."

Burr never liked the sound of "This is what we must do," especially from Jacob.

"My good friend, Wesley Goodspeed, owns The Gray Drake. He's going to take us fly-fishing on the South Branch during the Hex hatch."

Burr had no idea what Jacob was talking about.

"Surely you know what that is?"

Burr shook his head.

"It's the most famous hatch on the most famous trout stream at the most famous lodge east of the Mississippi." Jacob smiled at Burr.

Burr smiled back, waiting for the *quid pro quo*.

Jacob reached into his jacket pocket, pulled out a joint, and lit it.

"How can you be seasick one minute and smoke a joint the next?"

"It's the only thing that relaxes me." Jacob smoked the joint.

Burr had another glass of wine. The two of them looked at each other. Neither one said a word. They had played out this little drama countless times. Burr always outlasted Jacob.

Jacob licked his fingertips, put out what little was left of the joint, and put it back in his pocket.

"No reason to waste anything," Burr said.

Jacob ignored him. "If you aren't going to ask me, I'll tell you."

"Please," Burr said, triumphant.

"Wes has a daughter, Elizabeth. They call her Lizzie. She's the chef at the lodge. Her husband, Quinn, is a guide. The best guide on the river. And they have a boy of six."

"Of course," Burr said.

"*Was*, actually, the best guide," Jacob said.

Burr was afraid where this was headed but refused to say anything.

"It seems that last summer, Quinn drowned."

Burr arched his eyebrows.

"Yes, drowned. During the Hex hatch."

Burr finished his sandwich and poured himself another glass of wine. He drank half of it but didn't feel any better for it.

"As if that's not enough . . ."

Here it comes, Burr thought. He covered his ears with his hands.

"Stop that, Burr."

Burr kept his hands on his ears.

"I know you can hear me." Jacob spoke up, "Lizzie was just arrested for murder." He stopped for effect. "Murder. She's been accused of murdering her husband."

Burr dropped his hands from his ears. "I knew it. I knew it had to be something like this. I knew it when I looked down and saw you in the dinghy. God himself couldn't get you in a boat, let alone row yourself out to yet another boat."

"Then you'll defend Lizzie?"

Burr saw hope in Jacob's eyes. "No, I won't."

"You're the only one who can."

"Am I the only one who can help because I'm the only one who would take his fee in fishing?"

"Of course not."

"I'm not a criminal lawyer. No one knows that better than you. And I'm cash only."

"You'd do it for cash? Wes has plenty of money. I'm sure he'd pay us in cash."

"That's not what I said." Jacob started to say something, but Burr cut him off. "All I wanted for today was a little peace and quiet. I launched my boat. I motored out to this buoy. I rigged the main. I bought myself a sandwich and a bottle of wine. I took a nap. I'm trying to live a simple life. And you're trying to ruin it."

"A simple life?" Jacob said. The color came back to his face. "Burr Lafayette, you have the most complicated life of anyone I know." Jacob raised a forefinger. "You have an ex-wife to support." He raised another finger. "You have a young son. You have a rundown office building. You have this cur of a dog. You always seem to have a rundown sailboat. You hunt ducks. Women like you. And you have no money."

"You're going to run out of fingers, and it's too cold to take off your socks and shoes," Burr said.

"You wouldn't know peace and quiet if it hit you in the face."

Burr ran his hands through his hair, front to back.

"You always do that thing with your hair when you're troubled," Jacob said.

"I'm not troubled, and I'm not a criminal lawyer." He finished his wine.

"And you drink too much."

Jacob ran a thumb and forefinger down the crease of his slacks, a crease like the edge of a knife. Then he pulled the sleeves of his sweater down just beyond the cuffs of his jacket.

He's natty, Burr thought. *I'll give him that.*

"If you won't take this on, at least help get Lizzie out on bail. I'm sure Wes will pay cash."

Burr looked to the east again. The clouds, now black, were rolling in. "I'll take you to the dock, so you don't have to row back." He turned the key in the ignition, pulled out the choke, pushed the throttle forward and pressed the starter button. Four tries later, the engine kicked over.

* * *

Three days later, Burr sat in a packed courtroom waiting for the judge. He tap-tap-tapped his No. 2 yellow pencil, just as he had done for the past twenty-odd years. As far as courtrooms go, this one was like all the others, only shabbier. His table was dinged up, his chair wobbled, and there was a hole the size of a paper plate in the linoleum underneath his chair.

Elizabeth Shepherd to his left, Jacob to her left. Elizabeth Shepherd was an almost beautiful blonde. Her face was a little too long. Her nose was a little too pointed and her lips were a little too full, but her eyes were the color of robins' eggs and that made up for everything. She was wearing an orange jumpsuit, and she was the reason the courtroom was packed. Her father, Wesley Goodspeed, sat behind them in the front row of the gallery.

The bailiff entered, a slight young man struggling to grow a mustache.

"All rise. The Court of the Honorable Judge Harold F. Skinner is now in session."

At last, the judge entered and sat down. He was a short, square, neckless man. He looked like a cigarette machine.

Judge Skinner put on a pair of glasses with black frames and surveyed the courtroom. Burr thought the judge was pleased to have such a full house.

"You may be seated," the bailiff said.

"Counsel, you may begin," Judge Skinner said.

Burr stood again. "Burr Lafayette for the defense, Your Honor." He pulled down the cuffs of his shirt, a baby blue button-down, pinpoint oxford that did not need pulling down. He straightened his tie, a red foulard with blue diamonds that did not need straightening.

"Mr. Lafayette, when you have finished grooming, please begin."

Burr had been one of the best commercial litigators in the state of Michigan, but he had given up his practice and his marriage over a client almost young enough to be his daughter. Over an affair that hadn't turned out. After the year it had taken to ruin the previous twenty, he had moved to East Lansing and started an appellate practice—complicated, esoteric litigation that had made him famous in select legal circles but didn't always pay the bills.

"Your Honor, we are here to request bail for my client, Elizabeth Shepherd."

"The answer is *no*. I said *no* at the arraignment and the answer is still *no*." The judge raised his gavel and was just about to bring it down.

"Your Honor, my client has not been charged with murder. The preliminary exam isn't for another two weeks. If at that time—"

"No," the judge said.

Burr walked around the defense table and took two steps toward the judge. He thought that if he pulled one of Skinner's arms down, a pack of

Marlboros might pop out of his mouth. He looked back at his client. Lizzie looked down at her hands, just as he had coached her to do.

Burr took another step closer toward the judge. "Your Honor, as you know, there are two questions for determining bail, one." Burr raised his index finger. "Is the accused dangerous to the community? And two." He raised another finger. "Is the accused a risk to flee the jurisdiction?"

"Counsel, I ruled on this at Mrs. Shepherd's arraignment."

"May I finish, Your Honor?"

"Mr. Lafayette, I do not find your thousand-dollar suit persuasive," the judge said. "There are at least one hundred fifty people in here, and the air conditioning doesn't work very well. It's going to get ripe in about five minutes. Please get on with it."

"Thank you, Your Honor. My client has no criminal record. None whatsoever. She has never been charged with a crime." Burr paused. "She's never even had a parking ticket."

"Mr. Lafayette, Crawford County is ninety percent woods. There are no parking meters in Grayling."

There was a snicker from the gallery.

"Your Honor, Mrs. Shepherd is not a hardened criminal. She's not a criminal at all. And she is not a danger to the community."

"Objection, Your Honor." The prosecutor popped up. "John Cullen for the State. Mrs. Shepherd murdered her husband and then tried to make it look like an accident. She is most certainly dangerous."

"Thank you, Jack," Judge Skinner said. "Sit down."

Burr watched the prosecutor sit. He had a full head of curly blond hair and pockmarked cheeks, the remnants of an acne-filled puberty. What struck him most, though, was Cullen's smile. A big, wide smile that showed off straight white teeth. *Why does he smile when he objects?*

"Your Honor, my client is not going to commit a crime, and she is absolutely not a threat to flee the jurisdiction. She has a job and a six-year-old son. Since her husband drowned, she is the only parent and the sole breadwinner."

"Objection, Your Honor." Cullen stood up again, still smiling. "The sheriff stopped her headed south on I-75, fleeing the jurisdiction."

"Nonsense. She was on her way to Clare to see a friend," Burr said.

"She was running away."

Burr turned to Cullen. "Must you smile all the time?"

"That's enough, Mr. Lafayette. He can't help it," Skinner said.

"Your Honor," Burr said, "it is tragedy enough that Mrs. Shepherd lost her husband, and her son has lost his father. Please don't make it worse by keeping her in jail. You are making an orphan out of her son."

"That's because she killed his father," Cullen said.

"He drowned." Burr considered turning around, but he wasn't ready to deal with Cullen's smile. "We will post a bond, Your Honor."

Judge Skinner pressed his glasses back on his face.

"Your Honor, Elizabeth Shepherd ambushed her husband on the South Branch and murdered him with a canoe paddle. She is a murderess, and she is dangerous."

"You have no proof," Burr said.

"We'll see about that."

"Stop it. Both of you," Skinner said. "Mr. Lafayette, I take you at your word. Bail is set at one million dollars."

Burr didn't miss a beat. "Considering the circumstances, I think the bail is too high."

"Your client only needs to post ten percent," the judge said.

Burr felt Cullen's smile burning into the back of his head, but he turned around and looked at Wes. Wes shook his head *no.* Burr turned back to the judge. "Your Honor."

"If you're not going to post bail, I am going to adjourn." Skinner picked up his gavel. "The defendant will be returned to the county jail to await the preliminary exam." He cracked down the gavel. "We are adjourned."

"I'll pay the bond," said a voice from the back of the courtroom.

Burr turned around. A tall, thin man with silver hair stood. Other than the lawyers, he was the only one in the courtroom wearing a suit.

"Thompson, are you sure you want to do this?" Skinner said.

Thompson, whoever he was, smiled at the judge. A grim smile, Burr thought. "Who should I make out the check to, Hal?"

"Mr. Lafayette, please approach the bench."

The judge leaned over to Burr and spoke softly. "Counsel, the Main Branch is barely a hundred yards from my courtroom. There may be a blue-wing olive hatch this afternoon. I don't want to miss it. You have your bail. Are you satisfied?"

"Yes, Your Honor." Burr couldn't imagine how Skinner could possibly fit into waders, much less wade a trout stream.

Judge Skinner looked at the thin man. "Make the check payable to Crawford County."

* * *

Burr sat at his desk in his office, a cherry desk the size of a '64 Buick 225. To his left, a walk-in cedar closet held his most treasured possessions: waders, decoys, shotguns. Zeke napped on a leather couch against the far wall. Burr looked at an envelope on his desk and drummed his fingers.

There were two knocks on the door, followed by Eve McGinty, Burr's longtime, long-suffering legal assistant.

"That letter won't open itself," she said.

"I know what's inside."

"How many payments are you behind this time?"

Eve had been Burr's longtime, long-suffering legal assistant at Fisher and Allen. He had begged her not to follow him to East Lansing, but she had divorced well and said she wanted a house close to work that had a yard with full sun, so she could have a perennial garden. Burr said there must be a full sun garden somewhere near the Renaissance Center, but she wouldn't hear of it.

"I'm only three months behind."

"Let me." She grabbed the envelope.

Eve was a year older than Burr, which she didn't like, and which he didn't let her forget. She had a hint of crow's feet, which she also didn't like.

She ripped open the envelope and read the letter. Then she tugged at her earring. "This one is nasty."

"There is nothing to worry about until we get one by certified mail."

"Why you ever bought this building is beyond me."

"It seemed like a good idea at the time." Burr had bought the rundown Masonic Temple, circa 1937, when he moved to East Lansing. It was six stories, narrow, right in the middle of downtown East Lansing and had no parking. Replacing the elevator had almost bankrupted him. There was a restaurant on the first floor, his office and living quarters on the top floor and unoccupied in between.

"The elevator is broken again," Eve said.

"I don't take the elevator."

"How are you ever going to pay for all of this?"

"We have a new client. A rich client with a big problem. My favorite kind. Let me take you to dinner this evening, and we'll figure it all out."

"No, thank you."

He had been asking her out as long as they had known each other, and she had refused him every time.

Eve turned to leave just as Jacob burst through the door carrying a four-foot cardboard tube. He was dressed to the nines even though he spent all day doing research and writing in the bowels of the Lafayette and Wertheim Law Library.

"This is for you." Jacob handed the tube to Burr.

"Thank you, Jacob." He set it on his desk.

"Aren't you going to open it?"

Always suspicious of gifts, Burr looked at the tube. "I don't think so." He ran both hands through his hair, front to back.

"It's a gift. What could possibly be wrong with a gift?" Eve said.

"I have a bad feeling."

"Nonsense." Eve walked around Burr's desk, opened the top right-hand drawer and took out a pair of scissors.

"I was wondering where those were," Burr said.

She cut the tape off one end of the tube.

"I'll take it from here." Burr took hold of the tube and pulled out a crumpled newspaper. "The *Crawford County Avalanche*," he said. He took out more newspaper, then slid out a fishing rod.

"My goodness, it's magnificent," Jacob said.

"It looks like a fishing rod to me," Eve said.

"Eve, this is not just a fishing rod. It's a Sage. A six weight," Jacob said.

"Really," Eve said.

"This is the finest fly-fishing rod there is," Jacob said.

Burr had a sinking feeling.

"It's from our new client, Wes Goodspeed, the owner of The Gray Drake," Jacob said.

"This is from our new, rich client? Our new, rich client with a big problem is paying his bill with a fishing rod?" Eve said. She tugged at her earring.

15

"Burr, why don't you go ahead and catch up on your mortgage with this fly rod?"

"I thought we could help Wes and Lizzie this one time," Jacob said.

"Jacob, what on Earth do I possibly need this for?" Burr picked up the rod and was about to break it over his knee.

Jacob ran over. "Good God, man. What are you doing?" He wrenched the endangered fly rod out of Burr's hands. "This is a treasure."

Burr stood. "You said we would be paid in cash." He took a step toward Jacob, who took a step back.

"We simply must help Lizzie."

"I said I would. If we got paid. Stay right where you are, and hand me that rod," Burr said.

"You're going to break it."

"That's right, Jacob. In about two hundred little pieces. And then you're going to eat them."

The color drained from Jacob's face. "I can't possibly eat a fishing rod."

"That's right, Jacob. You can't eat a fly rod. I can't pay the mortgage with a fly rod. I said I would take on a criminal case if we got paid. In cash."

* * *

The next day, Burr sat at a corner table downstairs at Michelangelo's, facing the door. He wasn't in fear for his life. He didn't think anyone in particular was out to get him, but he didn't like having his back to the door. Any door. Zeke lay at his feet, on watch for what might find its way to the floor. The food at Michelangelo's was quite good, especially considering that Scooter, the proprietor, had blond hair, a pasty complexion and not a drop of Italian blood.

Burr sipped on Scooter's best Chianti. "It's quite good, Zeke." He picked up the glass, studied it, then drank the rest of it. He raised his glass and the waitress, a student no doubt, came over and set down a basket of breadsticks and refilled his glass.

"Are you ready to order, Mr. Lafayette?"

"No, but stand by with the Chianti."

She nodded and left.

Burr scratched Zeke behind his left ear, his favorite spot, but the dog had bigger plans. "I get it." Burr passed him a breadstick.

He took one more swallow, sighed and set down his glass. "This is silly." He reached over to the chair next to him and picked up the black three-ring binder that was none other than the Lafayette and Wertheim checkbook. Eve kept it hidden from Burr, but today Eve was mulching her garden and Burr had finally found where she had hidden it: in the law library behind the *United States Bankruptcy Code*. He stared at the checkbook. "There's nothing to be afraid of," he said out loud. Burr took another swallow and opened the checkbook, stubs on the left, long, light blue checks on the right, three to a page. He flipped to the last check that had been written. "Damn it all." He took one of the breadsticks, bit into it, then passed the rest to Zeke. "Damn it all," he said again, then slammed the checkbook shut.

At that moment, Scooter himself showed up. "Is something wrong, Mr. Lafayette?" The restaurateur had brought the bottle of Chianti with him.

"I'm upside down."

"I beg your pardon." Scooter looked a little nervous.

"About ten large. When the chickens come home to roost."

"I beg your pardon," Scooter said again.

"It's about money," Burr said. He finished off his wine.

Scooter looked a little more nervous. He refilled Burr's glass and changed the subject. "Mr. Lafayette, you know there are no dogs allowed in Michelangelo's."

"Scooter," Burr said.

Scooter raised a flabby, white hand and wagged his finger at Burr. "Mr. Lafayette, we have been through this many times." Scooter looked down at Zeke. "I know he is very talented, but he is not a seeing-eye dog. And you're not blind."

Burr turned the checkbook so that it faced Scooter and opened it. "Scooter, what we have here is the upside-down balance in the Lafayette and Wertheim checkbook."

Scooter looked very nervous.

"And the reason it's upside down, Scooter, is that you're six months late on the rent. And you owe me for the new oven I paid for. Which comes to about ten thousand dollars."

"I can't be the only reason."

"How are you going to pay me?"

"We can trade for the rent."

"I can't possibly eat that much pasta." Burr drank more of the Chianti. "Scooter, if you don't pay me, I'm going to get my padlock."

Scooter shuddered. "Not the padlock. How will I pay you if you lock me out?" He scurried away.

"Zeke, buying this building seemed like such a good idea at the time." Burr slammed the checkbook shut a second time.

* * *

Burr stewed over the stewed tomatoes on his clams with red sauce. He offered an angel hair noodle to Zeke, who sucked it in like he'd done it before. "Zeke, this is my own fault." Burr swirled the wine in his glass. "I spent all my money on wine, women, and boats. The rest, I wasted." He took a drink. "I know it's a cliché, but there is a place in the world for clichés." He finished the glass and stared out the window at MAC Avenue, the sidewalk empty, only the occasional car. Finals ended a week ago, and summer term hadn't started yet. "East Lansing is just about as empty as my wallet."

Burr almost jumped out of his skin. Elizabeth Shepherd stood right in front of him.

When he came to his senses, he stood, shook her hand and pulled out a chair for her. He sat back down.

"I wasn't expecting you," he said.

"I started at your office. Jacob told me where you were."

The waitress came to their table.

"Water for me," Lizzie said.

Burr switched to water, reluctantly.

"Will you help me?" she said.

"As much as I'd like to help you, I simply can't work for free."

"There's nothing free about that Sage."

"Your father owns the most famous fishing lodge on the most famous trout stream east of the Mississippi."

"That doesn't mean he has any money." She picked up her water. The glass shook in her hand, and she set it back down. "Will you please help me?" she said again.

"There are many fine lawyers," he said, although he didn't really believe it.

"I didn't kill my husband. My son doesn't have a father. I loved Quinn, and now he's gone." She reached for her water, but then she put her hands in her lap. "I'll find a way to pay you."

Burr felt himself caving in. Jacob would be delighted. Eve would be furious, but Lizzie did say she'd pay him. Of course, they all said that.

"You'll help me then?"

She has a little boy, like Zeke. I've come this far. I suppose I could help. Burr nodded. *Heaven help me.*

Lizzie reached across the table and put her hand on top of Burr's. "Thank you. Thank you so much. Now what do we do?"

Burr retrieved his hand. "Now we wait."

"We wait?" Lizzie tried to pick up her glass again, but her hand was still shaking. "It's been a year since Quinn died. Josh and I were just starting to get used to all this. And now I've been charged with murder."

"I need to know what evidence the prosecutor has. Until we know that, there is very little I can do."

"Don't you even want to know what happened?" she said.

"I read the coroner's report and the transcript of the arraignment. If that's all Cullen has, no jury will convict you."

Lizzie sat back in her chair. "Jury?"

Burr looked up at her. "The standard for indictment is low. Very low. To try you for murder, all Cullen has to show is that there is probable cause that you murdered your husband. That it's more likely than not that you killed him."

"I don't care about the ins and outs. I need you to stop it."

"According to the transcript of the arraignment, Cullen says he has the murder weapon. He says you were seen fighting with Quinn at a bar."

"I didn't kill my husband. I swear I didn't."

"At the moment, it doesn't matter if you did or didn't."

Burr watched Lizzie's cheeks turn red. She leaned in toward him.

"I'm about to lose what's left of my life, and all you care about are the rules."

"Unless someone can testify that you were with them the night Quinn was killed, it will be next to impossible to get the charges dropped at the preliminary exam."

Lizzie put her head in her hands.

For a lawyer with a silver tongue, I have just done a remarkable job of putting my foot in my mouth, he thought. "I'll do my best, but you need to be prepared for a trial."

She sat back up, put her hands on the table and studied them. She had long thin fingers and short fingernails, but the skin on her hands was dry and rough. She looked up at him. "I do all the cooking at the lodge. That's why my hands look like this."

"They look fine to me."

"They're dry and cracked. My fingernails are chipped. I love cooking. It's what I do."

Burr couldn't see where this was going.

"My son needs me, and so does my father. I want you to wake me up from this nightmare."

Burr looked out the window, then back at her. "Lizzie, I'll figure it out. Go back to the lodge. I'll get started right away."

"Thank you. Thank you so much."

Burr thought she looked relieved, but she was still scared. *But who wouldn't be?*

Lizzie left for The Gray Drake. Burr and Zeke took the stairs up to his office. He stopped at the landing on the fourth floor to catch his breath. "She said she didn't kill her husband, and she promised to pay." Burr looked down at Zeke. "That's what they all say."

When he got to his office, Eve was nowhere in sight. Burr put the checkbook back behind the Bankruptcy Code. Then he peeked in the library and saw Jacob hunched over a book of Michigan appellate decisions. *Keep up the good work.* Burr snuck into his office, shut the door quietly and lay down on his couch. He took a deep breath and smelled the leather. He kicked off his shoes and, with Zeke asleep on the oriental throw rug in front of the couch, readied himself to digest the clams and red sauce and sleep off the wine.

Burr woke up with Zeke licking his left cheek and Eve looking down at him, hands on her hips. He was groggy but awake enough to know that when Eve had her hands on her hips, things did not bode well. He scratched Zeke's left ear, considered sitting up but decided against it.

"It's bad enough that you're taking a nap on a Tuesday afternoon, but must you snore?"

"I don't snore," Burr said, who did and knew it.

"This cavalier attitude toward work and money will be the end of us."

"Jacob is hard at work on the Murphy appeal and I am about to bring in an important new case."

"You mean the fishing rod client?"

Burr was afraid he was going to have to sit up to defend himself.

"At the time, it seemed like a good idea to leave Fisher and Allen, but you don't pay attention to anything except Zeke and duck hunting. And I suspect you have another leaky sailboat," Eve said.

Burr sat up and swung his legs to the floor. Zeke retrieved one of his shoes, then the other.

"There is nothing better than a well-trained dog."

"You simply aren't paying attention to anything that matters."

"I am attentive to Zeke-the-Boy."

"It was lunacy to name your son after a dog. Why Grace went along with it is beyond me."

"Zeke is the finest retriever I've ever had."

"That's no reason to name your son after him."

"I thought it would be an honor to name my son after Zeke."

"I will never understand," Eve said.

Burr walked to his desk and looked out the window. "A fine spring day," he said. "All the leaves are out except the oaks." He turned to Eve. "They're always the last."

"Thank you, Aldo Leopold."

Burr sat down and studied the pile of papers stacked on a corner of his desk. It wasn't quite tall enough to hide behind.

"That stack of papers is about to fall over and you have no idea what's in there," Eve said.

"This is an archeological filing system. Bottom to top in chronological order."

"It's going to fall on you."

"We'll take care of it when I can't see over it." Burr studied the pile. "Where is the transcript of Lizzie's arraignment?"

Eve pulled a file from the stack. The pile swayed but didn't collapse. She handed the file to Burr.

* * *

Early the next morning, Burr slipped a padlock on the door to Michelangelo's on the way out of his building. Then, he and Zeke drove to Jacob's house. Jacob opened the passenger door of Burr's Jeep, and Zeke, riding shotgun as always, licked Jacob's cheek.

"There he is again." Zeke licked Jacob's cheek again.

"Zeke, back seat," Burr said.

The dog licked Jacob squarely on the lips and jumped into the back.

"That is the most disgusting thing that has ever happened to me." Jacob took a white linen handkerchief from his pocket and wiped off his face. He wiped off the seat. "There is dog hair everywhere."

"It's shedding season."

"He is a cur, and this is an abomination of a vehicle."

"It's perfect except for the back window." This one didn't work any better than the back window on his last Jeep, and it had the added disadvantage of having a windshield wiper. Rather than fix it when it broke, Burr had seized the initiative and broken it off before it could break. "And it's better than that silly Peugeot you drive."

"It's a Renault."

"If you're going to drive a small car, why don't you at least drive an American car? Like a Corvair," Burr said.

"A Corvair is a deathtrap."

"At least it's an American deathtrap," Burr said.

"The last Corvair was made twenty years ago."

Burr and Jacob didn't say another word until they arrived at The Gray Drake.

* * *

Burr and Jacob met Wes Goodspeed on the riverbank in front of the lodge. The river hurried by, cloudy from last night's rain. The sun was well over the trees. There was a clear blue sky, but raindrops still dripped from the leaves.

"The river's not fishable now, but it will clear up pretty quick." Wes kicked a stick into the river. "Thank you for helping us. We're very grateful."

"We're glad to help," Jacob said.

What have I gotten myself into?

"Lizzie can't be the one to take you down the river," Wes said.

"Mr. Goodspeed, Lizzie has to take me. I need her to show me where she was that night."

"She can't go," Wes said. He turned to Jacob. "You do agree."

"I'm afraid I agree with Burr," Jacob said. He was dressed like he had just stepped out of the Orvis catalog.

"Mr. Goodspeed...." Burr said.

"Call me Wes."

"Wes, there is nothing in the inquest that remotely hints that your son-in-law was murdered. And certainly not by Lizzie."

"That's because he drowned."

Burr looked over at Zeke, who had his eye on a chipmunk running in and out of a hole in the foundation of the lodge. "Zeke, stay." Burr looked back at Wes. "But that's not what the transcript of the arraignment says."

"None of it's true, and there's no reason to put her through this," Wes said.

"I need to know what happened, so I know what questions to ask at the preliminary exam."

"I'll take you. She's been through enough." Wes headed toward the parking lot. Burr and Jacob followed him.

"Zeke, heel," Burr said. The dog walked beside Burr. He looked back at the chipmunk but didn't break.

Wes climbed in a Suburban and backed it up to an Au Sable riverboat on a trailer. It had a forest-green bottom and three white seats, varnish everywhere else.

If this boat were a woman, she'd be a ten.

Lizzie came out from the lodge with a small boy, who didn't look a bit like his mother. He was dressed just like his grandfather, from his boots all the way up to his Patagonia fishing hat.

"I'll take them, Dad. You watch Josh." She dropped the trailer hitch on the ball, locked it down, and hooked the chains.

"I don't want to stay with Grandpa," Joshua said. "I want to go in the boat with you."

"I'm the one who was there that night. I'm the one who needs to go."

She took her son by the hand over to Wes, who put his hands in his pockets. "Take him. I'm the one who's accused." She stopped herself.

"Is this about Dad?" Josh said.

"No," Wes said.

"Yes, Joshua, it's about Dad," Lizzie said.

"Then I want to go."

Lizzie got down on one knee and hugged him. "I have to do this for Dad." Josh hugged her around her neck. She kissed him, then took his hand and put it in his grandfather's hand. "The pies need to come out in ten minutes." She kissed Josh one more time, then climbed into the Suburban. "Follow me," she said to Burr.

Burr and Zeke climbed into the Jeep. Seeing Lizzie with her son made Burr wish he was with his son.

Burr followed Lizzie through the woods, then past a scruffy-looking bar called the Two Track. *That must be the bar where Lizzie had the fight with Quinn that night.* About eight miles later, she turned into a gravel parking lot next to the river. Lizzie backed the trailer into the river and launched the boat. Just as Burr reached the boat, she climbed back into the Suburban.

"Follow me. We're going to drop off the trailer at Smith Bridge, then bring your Jeep back here."

When they got back to the Chase Bridge launch, Lizzie pushed the stern into the current, then pulled it to the bank, the bow facing downstream.

"Jacob, you take the middle seat. Burr, you take the bow. There really isn't room for Zeke but he can sit between you."

"Zeke can take my spot," Jacob said.

"How are you going to see where everything happened?" Lizzie said.

"Jacob, you look like you just stepped out of the Orvis catalog. Get in the boat," Burr said.

"I get deathly ill on all boats."

"How do you fish without being in a boat?" Burr said.

"I fish from the bank."

Jacob walked back to the Jeep. Lizzie sat in the stern, Zeke midships, Burr in the bow. Lizzie nosed the boat into the river. The current caught it and carried them through the runout. "The auction was over by ten-thirty. I dropped Quinn off here about midnight. I drove the trailer to Smith Bridge, picked up the Suburban and went home."

The river bent to the east. They floated over a sandbar, then past a marsh. After that, tag alders grew down to the river. Then the river took a sharp bend north. There was a thirty-foot bank on the east side, snags where the river ate away the bank, and the trees tipped over, their roots like so many snakes tangled up in each other. There were hardwoods and white pines on top of the bank.

"There's fish in this bend," Lizzie said. "It's deep here, maybe ten feet, but no Hex. There's not enough silt."

They floated on through riffles, runs, and holes. A beaver lodge on their left. A bald eagle, coasting in the wind, followed them downstream. There was a cabin every now and then, but it was mostly wild, river country.

Lizzie pointed with her paddle. "Over there. On the right. You can put a boat in there, but you've got to push it the last hundred feet. It's nothing you'd want to do in the dark."

Burr looked at his watch. They'd been in the river for a half hour.

"We're coming out of state land," Lizzie said. "Now it's mostly private. There are a couple holes here, but Quinn would have kept going. The best Hex hatch is up ahead."

There were a few more cabins now, mostly old, mostly rundown. But here and there, a well-kept log home.

"Do you know anything about the *Hexagenia limbata*?"

"What?" Burr said.

"The Hex." She pointed in about twenty feet in front of the boat.

"There's a hole in front of us. Some current but not too much, and the bottom is muddy. The Hex nymphs bury themselves in the mud. When the water temperature is right, they dig their way out and float to the surface. Those are the emergers. They drift a little in the current. Then they fly off. They're huge, especially for a mayfly. They swarm over the river and mate in the air. Then they die and fall back into the river. Those are the spinners. The trout get them as nymphs, emergers, and spinners."

Burr had no idea what she was talking about.

"They hatch at night. In the dead of night. That's why Quinn was here. The Hex hatch on the South Branch made The Gray Drake famous. That's how Wes got his Orvis fly shop. And all the sports wanted to fish with Quinn."

This seems like a lot of trouble just to catch a fish. I'd rather be sleeping in the dead of night. Burr turned and looked back at her. "If Quinn was murdered, someone must have met up with him on the river."

"Quinn drowned." She steered them around a deadhead in the current, then over to the bank. "There's at least twenty places you could walk in from the road. Four or five where you could bring a boat in on a two-track. But you'd have to drag the boat at least part of the way."

They passed a row of cabins on the west bank.

"Anyone from one of these cabins could have stopped him."

She nodded. "But no one did."

Burr thought she was awfully sure of herself. "Did Quinn have any enemies?"

Lizzie steered around a rock. "Quinn had rivals."

"Rivals?"

"He was the best guide on the river." Lizzie slipped the anchor chain over the side. The boat dragged downstream about ten feet, then the chain took hold. She pointed just past the bow. "See that? The dark water? That's Deadman's Hole, where Quinn drowned. The best Hex hatch on the South Branch comes off here. If you time it right."

How could Quinn have possibly drowned at a place called Dead Man's Hole?

"This hole's deep, maybe ten feet. And the current is tricky." She pointed with the paddle again. "And right there, that's where the riffles start. The hole ends just before there and the water shoals. That's where they found him. Cassie must have jumped out of the boat and swam to shore. Somehow she found her way back to the lodge."

"Cassie?"

"Quinn's dog."

Burr didn't know what to make of the dog. *Did she figure into this somehow?* Right now he needed to understand what happened on the river that night.

He swiveled in his seat and looked back at Lizzie again. The boat rocked. "Is this his boat?"

"No. The sheriff came and got it after they found the paddle." She ran her hand along the rail. "He loved his boat. *Traveler.*" Lizzie looked up at Burr. "Do you know who *Traveler* was?"

"Robert E. Lee's horse."

Lizzie nodded at him. "Lee said that was the best battle horse he ever had. That's how Quinn felt about his boat."

"What do you think happened?"

"I think he must have slipped and cracked his head on the rail." She ran her hand along the starboard rail again. "He must have been knocked out or at least dazed. The anchor chain got tangled on his ankle, and he fell over the side. Right about there." She pointed off to her right. "The chain didn't hold in the deep water, not with Quinn tangled up in it. The current dragged him and the boat downstream to the end of the hole, where the water shoaled." She pointed downriver about fifty feet.

Burr could see where the water changed color from coffee to sand.

"The chain hung up there. That's where they found him."

"Who found him?"

"A fisherman. The next day."

"How did he get in here?"

"He walked in from over there." Lizzie pointed to her left. "A two-track comes in from the west. By the time it gets to the river it's a path. There's another way in over there. Downstream." She pointed to the east side. "It's just a path."

Burr turned back around and looked at Lizzie. "How do you know he drowned?" Burr knew the answer, but he wanted to hear it from Lizzie.

She took off her sunglasses. Burr thought her eyes looked a little puffy.

"There was water in his lungs." She stopped. "It's so awful. I can't think about it." Her hands began to shake again. "I loved Quinn. More than anything. He loved me, and he loved fly-fishing. I never asked him to choose."

Burr needed to get back to what happened that night. "I assumed Quinn hit his head on the rail, but the transcript of your arraignment said you killed him with a canoe paddle."

Lizzie's voice broke. "Quinn and I had some problems, but I loved him. It wasn't a perfect marriage."

That was just about the most non-answer answer he'd ever heard. "When you got the boat back, was the paddle in it?"

"No."

"Did you wonder where it was?"

"I didn't really think about it. But it probably fell in the river and floated away. Things fall in every day, and nobody ever sees them again."

"We're going to have to think about it now."

"This was called Dead Man's Hole," she said. "Now they call it Quinn's Hole."

Lizzie pulled up the anchor chain, and they floated on.

"This paddle is going to be a problem. We're going to have to figure it out," Burr said.

Lizzie ignored him. "Over there," she said, "you can drive almost all the way in from there."

Burr looked to his right.

They kept going. Lizzie pointed out more Hex holes, but they didn't stop. A little further on, Lizzie pointed to the west bank. "There," she said. "That's Quinn's father's cabin."

Burr looked downstream. The river straightened out, higher ground with hardwoods and pines. This didn't exactly fit Burr's definition of a cabin. A two-story log home with shiny, varnished logs, paned windows and a shake roof. There was no grass, the yard filled with ferns, myrtle and wildflowers. There was a boathouse built on the dock with living quarters above.

"That must be worth a fortune," Burr said.

"Quinn's father lives there during the season," Lizzie said.

"With all that money, why was Quinn a guide?"

"That's how he could afford to be a guide," Lizzie said.

They drifted on. The river widened and flattened out. There were a few more cabins, but it was mostly wild again, low and swampy, full of willows, dogwood and tag alders. Smith Bridge lay just ahead. They drifted another hundred yards, then Lizzie leaned into the paddle and pulled them ashore.

"This is where we dropped off the trailer and where I left it that night. And this is where Quinn would have landed."

The boat nosed onto the shore. Zeke jumped out and found the nearest tree. Lizzie stepped into the river and pulled the boat over the bank. Burr stepped to the bow and onto the bank.

"How long would it have taken Quinn to get here?" Burr said. "In the dark."

"It depends on how much you fish."

"How about that night?"

Lizzie took off her sunglasses again. "That night, it took the rest of his life."

CHAPTER THREE

At ten on June 15th, a week after he'd floated the South Branch with Lizzie, Burr sat at the defense table in Judge Harold F. Skinner's courtroom. The air conditioning was working about as well as the last time he had been here.

Burr had floated the river. He'd seen where Quinn had drowned. He'd talked to Lizzie, Wes, and Thompson. He thought Quinn had drowned, but that's not what Cullen thought.

Burr tap-tap-tapped his No. 2 yellow pencil. *How did I get myself caught up in this?*

Lizzie sat to his left, Jacob sat next to Lizzie. Eve sat behind them in the first row of the gallery. Wes, next to Eve, looked decidedly out of place in a gray suit. Quinn's father, Thompson Shepherd, next to Wes, oozed money. The gallery was packed.

Lizzie had dressed as Burr had told her to—a black dress, knee length, no jewelry, no makeup.

The bailiff with the struggling mustache appeared. "All rise, the Court of the Honorable Harold F. Skinner is now in session." Judge Skinner shuffled in and sat down.

"Be seated," the bailiff said.

Skinner addressed the courtroom. "We are here today for the preliminary examination of Elizabeth Shepherd, to determine if there is enough evidence to bind her over for trial." He looked at Cullen. "You may proceed."

Cullen stood. "Thank you, Your Honor." Cullen turned to the defense table and then the gallery. His toothy smile lit up his pockmarked cheeks. The prosecutor cleared his throat.

"Early on the morning of June 22nd of last year, the defendant, Elizabeth Shepherd, snuck onto the South Branch of the Au Sable, ambushed her husband and murdered him. With malice aforethought." Cullen paused. "Not only did she murder him, she brutally murdered him. She smashed his head in with a canoe paddle. Then she…"

"Stop right there, Jack. Unless I am mistaken, this is a preliminary examination. There is no need for an opening argument," Skinner said.

"Yes, Your Honor," Cullen said.

"I suggest you call your first witness."

"Yes, Your Honor. The State calls Brian Bilkey."

After he was sworn in, Bilkey sat down and faced the courtroom. He had wire-rimmed glasses on a small nose, and his eyes were too close together. He was tan from his eyebrows to the tip of his chin, but his forehead was white.

"Another fisherman," Burr said, under his breath.

Cullen approached the witness. "Please state your name and address."

"Brian Bilkey, 530 Grosbeck, Lansing, Michigan."

"Thank you, Mr. Bilkey," Cullen said. "Would you please tell us what you were doing on the morning of June 22nd of last year?"

"I got up bright and early, and drove back to the Mason tract. I parked at the head of a two-track. Then I put my waders on, my vest, put my rod together and walked the two-track to the river. Then—"

Cullen raised his hand, palm out, to the witness. "Thank you, Mr. Bilkey. When you reached the river, what did you see?"

"See?" Bilkey straightened his glasses. "Well, I saw the river. That's where I came out. It was pretty clear, not too low. Which is good." He smiled at Cullen, who was not smiling.

"Mr. Bilkey, what else did you see?" Cullen raised his eyebrows. "On the river."

"Well, there was a nice seam in the current. Perfect place to float an Adams. I like a number ten."

"Mr. Bilkey, we're not here to talk about the kind of fly you used."

Bilkey nodded. "There was a boat, an Au Sable riverboat, out there at the end of the hole. Which ruined the hole. With the shadows and breaking up the current and all."

"Thank you, Mr. Bilkey. Was there anyone in the boat?"

"Not a soul."

"What did you think about that?"

"I was mad. Dead Man's is my favorite hole. I always catch fish there. Once in a while a chub but mostly browns."

"Chubs?" Cullen said.

"Yeah, I throw 'em on the bank for the raccoons. And the otters."

Burr had had enough. "Objection, Your Honor. While I have a keen interest in fly-fishing, I don't see the relevance."

"I agree, Mr. Lafayette," Skinner said. Then to Cullen, "You might pick things up a bit, Jack."

Cullen scowled.

If Cullen rehearsed this with Bilkey, this isn't going the way he planned.

"Mr. Bilkey, you testified that you didn't see anyone on the boat. Did you see anyone on the shore?" Cullen said.

"No."

"In the river?"

"No."

"Thank you, Mr. Bilkey. Then what did you do?"

"Well, I'd come all this way, so I thought I might as well give it a try." Bilkey rearranged his glasses again. "I waded upstream, then I drifted that Adams right through the hole. Nothing. So I switched to a Royal Wulff, then a Mickey Finn. There were a few fish rising, but I couldn't get 'em to do anything."

Cullen gritted his teeth.

"Then I switched to a Woolly Bugger. I cast it down and across and stripped it in. Three or four times. Then I got a strike. At least that's what I thought. This is a big one. I remember I said that."

"And?" Cullen said.

"It was a snag. A snag. But there's no snags in that hole. Unless something drifted in since I was there last." Bilkey stopped. He took off his glasses and studied them.

Burr saw Bilkey's eyes sink into their sockets. Little beady eyes. *Please put your glasses back on.*

At last, Bilkey finished studying whatever it was he was studying and put his glasses back on. He looked at Cullen. "I figured that my fly must be hung up on the anchor chain of that damn boat, which of course is upstream from the boat. I could have broken the fly off, but I tied it myself. I was really mad at whoever left that boat there."

Burr started to stand up and object, but he saw Cullen fuming. He thought it best to let the prosecutor stew in his own juices.

"Please continue, Mr. Bilkey," Cullen said.

Bilkey looked at Cullen like he was ruining his tale of the snagged fly. "I knew I wasn't going to catch anything there, so I thought I'd just wade out there and get my fly. I figured it was hung up on the anchor chain, and I thought I'd just reach down and get my fly off. And if the boat moves, who cares. There was nobody around anyway." Bilkey stopped again.

"Please, Mr. Bilkey. Continue."

"I waded out there. It was getting deep, almost over my waders. Finally, I got there. I looked down and the chain disappears, and I can't see my fly. I reach down, but I can't get reach down far enough without filling up my waders."

"Mr. Bilkey," Cullen said.

"So then I worked my way downstream along my fly line. Down to the leader. And then I had a hold of the chain. I got it up enough to reach my fly."

Bilkey stopped again. There wasn't a sound in the courtroom.

"I see it. There's my Wooly Bugger. But it's not caught on the chain. It's hooked on a man." Bilkey stopped again. "On his cheek." Bilkey touched his own cheek. "Just below his eye."

A woman in the gallery let out a little scream.

"The barb was buried in his cheek. His arms floated to the surface, and they're waving in the current." Bilkey waved his own arms like the body waved. "His eyes were bulging out of their sockets. And there were leeches on him. Leeches on his face but mostly on his lips. It was awful."

Lizzie buried her head in her hands.

Cullen stood off to the side of Bilkey, pleased with himself. Skinner looked over the courtroom. "Mr. Cullen, do you have anything further?"

"Yes, Your Honor. Mr. Bilkey, what was the condition of the man you found?"

"He was dead."

"Did you know the dead man?"

"No. Well, who knows? I might have, but he was so disfigured, I don't think I would have known him if I'd known him."

Cullen shook his head. "Mr. Bilkey, what did you do next? After you found a dead man in the river?"

"I got out of there as fast as I could. I ran to my car, went to a gas station and called the police."

"Then what?"

"I waited at the gas station. Then I took them down to the river."

"Then?"

"Then they took down my name and address and said I could go."

"Thank you, Mr. Bilkey. No further questions."

Bilkey had taken the long way around, but Cullen had gotten what he wanted. Burr pushed his wobbly chair back carefully. He walked up to Bilkey. "Mr. Bilkey, what do you do for a living?"

"Objection, Your Honor. Irrelevant," Cullen said.

"I'll allow it," the judge said.

Skinner turned to Bilkey. "You may answer the question."

"I'm a pharmaceutical sales rep."

"You sell drugs. Is that right?" Burr said.

"I call on physicians."

"And what is your territory?" Burr said.

"Northern Michigan. Everything from Clare to the bridge."

"So you have a full-time job?"

"That's right."

"But you were fishing on Monday, which is a workday. Is that right?"

Bilkey squirmed in his chair. "It's on the way."

"I wasn't aware that the South Branch of the Au Sable River was close to a doctor's office."

Cullen popped up. "This has nothing to do with anything."

"You may continue, Mr. Lafayette, but you need to show the relevance."

"Yes, Your Honor." Burr turned to the witness. "Mr. Bilkey, you were playing hooky that Monday morning." Burr paused, turned and looked at the gallery. "You went fishing and you snagged your fly."

"That's right."

"You testified that you snagged your fly on Mr. Shepherd. You were too shocked to help Mr. Shepherd. You were too shocked to see if there was any life left in him. Instead you ran for a phone." Burr paused and pulled his cuffs down again. "Is that right?"

"He was dead," Bilkey said, squirming.

"That's not what I asked."

Bilkey sat stone still in his chair.

"Answer the question, Mr. Bilkey," Skinner said.

"I went to get help."

"Mr. Bilkey, did you get your Woolly Bugger back?"

"I did."

"You didn't have the presence of mind to try to help Mr. Shepherd, but you had the time to rip your fly out of Mr. Shepherd's cheek."

Bilkey squirmed again.

"Is that right?"

"Objection," Cullen said.

Skinner pointed at Burr. "Approach the bench." Then he pointed at Cullen. "You, too."

Cullen stood in front of the judge. Burr joined him.

"What exactly do the two of you think you're doing?"

Burr had learned from situations like this that it was best not to say anything. He was quite sure that standing quietly and looking at his shoes was the best strategy.

The prosecutor had another plan. "Your Honor. As you know, in a murder case, there needs to be a body."

"Jack, you could have simply asked him if he found a dead man."

"I was establishing where he was found."

"And we didn't need all the fishing," Skinner said. "And you, Lafayette. What difference does it make what he does for a living?"

Burr looked up from his shoes. He thought it was time to answer.

"Your Honor, I don't believe that Mr. Bilkey is credible. And he never should have disturbed the body by removing the fly."

Skinner leaned over the rostrum to Burr and Cullen. "Listen to me, both of you," he said in a gravelly whisper. "All that needed to be done was to show that Quinn Shepherd was dead. Nothing more. No two-tracks. No flies. No snags. No arm waving. No jobs. Just a dead man. That's all we needed. You could have stipulated to it." The judge sat back down in his chair. "Do I make myself clear?"

"Yes, Your Honor," Cullen said.

"Yes, Your Honor. I have no further questions," Burr said. He walked back to the defense table and sat down. *If there was a trial, and if Cullen could shorten Bilkey's testimony without losing the leeches and the arm waving, Lizzie will be in serious trouble with the jury right from the start.*

"Call your next witness."

"The prosecution calls Sheriff Earl Starkweather."

Burr watched a thick man of about sixty settle into the witness chair. He had on his uniform, a dark brown shirt, tan slacks, and a shiny badge pinned to his chest. What struck Burr were the Sheriff's eyes. Or, rather, his eyelids. They were so droopy that they hung over the corners of his eyes. They made him look like he'd been sleeping.

Cullen approached Starkweather. "Sheriff, how long have you lived in Crawford County?"

"My whole life. Except for two years in the Army."

"And how long have you been sheriff?"

"Twenty-three years. I was a deputy for eight years before that."

Judge Skinner took off his glasses and looked at the prosecutor. "Mr. Cullen, I don't want to be presumptuous or do your work for you, but if we don't get on with this, it will be deer season before we know it." The judge looked at the sheriff, then back at Cullen. "Do I make myself clear?"

"Not exactly, Your Honor."

"I'll make it simple for you." Judge Skinner swiveled his head to the sheriff. "Earl, was Quinn, Mr. Shepherd, dead when you found him?"

"Yes."

Skinner turned back to Cullen and Burr. "Gentlemen, we have a body." Then to the sheriff, "Earl, you're excused."

"Your Honor—" Cullen said.

"Mr. Cullen, this is a preliminary exam, not a trial. We have a body. That's all we need." Skinner waved his glasses at the prosecutor. "Call your next witness."

Cullen stood. "The State calls Norwynn Potter."

"If that was my name, I'd change it," Burr said under his breath. He turned to Lizzie. "Who is he?"

"I don't know."

Burr watched a bull of a man lumber to the witness stand. He had a barrel chest, arms like tree trunks and a beer belly. His black hair and beard both needed a trim. *How can anybody who looks like that and has a name like Norwynn get through life without fighting every other day?*

The bailiff, dwarfed by the witness, swore Potter in. Potter sat and grabbed at the railing in front of him. His hands looked like baseball mitts. *What can he possibly have to do with Quinn Shepherd?*

Potter wore a white shirt that was too tight. If he sneezed, the buttons on his shirt would pop and somebody in the front row would lose an eye. He didn't have on a tie, but he'd buttoned his shirt all the way to the top. At least it looked that way; it was hard to tell because his beard hung over his collar.

"Mr. Potter, please tell the court what you do for a living."

"A living?" Potter's voice boomed like the horn on a semi.

"Your job."

"I don't have a job."

Cullen started over. "Mr. Potter, do you work?"

"Yeah."

"Where do you work?"

"I don't work. I own the Two Track."

"Is that the Two Track Tavern? On M-72, on the way to the Chase Bridge?"

"It depends on which way you're coming from."

Cullen bit his cheek.

"You said you own the Two Track Tavern?"

"Yeah."

"And is it between The Gray Drake and Chase Bridge?"

"Yeah."

Cullen needs more practice with Potter, too, but then again, this might be the best Potter can do.

"Thank you, Mr. Potter." Cullen continued, "And is the Two Track Inn a tavern?"

"It's a bar."

"Of course, it is."

"We serve food," Potter said. "Hamburgers mostly."

"Of course, you do," Cullen said. "Were you at the Two Track on Saturday night of June 21st, the night Mr. Shepherd died?"

"I'm there every night."

Burr leaned over to Lizzie. "Are you sure you don't know why Potter is here?" he said under his breath.

Lizzie shook her head.

"Is that a yes or a no?" Burr started chewing on his own cheek, then stopped himself. He looked back at Cullen and Potter.

"Mr. Potter," Cullen said, "on the night in question, was Mr. Shepherd at the Two Track?"

"Yeah."

"And who was he with?"

"Some woman."

"Was the woman his wife?"

"Not at first."

Burr leaned back to Lizzie. "I thought you said you didn't know him."

"I don't."

Burr didn't like the way this was headed. Cullen started over. *Apparently, he didn't like the way this was headed either, but for different reasons.*

"Mr. Potter, when you first saw Mr. Shepherd that night, who was he with?"

"A woman."

"And was that woman Mrs. Shepherd?"

"No."

"Mr. Potter, what was that woman's name?"

"I don't know."

"Who was she?"

"I don't know."

"Mr. Cullen," Judge Skinner said, "perhaps you could ask Mr. Potter just to tell us what happened. In his own words."

Cullen looked up at Skinner. "Yes, Your Honor. I was just about to do that." Cullen turned back to the man of few words. "Mr. Potter, would you please tell us, in your own words, what happened in the Two Track that night."

Potter looked at him, but he didn't say anything.

"Just as it relates to Mr. Shepherd."

"Oh," Potter said. "Well, Quinn comes in and sits in the corner. Where it's dark. He orders a shot. Then another one. He starts to get up when this woman comes over and sits next to him. Right next to him. She's a looker. In her own way. He doesn't act too happy to see her. He orders another shot. She puts her hand on his hand, then she whispers in his ear. And then his wife comes in."

"Whose wife?"

Potter looked at Cullen like he was a fool.

"Quinn's wife. Her." He pointed at Lizzie with a finger the size of a hot dog. "Anyway, she sees them in the corner and heads straight over. Before

I know it, there's shouting and screaming and chairs getting knocked over."
Potter gripped the rail again. His knuckles turned white. "They were starting
to go at it."

"Who was?"

"The two chicks."

"Do you mean the woman and Mrs. Shepherd?"

"Yeah."

"Then what happened?"

"Then I threw all three of them out."

Cullen nodded. "Did you hear Mrs. Shepherd say anything?"

Potter started to answer, but Cullen held up his own hand, tiny in compar-
ison to Potter's, and stopped him. "Before you threw them out."

Potter pointed at Lizzie again. "She said, 'If I ever see you with her
again, it will be the last time.'"

"Did you think Mrs. Shepherd might get violent?"

"Yeah."

"Objection," Burr said. He had to stop this, and Cullen had just given
him an opening. "The witness can't know what Mrs. Shepherd might have
done."

"I'll rephrase the question, Your Honor." Cullen flashed his teeth at Burr.
Then he turned to the witness, "Did she seem serious? Like she meant it?"

"Seemed that way to me."

"Then what happened?"

"She slapped him, and I threw 'em all out."

"Thank you, Mr. Potter," Cullen said. "Had you ever seen Mr. Shepherd
and this woman in the Two Track before?"

"Yeah. Plenty of times."

"How many, would you say?"

"Two or three. Maybe more."

"And were they affectionate? Did they seem fond of each other? Like
boyfriend and girlfriend."

"Yeah."

"Would you say they were having an affair?"

"Objection, Your Honor."

"In your opinion."

"I'd say so."

"Nothing further."

"Is this true?" Burr mouthed to Lizzie.

She whispered back, "Not the way he said it."

"It's so wonderful to be lied to by my clients," Burr said, under his breath. He stood and approached Potter, but stopped about six feet from him. "Mr. Potter," he said softly, "is it loud in the Two Track?"

"What's that?"

Burr spoke a little louder. "Is it loud in the Two Track?"

"What?"

"Speak up, Lafayette," Skinner said. "Norwynn can't hear you."

"That's right, Your Honor. He's deaf as a stone. He's so deaf, I doubt he could hear what anyone said to anyone in the bar," Burr said.

"I'm sure he could hear a screaming woman," Cullen said.

"I object, Your Honor," Burr said.

"Continue, Mr. Lafayette."

Burr spoke louder. "Mr. Potter, do you have a band in your bar on Saturday night?"

"Yeah."

"Are they loud?"

"Yeah. Kinda."

"Mr. Potter, is it possible you didn't hear Mrs. Shepherd clearly?"

"I know what I saw. And if looks could kill, he'd have been dead right then and there."

"Your Honor, I submit that Mr. Potter's testimony should be deemed unreliable. It was dark and he has hearing problems."

"Do you have anything further, Mr. Lafayette?"

"No, Your Honor."

Burr walked back to the defense table and sat. He was disgusted with himself, not because of Potter's answer but for his own stupidity. He should have stopped questioning Potter sooner. Jacob looked at him like he had just tipped over the punch bowl. Burr looked over at Cullen, who silently mouthed, *Thank you.*

"Mr. Lafayette and Mr. Wertheim, and you, too, Mr. Cullen. If the three of you are quite through with your little pantomime, I would like to continue. It is getting on to lunch."

Cullen called Joseph Gleason. He had unfashionably long brown hair, swept back over his head and curled over his collar. He had on a seersucker suit that must have cost at least two thousand dollars. *He either has money or knows where to get it.*

The bailiff swore in Gleason.

"Mr. Gleason, would you please tell us where you were the night of June 21st?"

"I was at the charity auction at The Gray Drake."

"And what did you do after the auction?"

"I went into the bar for a nightcap and then up to bed."

Cullen nodded knowingly. "So you stayed at The Gray Drake that night?"

"I did." Gleason stretched his arms and showed off gold cufflinks.

"Would you please tell us which room you stayed in."

"I was in my room, the one I always stay in. Number Sixteen. It's on the second floor. At the end of the hall, overlooking the river."

"Thank you, Mr. Gleason." Cullen beamed.

Gleason was the first of Cullen's witnesses who was actually following the script.

"Please tell us what you saw that night," Cullen said.

"Well, as I get a bit older, I have to get up during the night. Once or twice." It was Skinner's turn to smile. "Anyway, it was the second time I got up, about three in the morning, I'd say. I went down the hall. That's how they do it at The Gray Drake. Great place, but old-fashioned. Part of its charm, I guess. Anyway, when I got back to my room, I looked out the window and saw somebody coming up the path from the grass lot, the overflow lot off to the east."

"And who was it?"

Gleason lost his smile. "It was Lizzie. Lizzie Shepherd."

This can't be good.

"Was she with anyone?"

"No, she was by herself," Gleason said.

"And what was her demeanor?"

Gleason looked at Cullen like he needed a translation.

"Her actions. How was she walking. Her body language."

"Oh," Gleason said. "She was walking carefully, I'd say. Like she was sneaking."

"Objection," Burr said.

"Overruled. Continue Mr. Cullen," Skinner said.

"And then what happened?"

"I got right up next to the window and looked down. I watched her look around, and then she went around to the back and I lost sight of her. But I heard the back door close."

"No further questions, Your Honor." Cullen took his seat.

Burr walked up to the witness. "Mr. Gleason, may I ask what business you're in."

"I sell oil and gas interests through my company, Michigan Crude."

"Mr. Gleason, how do you know it was three a.m. when you saw Mrs. Shepherd?"

"I always wear my watch." Gleason showed off his watch, a gold Rolex on his left wrist.

That watch cost more than my Jeep.

"Mr. Gleason, are you nearsighted?"

"Yes," he said. "Yes, I am."

"Do you wear glasses?"

"Yes."

"And did you have your glasses on when you got up to relieve yourself?"

Gleason took a pair of glasses out of his inside jacket pocket and looked at them. "I don't remember."

Burr gave Gleason a steely look. "Then how can you be sure it was Mrs. Shepherd?"

"It was her." Gleason put his glasses back on.

"Mr. Gleason," Burr said, "assuming it was Mrs. Shepherd, is it possible that Mrs. Shepherd had been in the lodge, gotten up and gone to her car to get something?" Burr paused. "And you saw her when she was returning to the lodge?"

Gleason didn't say a word.

"Mr. Gleason, please answer the question."

"I saw what I saw."

"No further questions, Your Honor."

CHAPTER FOUR

"Call your next witness, Mr. Cullen." Skinner looked at the prosecutor's table, but there was no sign of him. He peered over the bench. "Mr. Cullen, what in the name of Mike are you doing under the table?"

Cullen was crouching under the prosecution's table with a package wrapped in brown paper. Cullen sat back up in his chair.

"There you are," the judge said. "Look here, it's lunch time. Are you quite through?"

"Not quite, Your Honor."

Whatever Cullen had been fiddling with was now on his table. The mystery package was about three-feet long, a foot wide, wrapped in plain brown paper and tied with a string. Cullen stood. "The State calls Margaret Winston."

Burr watched a vision of beauty walk to the witness stand. Willowy thin, but not starved. He thought she was in her late thirties. The adolescent bailiff, clearly taken with her, stuttered as he swore her in. She sat and crossed her long legs and pulled her navy-blue skirt down a quarter of an inch. She had no makeup except for rose lipstick, and sky-blue eyes behind glasses with black frames. *Her eyes are the same color as mine, but her glasses look a bit thick.*

"Ms. Winston." Cullen didn't seem nearly as taken with the witness as Burr and the bailiff. "Can you tell us what you were doing on the morning of May 9th of this year?"

"I was looking for woodcock nests."

"Woodcock?"

"In Crawford County," she said in a throaty voice. *An alto no doubt.* "There are a great many nesting woodcock."

"I see. And where were you?" Cullen said.

"On the east side of the South Branch. Near the river."

"And did you find anything other than woodcock nests?"

"I did."

Cullen looked like he was pleased with himself and the way this was all going. He strutted back to his table, picked up the mystery package, and walked back to Ms. Winston. He made a show of untying the string, which he rolled into a ball and stuck in his left jacket pocket. He unwrapped the brown paper, carefully. Very carefully.

"Mr. Cullen, unless I am grossly mistaken, Crawford County has a more than adequate budget for office supplies."

"Your Honor?"

"Get on with it."

"Yes, Your Honor." Cullen placed himself so that no one except the witness could see what he was holding. He took a quarter turn so the judge could see what he was holding. Burr still couldn't see what it was. *He's doing that on purpose.*

"What is that?" Judge Skinner said.

"Your Honor," Cullen said. "I am holding the murder weapon."

Burr jumped up. "Objection, Your Honor." He still couldn't see whatever it was, but he was damned if he'd let this go on any longer.

"Mr. Lafayette, there is no jury here, and I am not likely to be prejudiced by Mr. Cullen's theatrics," Skinner said.

"Your Honor, the State introduces this canoe paddle as People's Exhibit A."

"Mr. Lafayette?"

Burr stood and walked slowly to Cullen, who handed him the paddle. The blade was splintered along one edge and had a three-inch gash. "QS" had been carved into the throat of the paddle.

"Bailiff, enter this as evidence," Skinner said.

"I have no objection." Burr walked back to his table and sat.

"Thank you, Your Honor," Cullen said. "Ms. Winston, please tell us when and where you found this canoe paddle."

Margaret Winston nodded. "I was near the South Branch looking for nesting woodcock when I found this paddle." She stopped and pointed a long finger at it.

"Where was the paddle?"

"It was near the bank. By some dogwood." She took off her glasses, looked through each lens, then put them back on.

"And what did you do with the paddle after you found it?"

"I took it home and forgot about it. But then I remembered hearing about a man drowning on the river last year. So, I looked up the name, and I saw his name was Quinn Shepherd. I looked at the paddle again and thought the letters on the paddle might be his initials." She drew "QS" with her forefinger in front of her. "I thought it might be important, so I took it to the sheriff's office in Grayling."

"Then what happened?"

"That was the last I saw of it." She clasped her hands together and put them on her lap.

"Your witness," Cullen said.

Burr walked up to Ms. Winston. He hoped she kept her hands in her lap. She was easy on the eye, but he didn't like her as much as he did before he found out about the canoe paddle. "Ms. Winston, what do you do for a living?"

"I'm a professor of ornithology at the University of Michigan."

"So it's really doctor, not Ms.?"

"It's both." She made a two with the fingers of her left hand. Burr saw that she wasn't wearing a wedding ring.

"Professionally speaking, you are a doctor," Burr said.

"I am a professor. Professionally speaking, it is doctor."

"Are you a full professor?"

"I am."

"Well done," Burr said, smiling.

Dr. Winston did not smile back at him.

"Dr. Winston, are woodcock your specialty?"

"No."

"I see. And what may I ask is your specialty?"

"The Kirtland's warbler."

"But you were studying woodcock that day."

"I was."

"And why were you doing that near the South Branch?"

"I volunteer with the Department of Natural Resources. There are usually nests there."

"I see," Burr said, who didn't. "And how do you find the nests?"

"I use my dog."

"Your dog?"

She nodded at him. "It's next to impossible to find woodcock without a dog. To a dog, a woodcock smells to high heaven."

Burr's grandmother was the last person he'd heard say "smells to high heaven," and that was at least thirty years ago. He smiled to himself, then he said, "What kind of dog do you have?"

"Mr. Lafayette, how can it possibly matter what kind of dog Dr. Winston has?" Skinner said.

"It may be important, Your Honor."

Skinner shook his head. "You may answer the question."

"She's an English setter," Dr. Winston said.

"Thank you, Professor." Burr thought *professor* had a better ring to it than *doctor* and certainly better than *Ms*. "And your dog's name?"

"Saints preserve us," Skinner said.

"Finn. Her name is Finn."

"And Finn finds the woodcock nests, I assume."

"She does."

"Does Finn point them?"

She nodded.

Burr thrust his hands in his pants pockets and rocked back and forth. "So you were searching for woodcock nests near the river, and you found this alleged canoe paddle."

"Objection, Your Honor," Cullen said. "It's not an alleged canoe paddle. It is, in fact, a canoe paddle."

"Sustained." Skinner looked at Burr. "Would you please get to the point?"

"Yes, Your Honor." Burr looked back at the professor. "So Finn points the nests."

"Actually, she's pointing the woodcock sitting on their nests."

"Of course. And Finn is running around in the woods pointing the wood-cock sitting on their nests."

"That's right."

"And while she was doing that, you found the canoe paddle."

"Yes."

"In some dogwood near the river."

"Yes."

"Was it wet near the river?"

"Yes."

"Did your feet get wet?"

"I had on hip boots."

Burr moved in for what he hoped would be the kill. "Professor Winston, did you find the paddle in the dogwood, or did Finn find the paddle and bring it back to you?"

Professor Winston started to turn red. "Finn brought it back."

"Professor Winston, did you actually see Finn find the paddle, or did she just show up with it?"

"She brought it back from the dogwood next to the river."

"I thought you said you found it by the dogwood." Her ears were turning red.

"My dog found the paddle. She was by the dogwood when she gave it to me."

"Professor Winston, is it possible that Finn found the paddle somewhere else and the first time you saw her with it was at the dogwood?"

"No."

"Objection, Your Honor. This is irrelevant," Cullen said.

"Your Honor," Burr said, "for all we know, the dog took the paddle from another boat on the river, and brought it back along the bank, to the dogwood."

"That is not what happened," Dr. Winston said.

"It doesn't matter at all where the dog found the paddle," Cullen said.

"There is no way to know when the paddle was found or how it got there. For all we know, it could have been planted there. Your Honor, I object to the admission of the canoe paddle as evidence."

"I'm going to allow it. Do you have anything further, Mr. Lafayette?"

"No, Your Honor."

"Mr. Cullen, call your next witness."

"The State calls Boyd Wilcox."

A Michigan State Police sergeant in uniform marched to the witness stand. The sergeant turned and faced the gallery. He was short and thick, and had a square face below a blond flattop that you could land an airplane on. He had wire-rimmed glasses plastered on his face like they'd been surgically implanted.

The bailiff swore in the witness.

Cullen walked up to the witness box. "Sergeant Wilcox, would you please tell the court where you work and what you do."

"I work in the crime lab at State Police headquarters in East Lansing," Wilcox said, squeaking.

How could this fireplug of a man have a voice like a chipmunk?

"And what do you do in the crime lab?"

"I work on the evidence in criminal cases. I identify the salient characteristics of evidence and associate them with crimes."

Cullen chewed on his lower lip, this clearly too abstract to be of much use. He walked over to the evidence table and picked up the canoe paddle. "Sergeant, did you examine this canoe paddle?"

"I did."

"And what exactly did you do?"

"I examined the jagged edge of the canoe paddle."

Cullen ran his forefinger over the damaged part of the blade. "Here?"

"That's right."

"Sergeant Wilcox, did you find anything of interest on the damaged area?"

"I found strands of human hair tangled in the splintered area."

"Really?" Cullen said. "Human hair."

Burr was afraid he knew what was coming next.

"Sergeant, do you know whose hair it was?"

"It belonged to the deceased. Quinn Shepherd."

Whatever noise there was in the courtroom stopped. It was so quiet Burr could hear his teeth grinding.

"And how do you know it was Mr. Shepherd's hair?"

Wilcox pushed his glasses even more firmly onto his face. *If he pushes them in any more, he'll never get them off.* Then the Sergeant said, "I compared what I found on the paddle to known samples of Mr. Shepherd's hair."

"And they matched."

"They did."

"Are you absolutely sure?"

"There is no doubt in my mind."

"Thank you, Sergeant." Cullen turned to Burr. Burr thought the prosecutor looked like a self-righteous Cheshire cat. The prosecutor turned back to Wilcox. "Sergeant. How do you think the hair got on the paddle?"

Wilcox cleared his throat, but it didn't improve his voice. "I believe Mr. Shepherd was struck with the canoe paddle. A forcible blow that shattered this edge of the blade. Some of Mr. Shepherd's hair got bound up in the splinters."

"Nothing further, Your Honor," Cullen said.

"Your witness, Mr. Lafayette."

"Lizzie," Burr whispered, "did you go back to the river that night?"

"No. No, I didn't."

"Is that Quinn's paddle?"

Lizzie nodded.

"If you don't have any questions for Sergeant Wilcox, Mr. Lafayette, I am going to dismiss him so we can have lunch," the judge said.

Burr stood up.

"Sergeant Wilcox, do you have a college education?"

"Objection, Your Honor. The sergeant is an expert," Cullen said.

"An expert's qualifications are always subject to review," Burr said, starting toward the witness stand.

"Stop right there," Judge Skinner said. "For purposes of this hearing, I take judicial notice that the sergeant is, indeed, an expert."

"Thank you, Your Honor," Burr said. He turned to Wilcox.

"Sergeant, where, may I ask, did you get the hair samples from Mr. Shepherd that you used to compare to the hair found on the paddle?"

"From a hat that belonged to Mr. Shepherd."

"I see. And was there a search warrant to obtain Mr. Shepherd's hair?"

Wilcox replastered his glasses. "No."

"Your Honor, I submit that this evidence was illegally obtained. This is a clear violation of the constitutional right to privacy. Your Honor, I move that Sergeant Wilcox's testimony be stricken."

"Mr. Cullen?"

"The hat was hanging on a hook in the guide's room at The Gray Drake. The constitutional protection does not extend to evidence found in public places."

"Your Honor, the deceased had a legitimate expectation to privacy in the guide's room."

"Mr. Shepherd was dead," Cullen said.

"Your Honor, this violates every canon of the rules of evidence. Not to mention the Fourth Amendment."

"Mr. Lafayette, for purposes of the preliminary examination, I am going to allow all of the testimony of Mr. Wilcox. Do you have anything further?"

Burr turned and walked back to the defense table. He rummaged through his papers, found what he was looking for and held it up to Skinner. "Your Honor, the defense introduces the written report of the inquest as Defense Exhibit One."

The prosecutor looked down his nose at Burr. "I have no objection, Your Honor."

Burr walked up to Wilcox. "Sergeant, are you familiar with the findings of the county medical examiner as written in the inquest?"

"I am."

"And what did the coroner have to say about the cause of death?"

"Death by drowning."

"And did he say anything about the blood alcohol of the deceased?"

"I'm not sure."

"Let me refresh your memory. Dr. Fowler determined that Mr. Shepherd had a blood alcohol level of point one six." He looked up at Wilcox. "Twice the legal limit for driving a car. Dr. Fowler also noted the injury to Mr. Shepherd's head. Are you aware of that?"

"I don't remember."

"Read this." Burr handed him the report. "Start right here." He pointed about halfway down the page.

"Objection, Your Honor. Counsel is badgering the witness."

"The expert witness seems to have a poor memory."

Judge Skinner turned to the witness. "Sergeant, please read from the report."

"The deceased had a contusion on the right posterior portion of his skull, consistent with striking his head on the rail of his boat. He—"

"Stop right there." Burr took the report back. "Dr. Fowler, who examined the body immediately after it was found, determined that Mr. Shepherd was intoxicated. He got himself tangled in the anchor chain and then banged his head on the rail of his boat and knocked himself unconscious. He fell in the river where he drowned. Is that right?"

"That's not what happened," Wilcox said.

"But that is exactly what the autopsy done by the coroner says happened."

"Yes, but that is not what happened," Wilcox said again.

"Is that what the autopsy says happened?"

"Yes," Wilcox said.

"*Could* it have happened that way?"

"I suppose so, but the canoe paddle changes everything."

"Sergeant Wilcox, how could a canoe paddle stay in the river all winter, with rain, snow, and ice, and still have hair on it. Wouldn't it be washed clean by then?"

"Not necessarily."

"Sergeant, did you find the canoe paddle in the river?"

"No."

"Did you retrieve Mr. Shepherd's hat from the guide's room?"

"No."

"Sergeant, let's assume that you found the evidence on the paddle and the hat. Just as you say you did."

"That's exactly—"

Burr raised his hand to the now not-so-confident witness. "And let's assume that the hair on the paddle matches the hair on the hat." Burr stopped. "Even if all that's true, isn't it possible that someone put the hair on the paddle after it was found?"

"No."

"Oh, but it is," Burr said. "There was no control in the chain of evidence, was there?"

Wilcox sat there. Then he nodded.

"Sergeant?"

"No, there wasn't."

"Do you have anything further, Mr. Lafayette?"

"No, Your Honor."

Cullen stood up.

"Sit down, Jack."

"I have a closing argument."

"You don't need one." Skinner took off his glasses. "The court finds that there is probable cause that Elizabeth Shepherd murdered her husband, Quinn Shepherd, on the night of June 21, 1989. Elizabeth Shepherd, you are hereby charged with open murder. Bail is continued." Skinner banged his gavel.

Tears started to run down Lizzie's face. She didn't wipe them off. Jacob handed her his handkerchief.

"I object, Your Honor," Cullen said. "The defendant should not be out on bail when she's just been charged with murder."

The judge put his glasses back on. "Come up here, Mr. Cullen." He pointed at Cullen. "You too, Lafayette."

The two litigants stood before the judge. "She has a little boy. She isn't going anywhere. Quinn was probably the best fly fisherman I've ever known. I don't know what kind of husband he was. And now it's lunchtime. As for you, Mr. Lafayette, you are, without a doubt, the most argumentative lawyer I have ever had in my courtroom. I am delighted that I will never have to see you again. We are adjourned." Skinner banged his gavel and walked back into his chambers.

Lizzie ran out of the courtroom. Burr caught up with her on the courthouse steps and reached for her arm. "Not now," she said.

He followed her and the rest of the unhappy group back to The Gray Drake.

* * *

Burr, Jacob, Wes and Eve sat at a table by the window in the dining room.

Burr looked out the window and watched the river rush by. *It doesn't have a care in the world.*

Despite the fact she had just been indicted for murder, Lizzie started them off with a Washington State pinot noir—light, fruity, and well-matched with her watercress salad, the watercress picked from a cove on the South Branch just before it emptied into the Main Branch. After that, forest-floor soup—leeks and morels in a cream sauce with white wine. Then she served grouse-breast fillets in a cranberry sauce over wild rice and garnished with acorns. Burr had no idea how she could cook like this, or cook at all, after being indicted for murder. She stayed as far away from him as she could all through lunch, and then disappeared out the back door.

After lunch, Burr and Zeke followed Wes past the guides' room, down a hall, and finally to Wes's office. Wes sat behind a roll-top desk that faced the river. Two mahogany-colored leather wing chairs sat in front of the desk. Leaded windows ran the length of the wall that looked out on the river. The rest of the room was paneled in cedar. A worn Oriental rug covered most of the hardwood floor. Behind the desk, a fireplace stood between floor-to-ceiling bookshelves. The room smelled of cedar and leather.

Burr felt right at home. He took a seat in the one of the wing chairs. Zeke lay at his feet.

Wes looked up and over his reading glasses. "Now what do we do?"

"Now we're going to have to show it was an accident or figure out who killed Quinn."

Wes took off his reading glasses and looked out the window behind Burr. Burr turned around. A chickadee pecked at sunflower seeds from a birdfeeder.

"They're here all year," Wes said. "And they sing all year round."

Burr nodded.

"I lost my wife twenty-six years ago. Lizzie was seven. She sort of took over for my wife. Not then, but when she got older. I think maybe I should have done a few things differently." Wes stopped. "Don't move. There's a rose-breasted grosbeak out there. A female."

Burr turned around slowly.

"The male is the pretty one. Bright-red breast with a white belly." Wes paused. "I never should have let her marry Quinn."

Burr turned back to Wes, who was still looking out the window. "They have a beautiful song. Like a robin who took singing lessons," Wes said.

Wes looked at Burr. "My grandfather built the lodge in 1917. He named it the Au Sable Fishing and Outing Club. My father added on and changed the name to The Gray Drake. They hatch early in the summer. It's an easy fly to tie and easy to fish."

Wes looked back out the window, then at Burr. "This was all I ever wanted to do. I thought Lizzie would want to take over from me." Wes paused. "But I never asked her."

"I'm sorry all this happened," Burr said. *I'm not sure how much it helps me defend Lizzie.*

Wes nodded, then looked down at his hands.

"Do you have any idea who might have killed Quinn?"

Wes shook his head. "No, I wish I did." He looked back out the window.

"Did Quinn have any enemies?"

"Quinn?" Wes looked back at Burr. "No. No enemies that I know of."

This isn't going anywhere, but I've got to start somewhere.

"Can you give me a list of who was here at the auction?"

"This desk has been here since the lodge was built." Wes rummaged through his desk. Finally, he pulled out three sheets of paper and handed them to Burr.

There were about two hundred names on the list. *I won't get through this in my lifetime.*

"I suppose you'll want to know who else was there. The waitresses. The kitchen help. The string quartet."

"The string quartet?"

"They were quite good. And I suppose you'll want a list of the guides."

This will take two lifetimes. "Can you help me narrow this down?"

"The Gray Drake is a legend, but it's not the money-maker everyone thinks it is. It's old, a little rundown, and it always needs money. We all grew up here. Me. Lizzie. Now Josh."

Wes picked up his reading glasses and tapped them on his desk. "I know I shouldn't have sent you that Sage, but I should have some money by the end of the season."

Too many suspects and no money. He scratched Zeke's ear.

Wes tapped his glasses again and looked over Burr's shoulder. "Now they're both there. The grosbeaks."

Burr turned around, and the birds flew off.

* * *

Burr and Zeke headed for the North Branch. He had a list of the guests, the help, the guides, and no check. He needed to talk to Lizzie, and he was still hoping to get a check from her.

They drove through jack pine, then into aspen, and as they neared the river, hardwoods. Burr stopped three times to look at the directions Wes had scribbled in the margin of the day's menu. Burr had gotten turned around twice. He turned onto a gravel road. Then another, and another. Each one narrower and more rutted than the last. Finally, he turned on a two-track. A quarter mile later, the two-track turned south, and he found a driveway and a sign that read *Hemlock*. He drove another hundred yards and parked in front of a log cabin, but not just any log cabin. This one stood two stories. It had fresh chinking and a cedar shake roof.

They walked up to the house. Burr knocked on the door. No answer. He knocked again. And again. He reached down to scratch Zeke and found him sniffing an English setter, perhaps the most beautiful English setter he had ever seen. A tri-color. Black, chestnut and white. She had a black patch on her left ear, and long feathers on her legs and tail. The setter barked at him. "It's all right, girl." He bent down, and she came up to him. He scratched her ear, and she wagged her tail.

"You must be Cassie."

She ignored him and trotted off, around the side of the house. Zeke, smitten, followed, as did Burr, equally smitten. They found Lizzie sitting in an Adirondack chair looking at the river, her back to them.

"Cassie, where'd you go?"

"She was with us."

Lizzie jumped up. "My God, you scared me."

Burr walked past her to the river. The cabin had been built on a bend, a soft curve from south to east. The bank was about ten-feet high. Half-log stairs ran down to a dock. An Au Sable riverboat was tied to the downriver side of the dock. "There should be two boats," Lizzie said, "but one of Starkweather's deputies took *Traveler*. I think I told you that."

Burr looked out at the river. There were fish rising to flies in a pool just downstream.

"Those are caddis coming off," Lizzie said. "They come off most of the summer."

Burr nodded knowingly.

"It's a little early for them."

Burr thought there was a sad quality in her voice, as if what mattered when Quinn was alive didn't matter now. He nodded again. He looked over her shoulder at the cabin behind her. Two-story, plate-glass windows that faced the river. Lizzie joined him on the bank.

"It's beautiful, isn't it?"

"Business must be good at The Gray Drake," Burr said.

"Quinn's father is a generous man, although he never understood why we wanted to live on the North Branch. Quinn wanted to be here because it's out of the way. Away from everything. The fish are a little smaller, but they're all wild. There are big brookies and a few bigger browns. And the aluminum hatch doesn't really get this far north."

"Aluminum hatch?"

"Canoes. I love this place, and so does Josh, but I don't see how we can stay out here by ourselves."

"Where exactly are we?"

"Between Lovells and Jackson Hole. Closer to Lovells."

"It was generous of your father-in-law to post your bail," Burr said.

"Guides don't get rich. Or cooks."

"How did he get his money?"

"Banking."

"He's a banker?"

"His family started it. Now he owns it."

"Which one?"

"Peoples State Bank. It's the only bank in Hamtramck. It's Polish, and the Poles pay their loans on time," Lizzie said.

Burr kicked a stick into the river. He watched the current take it downstream. He heard a splash, and there was Zeke chasing the stick. Cassie watched from the bank. The stick turned around and around in an eddy. The current caught it again and took it downstream, Zeke still after it.

"Zeke. Come!" Burr watched the dog swim downstream after the stick.

"I suppose this isn't a social call," she said.

"It would have been helpful if you'd told me what happened at the Two Track." Burr turned back to Zeke. "He doesn't know a thing about currents." The dog had the stick in his mouth and was trying to swim upstream, but he was falling further and further downstream. *That dog is going to get himself up against a snag and drown.*

Burr started downstream. "Zeke, drop." The dog kept swimming, but he kept slipping further downstream. Burr ran along the edge of the river, his boots splashing. Zeke's head went underwater. He came up with a stick in his mouth, then went down again. Burr waded into the river after him. Zeke came up again. He turned downstream with the current and then to shore. Burr climbed out of the river. Zeke climbed out, shook himself off, ran up to Burr, and presented him the stick. Burr and Zeke followed Lizzie to the deck behind the cabin.

"Feet wet?"

Burr looked down at his feet. There were puddles around his shoes. *How am I going to figure out what happened if I can't even keep my feet dry?*

"It didn't take Zeke long to figure out the river."

"What about Quinn?" Burr said.

"It must have been an accident. I don't know how it could have happened, but it did. Quinn loved the river. He was the best fisherman I ever met, and he was far and away the best guide. He knew the river. He knew the hatches, and he knew where the fish were."

"Why does Cullen think you killed Quinn?"

"I've got to check on the chowder." She handed Burr a towel, opened the sliding glass doors and walked into the house, Cassie at her heels.

Burr dried off Zeke, wiped his boots on the mat and the two of them followed Lizzie and Cassie inside. Lizzie walked through the dining room, past a butcher-block bar and into the kitchen. She stopped at a massive stove, took the top off a soup pot, and stirred whatever was in it. Cassie lay down at Lizzie's feet. The pot smelled like rosemary and basil.

That's an Aga. Then out loud, "There's another thing that cost more than my Jeep."

Lizzie turned to Burr, spoon in hand. "What did you say?"

"That's a very nice stove," Burr said.

"It's an Aga."

Not only did it cost more than my Jeep, it's bigger.

"This is just about ready. It's fish chowder, Manhattan style. Would you like some?"

"I would."

"It needs a few more minutes and a little more basil." She took a step to the cupboard, but tripped over Cassie. "She's been underfoot ever since Quinn's been gone."

"And she was with Quinn that night?"

"Yes."

"How did she get back?"

Lizzie looked at him. "She showed up at the lodge late the next night. She was dirty, worn out and upset."

Burr looked down at the setter. "So she knows what happened."

"I guess she does."

"If only she could talk."

"Quinn said she always knew which holes had fish in them. That's why he called her Cassie. Short for Cassandra, in Greek mythology. Now all she does is bark." Lizzie reached into the cupboard and took out a jar of basil. "Cassandra could see into the future." Lizzie unscrewed the top and shook some of the spice into the chowder. She stirred, then sipped a spoonful. "A little more rosemary, I think." Two shakes of rosemary later, "It's Josh's favorite." She stirred the spices into the chowder.

"Where is Josh?"

"Quinn's father's house."

Burr walked up to the maple bar and sat on a stool. "The question isn't whether or not Quinn drowned. The question is, was it an accident or was it murder?"

"It was an accident. It must have been."

"That's not what Cullen thinks."

"Let's start at the auction," Burr said. "Did anything happen? Was anyone mad at Quinn? Did he fight with anyone?"

She stopped stirring. "No. Not that I know of. But I was in and out of the kitchen all night. I didn't see everything. I have no idea who would want to kill him." She looked at Burr. "I don't know what happened, and I need you to help me."

Burr looked down at the butcher block, the grain swirled and twisted. "All right then, what happened at the auction? Who bid on Quinn's trip?"

"Five or six guys, I think."

"Do you remember who they were?"

"A judge. A car guy. Three or four oil men. Quinn's dad."

"Who was the high bidder?"

Lizzie filled a mug with the chowder and handed it to Burr. "Be careful, it's hot."

Burr sipped and burned his tongue. "Too late," he said. He stirred his chowder. "Who was the high bidder?" Burr said again.

"Who won?" Lizzie chewed her lip. "Harley. He outbid Thompson."

"Harley?"

"Harley Hawken. He's an oil man from Traverse City."

"How much did he pay?"

"Twelve thousand."

"Dollars?"

"It was for charity." Lizzie got a mug out for herself.

"Who is Harley?"

"He made a lot of money in the Niagran."

"The Niagran?"

"It's a geologic formation around here. They're all around and they're full of oil. My father raises money to protect the river. Partly from drilling."

"Isn't it a bit ironic that an oil man would bid at an auction that would make it harder for him to drill for oil?"

"Quinn wasn't just any guide." Lizzie sipped on her chowder. "And it wasn't just any guided trip. It was the Hex hatch."

Burr took a spoonful of the chowder. It was full of tomatoes and spice. He blew on it, then slurped it off the spoon. *This was worth the drive.* He took a deep breath, "What did you do after the auction?"

"The auction ended about ten-thirty. Quinn was all wound up, and the hatch was on. So he wanted to fish it. I said I'd put Josh to bed, and my father would keep an eye on him until we got back to the lodge when he was done."

"What about the Two Track?" Burr said.

"We let him stay up for the auction. It usually takes a long time to get Josh to go to sleep. Stories, songs, prayers. He was wound up, but he fell right asleep. So I left. I saw the truck parked at the Two Track. Quinn was sitting over in the corner with that woman. When Quinn saw me come in, he got up and left. I followed him to Chase Bridge, and we launched the boat. That was the last time I ever saw him."

"I can't help you if you lie to me."

"I'm not lying."

"Potter said you fought with that woman at the Two Track."

"He's exaggerating."

"Why would he do that?"

"I don't know. He doesn't like us. He thinks we look down on him."

"Is that a good enough reason to say what he said?"

"Burr, please help me. I'm not lying."

Burr wasn't so sure. "Who was that woman?"

"I don't know."

"Had you ever seen her before?"

"I don't think so."

"You don't think so?"

"I don't remember seeing her until that night, but there's always people coming and going at the lodge. Especially at the auction."

"Did you ask Quinn about her?"

"I asked him at the river."

"What did he say?"

"He said he'd tell me later."

"What did you do?"

"I was mad. I slapped him."

"You slapped him?"

"It was the last thing I ever did." She paused. "He said there were things I didn't know, and he'd tell me later."

Burr didn't know whether to believe her or not.

"After I was done moving the trailer, I went back to the lodge. That's when Joe Gleason saw me." She reached down and petted Cassie.

Burr stirred his chowder again. He came up with a chunk of fish.

"It's brook trout," she said.

"Brook trout? In fish chowder?" Burr cocked his head to the side.

"Quinn kept a fish every once in a while. He said fishing was a blood sport."

* * *

Burr followed Lizzie to Thompson Shepherd's house on the South Branch. She had to pick up Josh, and Burr thought this was a foolproof way to find Thompson's house without getting lost. This was as good a time as any to ask Shepherd for a check. After all, Thompson Shepherd was a generous man.

They pulled into a circle drive. A fair stone maiden poured water from an urn into a stone fountain in front of the senior Shepherd's house. Behind the driveway, a two-story log home stood among sixty-foot white pines.

Burr left Zeke in the Jeep and followed Lizzie and Cassie up a brick path to a courtyard. The house had two wings angled away from the river and connected by a great room.

Lizzie knocked.

Thompson Shepherd opened the door.

Cassie barked at him.

"I'm sorry, Thompson. She's still not right."

"I know. I'll get Joshua."

He came back holding Josh by the hand. The boy ran to his mother and hugged her around her legs. Cassie barked again, then licked Josh on the face.

"Mr. Lafayette wants to talk with grandpa for a few minutes."

Josh looked back at his grandfather. "Bye, Grandpa."

"Goodbye, Joshua." The elder Shepherd nodded at Burr. "Please come in."

Burr walked into the foyer—slate flooring and hardwood paneling. Shepherd led him through the great room.

"Let's go down to the river." Burr followed Shepherd to a dock with a boathouse.

"Please sit down," Shepherd said.

Burr sat. He heard the river rushing underneath him.

"I generally don't like surprises, but I'm sure you have a good reason for showing up unannounced."

"I'm sorry to intrude, but I need some help."

Shepherd looked at the river, then back at Burr. "Quinn's mother died twenty-five years ago. I lost my only son. Joshua and Lizzie are all I have left."

"Do you think it was an accident?"

Shepherd looked back to the house again. "Joshua doesn't understand that Quinn is never coming back. Excuse me for a moment." He swatted at a mosquito, then disappeared into the boathouse that wasn't just any boathouse. Burr had seen plenty of houses that were smaller and not nearly as well done.

Shepherd returned with two cigars. He offered one to Burr, who declined. Shepherd sat back down, unwrapped a cigar and cut off the end. He rolled it around in his mouth, then lit it. Shepherd sucked on the cigar, blew the smoke out, then waved the cigar around him.

"Best mosquito repellent there is," Shepherd said. "But it's an expensive use of a Cuban cigar. Quinn was so at home on the river, I don't see how he could have drowned." Shepherd blew out a mouthful of smoke.

"Frankly, Mr. Shepherd, I need a few suspects." Burr coughed and waved the smoke away from his face. He thought he'd rather swat mosquitoes than choke on cigar smoke.

"Everyone loved Quinn." Shepherd pointed at a riffle on the near bank. "Look out there, Mr. Lafayette. Those are caddis coming off. It's mostly blue wings here, but we do have some caddis."

Why does everyone give me a lesson in entomology?

"Quinn and I fished that riffle every year." Shepherd paused. "We'll never do that again."

"I'm sorry, Mr. Shepherd."

"I must say, though, Cullen was persuasive."

"That's exactly why I need a suspect or two."

"If I thought Lizzie killed Quinn, I don't know what I would do. Joshua needs at least one parent."

"Who do you think might have killed Quinn?"

"I'm sorry, but I have no idea."

This isn't going anywhere.

"Mr. Shepherd, I need to find a suspect or two, someone who might have killed Quinn. That's why I'd like you to help pay for Lizzie's defense."

Shepherd sucked on his cigar again. Burr looked down at his slacks and watched a mosquito trying to sting him, right where the crease should have been.

Shepherd blew out more smoke. Burr slapped at the mosquito on his pants.

CHAPTER FIVE

The next afternoon Burr napped in the cockpit of *Spindrift*. The wind blew from the northwest at about fifteen knots, but the old cutter rode quietly on her mooring, sheltered by the bluffs. As luck would have it, the wind was coming from the direction of the late afternoon sun, and Burr, with his head at the cabin end of the cockpit, slept with his head in the shade. Zeke snored on the cockpit sole.

He woke up and propped himself against the cabin side. He ran his hand along the top of the gunwale in the cockpit—silky, varnished mahogany with four coats of Valspar. It would need a light sanding and another coat before the summer was over. He looked over at the teak deck, nicely oiled, which gave it a wet look, then past the tiller and the boom crutch to the harbor, now full of boats on their moorings. After Labor Day, they would all be put away until next year. In June, though, the harbor bustled with the boats owned by those with too much money and not enough sense.

He turned to starboard and looked over at the tip of Harbor Point, to Cottage 59, a magnificent three-story Victorian cottage that fronted both Little Traverse Bay and Lake Michigan. It belonged to his Aunt Kitty, his only living relative save Zeke-the-Boy. He would inherit Cottage 59 at the unfortunate time of his aunt's passing.

"Zeke, the cottage is free and clear. We could borrow against it." Zeke didn't acknowledge his master. "But that might not be such a good idea." Burr watched the patchy, cumulus clouds drift across the sky, turning the water from blue to black and back to blue as they passed overhead. Burr breathed in the lake air. It smelled like pines, sand and fish.

"I never thought for a moment that Skinner would dismiss the murder charge. He would indict Mother Teresa for jaywalking. Now we're going to have to figure out what to do," he said to the snoring dog. He ran his hand along the gunwale again. "But not today." He lay back down and pulled his hat over his eyes.

Burr woke from a most pleasant second nap to the sound of Zeke barking.

"Damn it all," he said. "Now what?" He pushed the bill of his hat off his face and saw Zeke standing on the deck looking over the side and barking. Probably ducks looking for another handout. "Quiet."

Zeke looked over at Burr and gave him an urgent look. He turned his attention and his barking back to whatever it was that was so important.

Burr lay there, then he heard what incensed Zeke. A knocking. It was a knock, knock, knock. Something or someone was rapping on *Spindrift*'s hull. Each time there was a knock, Zeke answered with a bark. Burr sat up.

"Come over here," said a voice.

Burr stayed put. It didn't sound like Jacob.

"This instant."

Burr thought the voice over the side had no understanding that Burr, as master of *Spindrift*, was a law unto himself, at least as far as the confines of his new boat.

"Come over here this minute."

Burr stayed put. The unwelcome visitor rapped. Zeke barked.

At last he could take it no more. He stood up and peered over the port side at a man in a dinghy. "Are you the Fuller Brush man of the nautical world?"

"I beg your pardon."

"Or perhaps you're selling the seafaring Encyclopedia Britannica."

"How dare you," the man said.

Burr took a closer look. Below him sat a severe-looking man in the most magnificent dinghy Burr had ever seen. Two-inch mahogany strips ran from a mahogany transom to a feathered bow covered with at least a dozen coats of varnish over a rich brown stain. He thought that dinghy probably cost more than *Spindrift*. If he was a salesman on the water, he was doing very well indeed.

"That dinghy is a thing of beauty." Now that Burr was fully engaged, Zeke stopped barking, his duty done.

In a white polo, khaki shorts, and Harken sailing shoes, the severe but handsome man looked every bit as good as his dinghy. He was in his mid-fifties with a deep tan, including his forehead. He must not fish, Burr thought.

"I am here for my money," said the unhappy man.

Just what I need, another creditor. The man, whoever he was, shipped his oars. Burr was sure he had never seen the man before, and he couldn't fathom how he could possibly owe him any money.

"I'm sure you're at the wrong boat," Burr said. "Now if you'll excuse me, I am rather busy."

"Do you know who I am?"

"Of course, I do," Burr said. "You're an annoying fellow in a very fine-looking dinghy."

"I am Aaron Carlson. Dr. Aaron Carlson, chief cardiologist at Munson Hospital in Traverse City."

"I'm not having any heart issues," Burr said, still confounded, but the name had a familiar ring to it.

"I am here for my money," said the cardiologist.

"A cardiologist," Burr said. "Now I understand your attitude. You sit at the right hand of God."

Dr. Carlson pointed a long, manicured finger at Burr. "*Spindrift* was my boat, which you bought on a note, which is in default."

Burr looked astern at his dinghy, plywood, painted white with a firehose rub rail. He remembered how he knew Carlson's name. He had bought *Spindrift* from a broker and had never met the owner. All he had done was sign a note. Burr was fairly certain he had overplayed his hand, especially the part about the Fuller Brush man.

Burr scratched Zeke's left ear, the ear he liked having scratched. Burr loved his new boat. In point of fact, Burr loved all boats. And women. And dogs.

"I'll tell you what I'll do. Bring the note current and I'll row back to shore. Let's call it four thousand even. You may keep *Spindrift* as long as you stay current."

Burr disappeared down below. He fished out his wallet and took out a folded piece of paper. A long, blue Lafayette and Wertheim check. He filled in the past-due amount and signed his name with a flourish. Back on deck, he passed the check to the good doctor.

"It is a felony to pass a bad check."

"It will clear," Burr said.

Dr. Carlson folded the check and put it in his shirt pocket. He pushed off, turned the stern of his dinghy to Burr, and rowed away.

Burr read the transom and laughed despite himself. Heartache.

His nap ruined but still master of *Spindrift*, at least until the check bounced, Burr sat in the cockpit and scratched Zeke's left ear again. The dog sighed. Burr's favorite coffee mug read, "If dogs could purr, there would be no need for cats."

Burr caressed the satiny varnish on the gunwale again, then reached down and ran his fingers on the oiled teak cockpit sole. Then he looked up at the spindly mast, all forty-seven feet of it. *Spindrift* had more rigging than a clipper. He thought it would have been simpler to use a bigger tree for the mast.

"Zeke, this is a fine mess." He looked at his watch. "There's only one thing to do." He scurried down below and pried up one of the floorboards. There, where some of the ballast should have been, were three-dozen bottles of wine in all shapes and sizes, but mostly reds and mostly Bordeaux. Burr picked out his favorite. It was mostly Cabernet, but it had some Merlot and a pinch of Cabernet Franc. There was a little water in the bilge, but nothing to worry about, and it kept the wine nicely cooled. He replaced the floorboard and stepped forward to the galley.

Spindrift was his first boat with a midships galley. She had an alcohol stove, an icebox, a food locker and one drawer. He rummaged through the drawer until he found the corkscrew. He uncorked the Bordeaux and took three steps back to the main salon. He sat down on the starboard bunk and waited for the wine to open. Zeke lounged on the port bunk. Burr smelled the boat smells: the mildew, the gas in the bilge, the varnish. He couldn't wait a moment longer and poured himself a glass.

Three glasses later, Burr lit the alcohol stove. He watched the blue flame and smelled the burning alcohol. The wind had shifted around to the southeast. *Spindrift* bounced up and down on her moorings, but the stove, mounted on gimbals, barely moved. He opened a can of baked beans, dumped them into a small pot and put them over the flame. He stirred the beans, Bush's Original, then sliced two hog dogs, Koegel's Viennas, over the pot. He lit the kerosene lamps in the main salon. They also swung on gimbals. He dropped down the table mounted on the mast and served himself a plateful of beans and franks. He poured himself another glass of wine.

He scooped up a spoonful. "Zeke, I love a good Bordeaux with Bush's and Koegel's," he said. "This is the life." Except that, at the moment, it wasn't. He drank from his wine glass.

There was the small matter of the check. Burr passed Zeke a piece of the hot dog. "Be careful. It's hot." Zeke wolfed it down, either not noticing or not caring. Burr drained his glass.

* * *

At six the next morning, Zeke licked Burr on the cheek. He knew exactly what Zeke wanted, there being certain inconveniences to keeping company with a dog on a boat. Burr threw on his clothes and grabbed his canvas bag. He put on his Sperry rain gear and climbed into the dinghy, Zeke at his heels.

A low had drifted in overnight and the rain had started at about two in the morning. Burr quite enjoyed sleeping while it rained, especially on a sailboat. The sound of the rain tapping on the cabin top soothed him, but *Spindrift* had her share of leaks, actually more than her share. No matter where he moved, the rain dripped on him.

Burr rowed from midships. Zeke sat in the stern. As soon as Burr beached the dinghy, Zeke leapt over him and found the nearest tree. Burr put his soggy dog in the Jeep and showered in the boater's head. He walked up the hill to Mary Ellen's, an old-fashioned diner on Main Street and ordered the Mary Ellen: two eggs over easy, sausage, hash browns, toast, and coffee.

More or less revived, but still a little foggy from the Bordeaux, he and Zeke set off for East Lansing.

* * *

Burr sat behind his desk in his leather chair. Zeke was curled up on the couch.

Burr turned and looked out the window at downtown East Lansing. It was August, and the end of summer term at MSU. No traffic to speak of, and no one on foot.

Burr swiveled back to his desk. He had put this off as long as he could. He had the accursed Lafayette and Wertheim checkbook in front of him. He started to open it, but thought better of it. Instead, he opened his top desk drawer and took out yet another No. 2 yellow pencil. He tapped it on his desk. He put the pencil down. "Here we go, Zeke."

Burr opened the checkbook and flipped through the stubs to the last check written. Consumers Power for seven hundred twenty-nine dollars and seventeen cents. How could it possibly cost so much to heat his building in the summer when the heat wasn't even on. Thompson Shepherd had said he'd think about giving Burr a check. Burr hoped he wouldn't think about it too long. Without some money from somewhere, the check he had written to Carlson would surely bounce.

At that very moment, Eve walked in, Jacob at her heels.

"What goes on with the checkbook?" Eve said.

"Just making sure we're still solvent."

"We may be liquid, but we haven't been solvent for quite some time," Eve said.

The finer points of finance annoyed and confused Burr, who preferred to live by the how-can-I-be-out-of-money-if-I-have-checks philosophy. He reached into his pants pocket and pulled out the lists Wes had given him.

Burr tapped the list with his pencil. "These are lists of everyone who was at the auction."

"The auction?" Eve said.

Jacob picked an imaginary dog hair off his slacks. "At The Gray Drake. The night Quinn Shepherd was murdered."

"He may have been murdered, or it may have been an accident." Burr tapped on one of the lists with his pencil. "These are the guests." He tapped on another list. "This is the help, waiters, waitresses, bartenders, busboys, dishwashers, cooks." He tapped on the third list. "And this is the string quartet. From what I'm told, they are quite accomplished."

"A string quartet?" Eve said.

"They play the *Four Seasons*. All four movements," Jacob said.

"And here is a list of the guides," Burr said.

Eve leaned over the desk, turned the lists so they were facing her. "There must be two hundred names on these lists."

"I think it's closer to three hundred," Burr said.

"It would take months to go through this list, and money," Eve said.

"We have to start somewhere," Burr said.

Jacob picked up the list of guides. He ran his finger down the list. "Here he is. Billy McDonough. He's the oldest guide on the river. Knows everyone. I'd start with him."

Burr and Zeke walked down the stairs, past Michelangelo's, the padlock still on the door, and outside to his Jeep. He pulled a parking ticket out from under the windshield wiper and crumpled it into a ball.

* * *

Just after five-thirty, Burr found Billy McDonough's house, a small cabin with peeling gray siding. Burr knocked. No one answered. But there was a red Ford F-150 with rusted quarter panels parked in the driveway.

They walked through the yard, mostly ferns, shaded by fifty-year-old oaks. Not a blade of grass in sight. He saw a boathouse that was bigger than the cabin. "That figures." Burr knocked on the boathouse door. No one answered. He knocked again. Still no answer. He turned the knob and opened the door about a foot. It was dark inside, except for a light in the corner. The smell of the river seeped up and out the door, along with something else. What was it? Burr took a deep breath. Wood, the smell of wood. Wood shavings and sawdust. He stepped in and saw a light in the corner. "Anybody home?"

A dog barked and ran at him and Zeke, its nails clicking on the concrete floor. The dog looked at him and then growled at Zeke. Never one to back down, Zeke growled back. The hair on his back stood on end.

The dog, a bull of a German Shorthair, launched himself at Zeke. Zeke snapped at the shorthair. Burr grabbed Zeke by the collar.

"What the devil is going on?" said a tall, thin man with a white ponytail. "Jake, no."

The shorthair backed off.

"Jake, heel." The dog moved to the left of the tall man and sat at his side.

Zeke lunged at the pointer, but couldn't shake free of Burr's grip. "Stop it, Zeke."

"Get that dog out of here and take yourself with him."

"I'm sorry, Mr. McDonough," Burr said. "You are Billy McDonough, aren't you?"

The man nodded. His white ponytail reached his shoulders and matched his mustache and his eyebrows. He had a lined, leathery face, and yellow teeth.

"You better have a good reason for breaking in here like this."

"I'm sorry, Mr. McDonough. I knocked twice, but there was no answer."

"So you barged in?"

"I saw a light in the corner."

"Sometimes I don't hear anything when I'm working."

Zeke squirmed and tried to slip out of his collar.

"You better get control of your dog."

Burr put Zeke in the Jeep and went back to the boathouse. Burr walked toward the light and found himself standing in a pile of lumber, wood shavings and sawdust. There was a table saw to his left, a lathe to his right. McDonough was at a workbench, sharpening a knife.

"Don't say anything until I finish this. If there's one thing I've learned, it's that if you've got something sharp in your hands, you better pay attention to it."

Burr stood behind McDonough and watched him slide the blade, all nine inches of it, back and forth along a sharpener. McDonough made it look like an art form. He finished sharpening and sheathed the knife.

"Mr. McDonough, my name is Burr Lafayette, Elizabeth Shepherd's lawyer."

"I'm busy."

"Do you know anyone who might have had a reason to kill Quinn Shepherd?"

McDonough looked up at Burr. "Other than Lizzie?"

"Why would Lizzie kill Quinn?"

"She had all the reason in the world—what with his cattin' around and the drugs."

Burr kicked at a scrap of wood. "The drugs?"

McDonough turned on the overhead lights. To Burr's left, the skeleton of an Au Sable riverboat sat on sawhorses. The boat's naked ribs made it look like a dinosaur lying on its back.

"He couldn't live like that on a guide's wages." McDonough walked over to the frame and disappeared under the sawhorses.

Burr crouched, so he could see McDonough. "I thought his family had money."

"Maybe they do. Maybe they don't. But that's how I think Quinn made his money. Sellin' drugs to the sports. There's so much oil money around here now, they got nothin' else to spend it on. Then there was that woman. So I'd say Lizzie just got tired of the whole thing."

"So you think it was drugs?" Burr said. "Drugs and women?" *This is just what I need.* "Could it have been an accident?"

"No." McDonough crawled away from Burr. "Quinn might have been a lot of things, but he was no fool on the water."

"What if he were drunk?" Burr said.

"Drunk or sober, nobody could fish like him, and nobody was better on the river."

Burr was tired of looking at McDonough from behind. He walked around the soon-to-be-boat, so he could at least talk to the top of McDonough's head.

"I been building these boats for almost fifty years and floating the Au Sable longer." McDonough looked up at Burr. "I been down every foot of the river, and I never seen anything like Quinn Shepherd." He turned his back to the boat. "This is the only place in the world these boats are used. The loggers used them, and then somebody got the bright idea to use them for fishing."

Here we go again.

"And the water where this boathouse sits is in the Holy Waters," McDonough said.

"The Holy Waters?"

"Catch and release. DNR fought us over it. But we got it two years ago. Wes and his damned auction had a big part in it. I'm pretty sure he has his crippled-up hand in the cookie jar. Anyway, this is the place, and I'm here to fish it. And guard it."

"Mr. McDonough—"

"And while I'm giving you some history, T. U. was started just down-stream from the lodge."

"T.U.?"

"Trout Unlimited. So here's my point. You get up on the South Branch during the Hex hatch, and anybody who can throw a fly the size of a paper plate can catch a brown. But down here you got to match the hatch."

"Mr. McDonough—"

"Let me finish. So Quinn goes up there that night, and Lizzie does, too.

And she's had enough." McDonough started to stand but cracked his head on the boat frame. "Damn it," he said. "And who could blame her?"

"Mr. McDonough."

"You might as well call me Billy." McDonough rubbed the back of his head.

"I don't see how any of this proves Lizzie killed her husband."

"That's not my point," McDonough said. "My point is he was the best fisherman I ever met, but he was still strung out on catching those big browns, not the art of it."

Burr still had no idea where this was going.

"Don't you see? If Quinn don't get greedy about those browns, he don't go up there that night. If he don't go up there, Lizzie don't kill him."

McDonough had Burr thoroughly flummoxed.

"This is about the river," McDonough said. "It's not about the bugs. It's not about the fish. It's about the river. It's always been about the river."

"I see," Burr said, who didn't see. He chewed on his lip. "Do you know who might have sold Quinn drugs?"

* * *

Burr and Zeke had gotten back to East Lansing after dark and gone straight to bed. Burr had no better idea who might have killed Quinn than he did before he'd left. And he had no idea at all who might have sold Quinn drugs.

Scooter found Burr early the next morning and handed him a shoebox. Burr went downstairs and took the padlock off the door. On their way back upstairs, Burr stopped to catch his breath on the landing on the fourth floor, the shoebox cradled in the crook of his left arm.

Two floors later he walked into his office. Eve and Jacob were already there. He sat down at his desk and set down the shoebox. He gave them his biggest, friendliest smile, which was not returned.

Zeke strolled over to Jacob and licked his unsuspecting hand. Jacob jumped up. "Get that cur away from me."

"*Cur*," Burr said. "I love that word."

"Why are we here?" Eve ran her hands across the knees of her jeans.

"It is a workday." Burr gave her jeans a disapproving look.

"It's not a workday if I don't get paid," Eve said.

"That's about to change." Burr threw off the top of the shoebox.

Eve leaned back in her chair.

Jacob peered into the shoebox. "My God, it's full of money." He started to reach in, but Burr slapped his hand.

"In due time," Burr said.

This was too much for Eve, who popped out of her chair and bent so far over the shoebox her earrings brushed the cardboard. "What did you do this time?"

Burr reached into the shoebox and pulled out a fistful of cash. He started counting and made three piles. "Today is payday."

"'What about the withholding?" Jacob said.

"Be quiet, Jacob," Eve said. "Where did you get this money?"

Burr started counting. The stacks got higher and higher. Finally, he stopped. He slid one stack to Jacob and one to Eve. Jacob reached for his stack, which tipped over into a go-fish-looking pile of playing cards.

"Eve, I believe you are now current."

"We're still overdrawn."

Burr put the lid back on the shoebox. "There is more money in here." He slid her the shoebox.

"Where did you get all this money?" Jacob said.

"From Scooter."

"The padlock," Jacob said.

"Exactly."

"There's still not enough to pay the mortgage," Eve said.

"We have not yet received a certified letter."

Burr and his four-legged friend left the way they had come, a certain jauntiness to their step.

* * *

Burr stopped at the bank and deposited the rest of the cash. The check he had written to Carlson would clear after all. He didn't know what to think about Billy McDonough. If what the guide had told him was true, maybe Lizzie had finally had enough. But if that was true, she was a convincing liar. Maybe she was or maybe Quinn's drug supplier had murdered him or maybe it was one of the sports he was selling to. Either way, he had to keep going.

He and Zeke drove north to Traverse City and the Park Place Hotel. It was art deco, built in 1937, and at ten stories, the tallest building in northern Michigan. It was also the priciest hotel in northern Michigan, way beyond Burr's means, but he had a little room on the Lafayette and Wertheim credit card.

After bribing the desk clerk with a twenty, Burr and his faithful companion took the stairs to the eighth floor. He called room service and ordered dinner for himself and Zeke. He had the chicken piccata. Zeke had the house dog food, two hamburgers.

The next morning, Burr and Zeke started up Michigan's little finger on M-22. About two miles up the road, he pulled into the parking lot of Reef Oil and Gas. It was three stories of glass and steel hanging over Grand Traverse Bay. An eyesore. This was the place of sunsets, blue skies and blue waters.

Armed with the program from the auction, he announced himself to the receptionist, a twenty-something brunette who showed him to the elevator.

"I'll take the stairs."

Three floors later, he presented himself to a matronly-looking woman guarding Harley Hawken's office. She disappeared through an oak door about the size of a barn door. A few minutes later, she reappeared. "Mr. Hawken will see you now."

Burr walked in. There sat Harley Hawken bent over an old-fashioned adding machine, the kind with the keys, the levers and the tape. He either didn't notice Burr or he didn't care.

His reading glasses were perched on a broad, not hawk-like nose. He had salt and pepper hair with a matching full beard, neatly trimmed. He punched away at the keys on the adding machine.

"Mr. Hawken."

Hawken raised his non-adding machine hand and shushed him.

Burr already didn't like Hawken. He looked out at the cat's paws on the bay, the wind filling in from the north. He walked over to the floor-to-ceiling window. A sixty-foot powerboat was tied up at a slip behind the building. The transom read *Pay Zone*. Burr liked Hawken even less than he didn't like him before.

"Don't walk behind me," Harley Hawken said.

Burr completed the circle of the preoccupied oil man and sat in an oversized, overstuffed chair facing Hawken. He scooted over to the left side of the chair. He thought there was room for at least two more people.

Hawken rang the lever one last time and ripped off the tape in triumph. He stared at Burr. "What is it that you want?"

"I represent Lizzie Shepherd."

"What does that have to do with me?"

"I thought you might be able to help," Burr said.

Hawken glared at him over his wire-rimmed reading glasses. Then he looked down and studied the tape again.

"I'll get right to the point," Burr said. "Who do you think might have murdered Quinn?"

"Other than Lizzie?"

You're the second one to say this. Burr reached in his pocket and pulled out the auction program. "Mr. Hawken, you were the winning bidder on Quinn's guided trip."

"Which I'll never collect on."

Burr took a deep breath and let it out slowly. "Twelve thousand dollars is a little steep for a one-day float."

"It was for a good cause. And Quinn was the best fly fisherman I've ever met."

Burr looked back down at the program. "How about Noah Osterman, Mickey Malone and Joe Gleason? They all bid."

"No."

Burr looked up at Hawken. "No, what?"

"Noah Osterman is my lawyer. Mickey Malone is a land man. A damn good one. Joe syndicates my deals." Hawken's teeth peeked through his beard. Burr saw the first hint of a smile. He waved his arm in a semicircle around the room. Burr followed his arm. Where he might have expected to see art, or at least a picture of a setter on point or a lab with a duck in its mouth. Instead, Hawken had filled his walls with pictures of oil rigs. In all four seasons.

"Would any of those men want Quinn dead?"

"No."

"Do any of them use drugs?"

"What does that have to with anything? Certainly not."

"Mr. Hawken, where were you after the auction, when Quinn Shepherd was murdered?"

Hawken ripped off his glasses. "Get out."

Burr didn't budge. "Does that mean you don't have an alibi?"

Hawken pointed to the door. "Now."

Burr slid across to the other side of the goliath of a chair.

"I said out."

Burr sat there.

What little skin showed between Hawken's hair and his beard turned a violent shade of red.

Burr made no move to move.

Hawken put his glasses on and turned his attention back to his adding machine. It clattered to life.

Burr slid back to the other side of the chair and waited.

Finally, the clattering stopped, and Hawken looked up at him. "I was with Noah Osterman in the bar at The Gray Drake. Then I went to bed. In Number Seventeen. I have that room from the last Saturday in April through Labor Day."

"Did you buy your drugs from Quinn? Cocaine is fashionable," Burr said.

Hawken folded and folded the tape from his adding machine until it was as thick as a matchbook. "You may leave now."

Burr sat in the chair-big-enough-for-three long enough to make sure Hawken was thoroughly put out. Then he got up and left.

* * *

Burr and Zeke headed back down M-22 into Traverse City. He parked at a meter on Front Street and looked over at his dog.

"Zeke, if a meter reader comes by, put a quarter in."

Fifty feet later, he opened the door to Osterman and Krueger, Attorneys and Counselors. The door was two sizes smaller than Hawken's. He nodded at the receptionist, found Noah Osterman's office and let himself in.

The attorney and counselor was looking out the window, his back to Burr.

"I find it almost unbelievable that all of these buildings back up to the

Boardman, like it's nothing more than an alley. It's such a fine trout stream," Osterman said, his back still to Burr.

Burr didn't say anything.

"Unless you own one of these buildings, you can't even get to the river from here. A shame, I suppose. I don't really care, though. It's good not to be the hoi polloi." Osterman swiveled in his chair. "You are not my eleven o'clock appointment."

Burr sat and faced Osterman in a wing chair built for one.

"I beg your pardon." Osterman had a mouthful of smoke-stained teeth below a trimmed mustache, wire-rimmed glasses and eyes the color of the barrel of Burr's shotgun. He had a red face, florid actually. Burr thought Osterman looked like he could drop dead from a heart attack at any moment. He could picture Osterman wearing Bismarck's helmet, the Prussian's Prussian.

Burr stood and stuck his right hand at Osterman. "Burr Lafayette," Burr Lafayette said. "And you must be Noah Osterman."

"Osterman. With a long *O*."

"So it rhymes with toaster," Burr said. "Like *Toaster*-man."

"Not only am I sure we haven't met, I have no intention of meeting you now," Osterman harrumphed.

Burr sat back down. "I represent Lizzie Shepherd."

"Good for you."

"She has been indicted for murdering her husband."

"Good for her." He pointed to the door. "You may leave now."

Burr had been treated worse by worse people. He saw no reason to leave.

"Mr. Osterman, you were one of the bidders on Quinn's float trip. You obviously knew him. I was hoping you might have an idea who might want to kill him."

Osterman reached into his desk drawer. He pulled out a pack of Winstons and lit a cigarette without offering one to Burr. "No."

"No, what?" Burr said.

Osterman blew the smoke out through his nose. "I don't recall being under oath."

"Are you always so rude?"

"Only to the uninvited."

"Touché. Who do you think might have wanted to kill Quinn?" Burr said.

"I have no earthly idea." Osterman gave him a nasty smile.

At least he didn't say other than Lizzie.

"Mr. Osterman, where were you after the auction?"

"I don't remember."

"You don't remember?"

"Actually, I don't know." Osterman sucked on the cigarette. "No, that's not it. I forgot." He blew out the smoke, this time from his mouth.

"Mr. Osterman—"

Osterman cut him off, waving with his right hand, the one with the cigarette, smoke trailing.

"You're a litigator, Lafayette. Even if it's only criminal law. You surely know the three things we tell our witnesses to say." The Prussian lawyer raised his beefy index finger. "I don't remember." His middle finger. "I don't know." Now his ring finger. "I forgot. It's hard to get in trouble with those three little pearls."

"Who said you were in trouble?"

"If I did remember, and I did know, and I hadn't forgotten, I'd say I was with Harley Hawken in the bar at The Gray Drake. I then retired to my room right next to his."

"Mr. Osterman, did you buy your drugs from Quinn?"

"Get out."

Osterman's receptionist stuck her head through the door. "Mr. Hawken is on the phone again," she said. "And your eleven o'clock is here."

Burr started for the door. Osterman stubbed out his cigarette and picked up his phone. "Harley, is that you?"

* * *

Burr reached for the parking ticket stuck under his windshield wiper and dropped it in a trashcan. He shooed Zeke off the driver's seat. With Zeke back at shotgun and order restored, he climbed in. He hadn't found out a thing from either Hawken or Osterman other than Hawken liked money and Osterman would be the worst witness he'd ever had.

He drove north on US-31, past Charlevoix. They turned on the road to

Walloon Lake and then into a driveway with a wooden sign nailed to a tree. The sign was cut in the shape of an oil drum and read "Barrels."

He parked in front of a two-story, gray-planked cottage with navy trim, circa 1930. Beyond the cottage, the north end of the north arm of Walloon Lake— deep, clear, and spring-fed. Walloon Lake was the ritziest, snootiest inland lake in Michigan, public access virtually non-existent. You could use the lake if you could get to it, but you couldn't get to it.

A fortyish man answered the door. His hairline started halfway across the top of his head, and he had a big smile that made him look like a Halloween pumpkin. Wraparound sunglasses completed the look. All in all, Burr thought he looked like a balding jack-o'-lantern posing as a movie star.

He pumped Burr's hand. "Mickey Malone. So glad you could come." Malone started off around the house toward the lake. "Right this way."

Burr followed the balding pumpkin to the lake side of the house. The lawn fell away to the beach. A white dock ran to the edge of the drop-off, a pontoon boat on one side of the dock, a ski boat on the other, patio furniture in between. Malone led him out to the end of the dock.

They sat and Malone took out two highball glasses from a wicker basket and handed one to Burr. He reached into a cooler and pulled out a pitcher of what Burr assumed was iced tea. He filled Burr's glass, then his own.

Burr took a sip. He coughed.

"Long Island iced tea," Mickey said.

A couple of these could get me in serious trouble.

"And how may I be of service?"

Once more, Burr reached in his pocket for the bidding list and unfolded it.

"You bid on Quinn Shepherd's trip. At the auction."

"I didn't bid on it, but if I'd wanted to, I could have been the highest bidder."

"But you weren't."

"I always let Harley win." Malone drained half his glass into his jack-o'-lantern mouth. "Do you know what a land man is?"

Burr did know, but he shook his head *no*.

"I lease drilling rights from landowners. Farmers, government, anybody. I bid at auctions. I work for oil companies. They pay me in cash. But, every once in a while, I take a slice of the working interest." Malone paused.

"That's what I did with the Crawford-Olsen. It paid for this little slice of heaven."

Burr nodded but had no earthly idea how an oil well had the remotest connection with the auction.

Malone finished his drink and refilled his glass. He drank off the top half again. "The Crawford-Olsen is Harley's well. And it just wouldn't do to outbid him." He finished off his drink. "Now would it?"

There's always a pecking order. "I suppose you were in the bar that night with Harley, Osterman and Gleason." It was Burr's turn to drink. "And your room was two doors down from Harley's?"

Malone took off his glasses. "How did you know?"

Burr watched Malone's pupils shrink from teaspoon-sized to pinpricks. *Alcohol, drugs, or both*, Burr thought. This wasn't going anywhere, other than Burr was getting an education in the ins and outs of the Michigan oil business.

"Who do you think might have killed Quinn?"

"I thought it was an accident."

This isn't getting me anywhere. "Did you buy your cocaine from Quinn?"

Malone put his sunglasses back on.

* * *

Burr reconvened the brain trust in his office. "I've talked to three of the four highest bidders on Quinn's trip. And they all have each other as an alibi."

"So they're all out," Jacob said.

"Or they're all lying," Eve said.

"Right," Burr said.

"So one of his customers could have killed him," Eve said.

"Why would they?" Jacob asked.

"Maybe Quinn took the money and didn't deliver the drugs," Eve said.

"Right again. So where does that leave us?" Burr said.

"I think this leaves us worse off than we were." Eve handed Burr a single sheet of paper.

Burr read it and collapsed into his chair. "Damn it all."

"What is it?" Jacob said.

Burr passed it to Jacob.

"It's a show cause. Cullen wants to exhume Quinn Shepherd's body," Jacob said.

"When is the hearing?" Burr said.

"July 25th," Jacob said.

"When is that?" Burr said.

"That would be tomorrow," Eve said.

"Jacob, we have work to do."

"*We?*"

"You."

"I don't know anything about the law of exhumation," Jacob said.

"You are about to," Burr said.

"Why does Cullen want to dig up poor Quinn?" Eve said.

"He wants to match the wound on Quinn's skull with the canoe paddle. If they match, it's very bad for Lizzie."

"That wouldn't be conclusive," Jacob said.

"No, but it would be connective," Burr said.

"What do we do?"

"We oppose the motion," Burr said.

"What if there is no match?"

Burr ran his hands through his hair, front to back. "We can't take the chance."

"Let's ask Lizzie," Jacob said.

"Who knows if she'd tell the truth," Burr said.

"Would she lie to us?" Jacob said.

"Lawyers lie. Witnesses lie. And most especially, clients lie," Burr said.

"You haven't given me one good reason why we should be against this motion."

"Because Cullen is for it," Burr said.

* * *

The next day, Burr found himself in the Crawford County Circuit Court. After Skinner had charged Lizzie with murder, her case moved up from the district court to the circuit court. Everything about her case would be decided here in this courtroom, just down the hall from Judge Skinner's. This one was much like the other, slightly less threadbare, but not by much. At least Burr's chair rested squarely on all four legs.

According to the nameplate outside the courtroom, the judge was also named Skinner. Lawrence G. Skinner. *Are they brothers?*

Cullen sat across the aisle from Burr. Lizzie sat to Burr's left, Jacob next to her. Eve sat behind him along with Wes and old Thompson. There was no one else in the gallery.

"All rise," said the bailiff with the wispy mustache. "The court of the Honorable Lawrence G. Skinner is in session."

A youngish man, no more than thirty-five, appeared from the judge's chambers. He was tall, thin, and hunched over, as if the ceiling was too low for him to stand up straight. He sat, still hunched over.

The bailiff cleared his throat. "The circuit court for Crawford County, the Honorable Lawrence G. Skinner presiding, is now in session. Be seated."

He's just a boy.

Judge Lawrence G. Skinner, as tall as his father was wide, looked up at Cullen, at least his eyes did. His chin disappeared into his Adam's apple.

"Mr. Cullen, your motion looks all right to me. So does the certification from the health department. They want you to rebury Quinn as soon as the examination has been completed."

"Your Honor." Burr stood.

Skinner the younger looked at Burr without moving his head or his neck. "And you are?"

"Burr Lafayette, Your Honor. Counsel for the defense." He went through his cuff pulling and tie straightening ritual.

Judge Skinner moved his eyes without turning his head. "What are you doing with your shirtsleeves?"

"Your Honor, the law does not favor exhumation. In fact, there is a presumption against exhuming a body."

"Mr. Lafayette, I am going to grant Mr. Cullen's motion."

"Your Honor, not only is exhumation not favored, it is rarely granted against the wishes of the family." Burr picked up a piece of paper in front of him. "Your Honor, I would like to introduce the affidavit of Elizabeth Shepherd, wife of the late Quinn Shepherd and the closest living relative of the deceased. She objects to the motion of exhumation."

The boy judge pressed the tips of the fingers of each hand against the other. He tapped them against each other. "My father warned me about you."

Burr thought it best to stick to the legal arguments. This particular Skinner didn't seem nearly as bright as his father, and the senior Skinner wasn't exactly law-review material, either.

"Your Honor, the autopsy is a clear written record of the examination of Quinn Shepherd. There is no evidence that he was struck by a canoe paddle. None whatsoever."

"Mr. Lafayette, I am interested in what really happened. And the best way to find out what happened is to exhume the body."

"Your Honor, I object," Burr said.

The judge turned to the prosecutor. "Mr. Cullen, approach the bench."

Cullen handed Skinner the motion, which he signed.

Burr looked at Lizzie. She had her head in her hands.

She looked up at Burr. "Do you have any idea how terrible this is?"

"I think I do."

"It's bad enough to think of him in a grave, but to think of that awful Cullen having him dug up and then opening the casket…"

"I'm so sorry," Burr said.

"This is so awful."

"What is Cullen going to find?" Burr said.

"Nothing." She looked away from Burr. "I don't know."

"Is he going to find out that you hit him with the paddle?"

She turned back to Burr. She wasn't crying yet, but she was about to.

* * *

Cullen hadn't wasted any time, but then again, neither had Burr. The next afternoon, he drove to Elmwood Cemetery, about five miles east of The Gray Drake, the graves under a canopy of maples and oaks, not an elm to be seen. The grass barely grew, and the only flowers were faded plastic bouquets, almost all of them blown over. He didn't like cemeteries in the first place, and the plastic flowers made it worse.

To his left, the gray marble headstone lay flat on the ground, the inscription facedown. There were at least five other headstones, grand by Elmwood Cemetery standards, that had *Shepherd* on them.

The casket hung on a chain from the bucket of a backhoe. A hearse stood by, its rear doors open, waiting. The backhoe operator lowered the casket to the ground. Four men got out of the hearse. They picked up the casket, caked with dirt, its handles tarnished, and slid it in the back of the hearse. The workers shuffled their way over to the hearse and slid the casket in back.

Burr bolted out of the Jeep and ran over to the hearse. He handed a piece of paper to a chubby, jowly man. The man studied the paper, handed it back to Burr and climbed into the hearse. Burr ran to the door of the hearse and knocked on the window. The man looked out at Burr.

"Get out," said the jowly man.

He started the engine.

Burr pounded on the window.

The driver started off.

Burr ran to the Jeep, climbed in and followed the hearse through the cemetery. He couldn't pass the hearse unless he drove over graves and knocked over headstones. When they reached the road, Burr gunned the Jeep past the hearse and slammed on the brakes, the Jeep sideways to the hearse.

The hearse lurched to a stop. Burr let out the breath he didn't know he was holding. He watched the driver pop out, spry for someone so chubby, and up until now, not interested in anything that had anything to do with Burr. The driver ran to the Jeep and pounded on the window. Burr looked out at him, but he didn't roll down his window. The driver pounded again. Burr smiled at him, but still didn't roll down his window.

The driver pounded harder. *If he breaks the window, it will cost me a fortune to get it fixed, not that it works that well to begin with.* Burr opened the door and pushed the driver out of the way with it.

"What the hell do you think you're doing?" The jowly man pulled out his own piece of paper. "It's a crime to interfere with a disinterment."

Burr reached back into the Jeep for his piece of paper. "Do you have a name?"

"Jenkins," he said. "Norman Jenkins."

"Mr. Jenkins, it is a bigger crime to interfere with an order from the Michigan Court of Appeals." Burr, not at all sure how literate Jenkins was, unfolded the court order. "This, my jowly friend, is a stay of Judge Skinner's exhumation order."

"I got my orders from Mr. Cullen."

"This trumps yours," Burr said. "If you violate it, I will see to it that you are put in jail. Your friend Mr. Cullen will prosecute you for contempt."

Jenkins glared at Burr. The driver got back in the hearse and said something to his helpers. Burr got out and knocked on the driver's window. It slid right down. "After you rebury Mr. Shepherd, fill in the hole, and put the headstone back where it belongs." The window went up. The hearse turned around and rolled back to the cemetery.

* * *

Burr had had quite enough of the law and judges, not to mention clients. He and Zeke-the-dog pulled up at his former house at Sunningdale-and-Wedgewood in Grosse Pointe Woods. Grace met them in the driveway, Zeke-the-boy holding her hand. Burr was not allowed in the house since the divorce, and he didn't blame her. He had ruined their marriage with his foolish affair, and she had never forgiven him.

It hadn't been a perfect marriage. Grace had had occasional run-ins with depression. Burr worked more than he should have and hadn't always been there. They both wanted a large family, but Zeke-the-boy was all she could manage. Burr knew full well that was no reason to end a marriage.

Too much work, too much ego, and too much Suzanne had done him in. She had worked for an ad agency client of Fisher and Allen, and had gotten the agency in trouble over some over-the-top copy. Burr had called it "permissible puffery" and won the case. In the process, he had fallen in love with Suzanne, ruined his marriage, and made a fool of himself at the firm.

Looking back on it, he knew that Suzanne had been a colossal mistake. His ego wouldn't let him say he was sorry, and now here he was. He had an esoteric law practice that sometimes paid the bills. He drank too much, and he was a part-time father. He couldn't put Humpty Dumpty back together again, but he was determined to do his best as a father.

Grace did give him a hint of a smile. She had a long narrow face and shoulder-length dark brown hair with auburn highlights. She was pretty when he married her, and she was pretty now.

"I'll take the other Zeke." Grace refused to call either of the Zekes, Zeke-the-boy or Zeke-the-dog, but Burr was sure Grace liked Zeke-the-dog better than she liked him, which wasn't surprising.

They exchanged Zekes, and Burr watched her walk back to the house. *She looks good in those jeans.*

By Sunday evening, Burr was sure he'd be ill if he ever saw another cheese pizza, his son's favorite food and perfectly suitable for breakfast, lunch, and dinner, at least according to his sole heir.

* * *

At 10:30 Monday morning, Burr left an annoyed Zeke-the-dog in the care of a more annoyed Eve. He got into the Jeep yet again and took I-96 to Grand Rapids. At noon, Burr parked in a no-parking spot on Ottawa Street in downtown Grand Rapids. It was a perfectly good place to park, and for the life of him, he couldn't see why he shouldn't park there.

Burr walked into the Pen Club and took the stairs to the third floor. The Peninsular Club was Grand Rapids' oldest downtown club. It had a grill, dining room, hotel, locker room, gym, handball courts, you name it, yours to use as long as you were from the Grand Rapids upper crust and paid your dues on time. It helped if your last name started with *Van*, *Ver*, or otherwise had a Dutch ring to it. And most importantly, you needed to be well-heeled. He opened the fortress-like, mahogany door to the Men's Grill.

The maître d', a young man whose collar was much too big for his not-so-big neck, took Burr into the dining room and found Gleason, his face still tan and lined.

Burr didn't think Joe Gleason was truly well-heeled. He suspected the oil and gas promoter frequented the Pen Club to solicit checks from the unwary.

Gleason pumped Burr's hand as if they were old friends or, more likely, Burr thought, as if he were just about to write him a check. The grilling at the preliminary exam forgotten.

A career waiter, sixty, with a puffy face, a puffy mustache, and a belly to match, immediately appeared at Burr's side. "Something to drink, sir?"

Burr, for once nonplussed, said, "I'll have what he's having."

The waiter returned with a highball glass full of ice and bubbles, garnished with a lime squeeze.

Gleason raised his glass. "May we find oil at the bottom of the hole."

Burr raised his glass, hoping that this was a gin and tonic and not a vodka and tonic. He took a sip. It was Perrier. Perrier with a lime squeeze. He set it down immediately. It was worse than vodka.

"Anything wrong?" Gleason said.

"No. Everything is fine."

"I find Perrier refreshing."

"I do, too," Burr said, who didn't. In fact, the only time Burr could drink Perrier was when he had a hangover, which he didn't have at the moment.

The waiter reappeared, and Gleason ordered the liver and onions. Burr ordered the special of the day, sockeye salmon with rice pilaf.

"How can I help?"

"I'm trying to figure out who was where the night Quinn died," Burr said.

Gleason lost his salesman's smile. "And you think I might have killed him?"

"Not at all."

"I was the one who saw Lizzie come in. There wasn't time for me to have a drink, go to the river, and get back in time to see Lizzie."

How convenient. "I suppose not."

"Do you know anything about Quinn selling drugs?"

Gleason took a swallow of his Perrier. "There were rumors about drugs, but I never saw any."

"So you didn't buy any."

"Drugs aren't my poison. I like vodka. That's why I'm drinking Perrier today. Can't stand it otherwise."

"Did Quinn have any enemies?"

The waiter arrived with their lunches along with a striking, peroxide blonde, who had spent too much time in the sun. "I am so sorry, Mr. Gleason. I told her that women were not allowed in the men's grill."

Gleason's face turned a malarial shade of tan. "Don't even think of putting those plates down," said the too-tan blonde. The waiter cowered, plates in hand. She produced a checkbook from her saddlebag-sized purse.

It looks like my checkbook. He shuddered.

"Meet my wife, Suzy," Gleason said.

She slammed the checkbook down in front of Gleason and opened it. She had long red fingernails, leathery hands to match her face, but striking features. She was at least fifteen years younger than Gleason, except for her skin. She handed Gleason a pen and pointed at a blank check with what Burr thought looked more like talons than fingernails. "Sign here."

Joe Gleason signed the check. Suzy Gleason ripped it out of the checkbook and stuffed it in her purse, along with the checkbook. "How do you do," she said to Burr. She left before Burr could say anything.

"I have no idea how she found my checkbook." Gleason looked at Burr. "Three wives, five kids. Are you married?"

"Not anymore."

"I should have stopped after one. That little tornado was strike three. I think we're ready for lunch now," Gleason said to the still-quaking waiter.

CHAPTER SIX

The Jeep crawled through the woods.

"Zeke, we've spent the entire summer lost on these damned two-tracks." But in another quarter of a mile, he'd know where he was. Actually, he had no idea where he was, but he knew he was in the right place. There were two forest-green DNR pickups pulled off to the side. And a black Explorer.

There wasn't a soul in the trucks, but he heard voices off to his right and a humming sound underneath the voices. Burr and Zeke followed a trail through the woods. Jack pines, five-to-ten-feet tall, grew out of the sandy soil—row upon row of trees, grass and weeds in the understory.

A hundred yards in, Burr and Zeke came upon four young men wrestling a net filled with birds, directed by Burr's favorite ornithologist, Margaret Winston.

"Get that one out of the net. That's a brown thrasher, not a cowbird," she said.

Burr watched while a young man untangled what Burr could only suppose was the brown thrasher.

"Dr. Winston."

"I'm busy," she said.

Burr shifted his weight from his right foot to his left. "I was hoping we might talk a little. Just for a moment." He kicked at the sand with the toe of his left boot.

"Not only am I busy, I don't ever want to speak with you. Unless you have a subpoena."

"I was hoping that wouldn't be necessary."

She had tucked her hair into a Detroit Tigers baseball cap, her only makeup, a smudge of dirt on her nose. And she was still a vision of beauty.

An English setter ran up to her, ginger-and-white, its feathers combed out on its legs and tail.

"This must be Finn."

Zeke had figured that out, sniffing and prancing around her. Finn ran back down the path, Zeke right behind her.

"How on earth did you find this spot?"

"The DNR office in Roscommon has a schedule for the Kirtland's warbler project, but you probably know that." Burr looked over at the net full of birds. "Isn't that a little hard on them."

"Those are cowbirds. I take it you've never seen a Kirtland's?"

"I don't think I have."

She turned to the bird wranglers. "Let's get the net to the trucks." Then to Burr, "There are only one hundred seventy-two nesting pairs left. We may already be too late to save them."

"And you're doing it with cowbirds?"

"Cowbirds don't make nests. They lay their eggs in the nests of other birds. Out here, they lay them in Kirtland's nests. The cowbird chicks are much bigger and much more aggressive than the Kirtland's. They eat all the food that the adults bring back to the nest. The Kirtland's chicks starve to death. So the Kirtland's parents end up raising the cowbirds."

"I see," Burr said, who once again didn't. *It's a different world up here.*

"These are pine barrens. About the only thing that will grow here is jack pine. Like these. Except that these were planted."

She bent over and pulled a pinecone off one of the trees. She stood up and tossed him the cone. "It takes about five hundred degrees to open the cone up to spill out the seeds. And that takes a forest fire."

Burr had no idea where this was headed, but he did what he always did in these situations. He looked down at his feet and didn't say a word. Then he looked back up at the winsome professor.

"The Kirtland's warbler only nests in jack pine and only when they're scrub, like these. Now that we've pretty much stopped forest fires, they have no habitat. Unless we make it by cutting or burning. If you'll excuse me, I have to attend to the cowbirds."

She started off, then stopped.

"Do you hear that droning off in the distance?"

Burr nodded.

"That is an oil rig. Drilling in the Niagran. If the cowbirds don't get the Kirtland's, the oil men will."

"There is much to admire about your work," Burr said.

"Thank you," she said, turning to him.

Did she just smile at me?

"I was hoping you'd show me where you found the paddle."

"I'm much too busy. As you so cleverly pointed out, it was Finn who found the paddle."

It must not have been a smile. "It might save a life from being ruined."

She called Finn.

The English setter, with Zeke right behind, ran out of the jack pines.

"What are you going to do with the cowbirds?"

She started down the trail with Finn. She looked back at him. "We're going to kill them."

* * *

Burr and Zeke drove to Harbor Springs and rowed out to *Spindrift*. He hadn't had any time on his boat, and he was going to enjoy it while he could.

He ducked below, pried up a floorboard, and retrieved another bottle of his favorite Bordeaux, nicely chilled in the bilge. He uncorked the wine and started on a Labatt while the wine opened.

He nursed his beer as long as he could, then, "Zeke, it must surely be open by now." He poured himself a glass, swirled it and raised it to his lips.

"Burr."

Zeke barked.

Burr ignored the barking and the voice, convinced or at least hoping he was hearing things.

"Burr. I know you're there."

Burr swirled again.

"Come up this minute."

Zeke barked. Burr peered out of the cabin.

"For God's sake, man, I'm going to drown," Jacob said.

He stuck his nose halfway in and breathed. He took a sip. "Almost perfect." He climbed up the companionway and peeked over the side. There was Jacob in the dinghy, again. Zeke barked.

"Quiet, Zeke." Burr took another swallow. "Yes, Jacob?"

Jacob looked up from the dinghy. He had on a red-and-white-striped polo and blue Bermudas.

"You look like an American flag." The dinghy bumped against *Spindrift*. "Fend off."

"I beg your pardon."

"You're going to ding up the hull."

"Skinner wants to see you."

"The boy judge?"

"He wants to see you. Tomorrow morning."

Burr climbed out of the cockpit. He put his wine glass down, sat on the deck and kept the dinghy off *Spindrift* with his feet. He picked up his wine, swirled and drank.

"Why didn't someone call me?"

"You have no phone on this blasted ship."

"Exactly."

"He wants to meet with you and Cullen."

"Jacob, would you like to join me for dinner on *Spindrift*?"

"I would be violently ill."

Burr pushed the dinghy away with his feet.

* * *

Burr sat next to Cullen and across from Skinner, who was hunched over behind a desk the size of a pickup. For all the shabbiness of the Crawford County Courthouse, Skinner's office had the trappings of a king. Diplomas and awards filled the walls. Light streamed in through the windows.

"I'll get right to the point," Skinner said.

Burr certainly hoped so.

"Let's get going with this trial. I want to get the scheduling order out."

"Your Honor, I'm afraid we can't schedule anything until the Court of Appeals rules on the exhumation," Burr said.

"That's why you're here. I want you to dismiss it."

"I'm afraid I can't do that, Your Honor."

"Of course, you can. I know the law. I was elected just like my father."

Burr sat straight up and shook his head *no*.

"It is a perfectly reasonable request. Then we can wash our hands of this." Skinner did just that with his hands. "Overruled by those idiots in

Lansing. Their preliminary injunction will be overturned." He pointed a long, skinny index finger at Burr. "And an *ex parte* order, to boot." Skinner pronounced it *ex part*, and not *ex part-A*.

"Your Honor, Michigan law does not favor exhumation. I said that at the hearing."

"I said get that *ex part* order dismissed."

Burr did not suffer fools gladly, even when he knew he should. "Respectfully, Your Honor, it is '*Ex Part A*.' The 'e' is not silent. It is pronounced like a long '*A*'. Ex Part *A*."

"Out." Skinner pointed at the door.

* * *

"All rise," the bailiff said.

Those two little words always got Burr going. He loved to litigate. He loved to fight with words. Armed only with his No. 2 pencil and his legal pad, he loved to meet the enemy and win the day. Today's would be a battle royal, but thanks to Squire Jacob, Burr was well armored. He stood, as did his foe.

The three judges entered from the back of the courtroom and sat.

"The Court of Appeals for the State of Michigan is now in session," the bailiff said. "You may be seated."

For all the shabbiness of the Crawford County courtrooms, the Court of Appeals was nothing if not elegant. It was on the second floor of the Prudden Building in downtown Lansing. The courtroom had oak paneling, the varnish so old it had turned almost black, covering all but the brightest of the grain in the oak. It had so many coats of varnish, you could see your reflection in it. Tapestries framed the windows. There were walnut desks for the judges, matching walnut tables and chairs for the litigants, walnut pews for the gallery.

It was a grand setting for grand-and-weighty matters of law, although the subject matter today tended more toward the macabre than the esoteric.

Once again, Lizzie sat on Burr's left, Jacob next to her. Cullen sat across the aisle. Eve was the only one in the gallery.

"We are here today to decide whether that certain *ex parte* order, issued by this court, in the matter of the People versus Shepherd shall become a permanent injunction. The court notes that the temporary restraining order was granted by Judge Gunnison." This said by Chief Judge Miriam Florentine, a petite, attractive, white-haired woman in her sixties. Burr had argued before her many times and had great respect for her intellect.

"Counsel, I must say that I find it highly irregular for this court to grant an emergency *ex parte* order."

Burr himself had found it highly irregular and was shocked, not to mention delighted, when Judge Gunnison granted the order. Judge Delton Gunnison, referred to by Burr as Tweedledum, and his counterpart on the other side of Judge Florentine, Judge Wilton Franklin as Tweedledee, were living proof that judges should be appointed, not elected. Burr, though, had cultivated relationships with all of the appellate court judges, and he usually won the close calls.

"You may proceed, Mr. Lafayette," she said.

Burr stood. "Thank you, Your Honor. As I'm sure you're aware, and as noted in my brief, Michigan law does not favor exhumation. The policy of the state is not to disturb the remains of the dead." He paused and pulled on the knot of his tie. "Moreover, the wishes of the relatives are also of paramount importance, and Mrs. Shepherd, the widow, does not want the remains of her husband disinterred. These two principles have been affirmed in case after case. For example, in Shumway versus—"

Tweedledee, a stout man with a fringe of black hair and bifocals, raised one hand, palm toward Burr. "Stop right there, Mr. Lafayette. We have all read your most able brief."

"Yes, Your Honor."

"Mr. Wertheim's legal scholarship is without peer."

"Thank you, Your Honor," Burr said.

"Having said that, there are other factors that weigh in the decision." Tweedledee turned toward Cullen. "Sir, do you have anything you would like to add?"

Cullen bolted out of his seat, smiling his inane smile. "Thank you, Your Honor. Counsel is correct, as far as he goes." He looked over at Burr. "The policy of the state and the wishes of the relatives are trumped by certain circumstances such as, if a crime has been committed."

"Quinn Shepherd drowned," Burr said.

"Please be quiet, Mr. Lafayette. Continue, Mr. Cullen," Judge Florentine said.

"As I was saying, exhumation is permitted if the *possibility* exists that a crime has been committed. Especially if new evidence is brought forth that suggests a crime has been committed. In these circumstances, the interests of the state outweigh the interests of the relatives."

"There is no justice in what you're doing," Burr said.

Judge Florentine pointed at Burr. "I'm going to ignore your last comment, Mr. Lafayette, but if you have one more outburst, I am going to eject you, and then we will hear from Mr. Wertheim."

Jacob cringed.

"Now then, Mr. Cullen."

"The case law is clear on this. In Spencer versus—"

"I read your brief. What is your point?" Tweedledee said.

"My point is, Your Honor, there is new evidence. Shocking new evidence. We have a canoe paddle with a shattered blade. And the blade has traces of Mr. Shepherd's hair. If we are allowed to examine Mr. Shepherd's body, we will be able to show that Mrs. Shepherd struck Mr. Shepherd on the head with the canoe paddle, thereby causing his death."

Burr couldn't take it anymore. He looked at the pencil in his hand and snapped it in two. All three judges looked at him.

"Excuse me," Burr said. He studied his broken pencil, then stood. "Your Honor, if I may—"

"If you must."

"The coroner ruled that Mr. Shepherd drowned. The autopsy described Mr. Shepherd's injury in detail. It determined that Mr. Shepherd struck his head on the rail of his boat. It did not even suggest that he was struck by a canoe paddle." Burr looked at Cullen. "While Mr. Cullen is correct as far as he goes, the case law is also clear that there must be an overwhelming reason to disinter. There is no overwhelming reason here. Mr. Shepherd's injury was analyzed in painstaking detail at the autopsy."

"The medical examiner did not know about the canoe paddle," Cullen said.

"The canoe paddle was found almost a year later," Burr said. "By a dog."

"A dog?" Tweedledee said.

"The paddle has Mr. Shepherd's hair on it," Cullen said.

"Sit down, Mr. Lafayette. You too, Mr. Cullen," Judge Florentine said.

"Gentlemen, I have quite enjoyed the lively discussion and the education regarding the law of exhumation. I now know much more about the law of exhumation than I care to. In fact, I fear that if I learn anything further I will know less than when we started. But, I am afraid that all of you, including my learned colleague, have missed the point."

Judge Florentine cleared her throat. "We are not here today to decide whether the body of the late Mr. Shepherd is to be exhumed. On the contrary. We are here today to determine whether the *ex parte* temporary restraining order should become a permanent injunction. This is a procedural question not a substantive question."

The chief judge continued, "Mr. Lafayette, I do find that you have met certain of the requirements of a preliminary injunction. It is certainly the case that money damages would not be an adequate remedy."

Burr nodded at the judge and smiled, Cullen's smile noticeably absent. "As to the test of irreparable harm, the family, particularly Mrs. Shepherd, has already suffered harm from an exhumation. Will it be irreparable? I don't know, but the decision does not rest on this point."

Both Tweedledum and Tweedledee nodded. Burr was sure they had no idea what they were nodding about. He was afraid he did.

"The point of decision, Mr. Lafayette, rests on the matter of prevailing on the merits. That is, are you likely to win at trial? Is the trial judge likely to decide that the wishes and interests of Mrs. Shepherd in preventing the exhumation outweigh the interests of the state in obtaining justice? Particularly, when there is new evidence. I am afraid, Mr. Lafayette, that on this point, you must fail."

"Your Honor," Burr said, standing.

"Sit down, Mr. Lafayette."

Burr sat down.

"It is not clear that you would win at trial. Therefore, I find that this matter does not warrant a preliminary injunction. The temporary injunction is dissolved."

"Your Honor," Burr said, standing once more.

"Mr. Lafayette, you have two choices. You may either appeal to the Supreme Court of the State of Michigan or you may take this up with the trial judge, Lawrence G. Skinner, and have a trial on the merits."

Burr started to sit back down.

"You might as well keep standing. We're leaving now. We are adjourned." She hammered her gavel and left, followed by Tweedledum and Tweedledee.

* * *

Burr rarely mourned a loss. There was always the next battle, and, for that matter, he hardly ever lost. After this loss, they adjourned to Jim's Tiffany Place. The food wasn't great, but Jim's had the great advantages of being close to the Court of Appeals, and having a good wine list. They sat in the atrium, the September sun pouring in, and as far away as Burr could get them from the schmaltzy Tiffany lamps that littered the restaurant and gave it its name, but had nothing to do with the Greek food it was known for.

Eve ordered Greek samplers for all of them. Burr didn't like Greek food, and he especially didn't like samplers, but the food was secondary to the wine, and the wine was secondary to the matter at hand.

Lizzie sat across from him, her stuffed grape leaf untouched. "So they're going to dig up Quinn?"

"No, they're not," Burr said.

"I thought we just lost."

"Judge Florentine said we can either appeal to the Supreme Court, or we can have a trial in front of Skinner."

Lizzie picked at the grape leaf with her fork. "What's going to happen?"

"We'll probably lose. In both forums," Burr said.

"Then why should we do it?"

"We can't give in to Cullen. If we fight long enough, we'll win," Burr said.

Jacob straightened his tie. "It will be expensive."

"Not that expensive," Burr said.

Eve, director of finance, poked Burr on the wrist with her fork.

"Burr, sometimes I think that you fight for the sake of fighting," Lizzie said. She stabbed the stuffed grape leaf, put the fork to her mouth, then set it back down. "I'm tired of fighting about this, especially if we're going to lose anyway."

Burr, who never gave an inch, gave an inch. "What would you like to do?"

"I don't want to fight about this anymore."

* * *

Back in his office, Burr leaned back in his chair, hands clasped behind his head, feet propped up on his desk. Zeke napped on the couch. Eve out front, Jacob in his office.

"Money." Burr said, loud enough for all to hear. "Money," he said again. "Jacob, it's time we started looking for the money."

"What did you say?" Jacob said from his office.

"How about a few suspects?" Eve said from her desk.

"My point exactly." Burr righted his chair. "Jacob, let's look for the money."

"We're going to look for money?" Jacob said.

"Who has it. Who doesn't. What they do with it."

"I beg your pardon," Jacob said.

"Whose money?" Eve said.

Burr was getting tired of talking to people he couldn't see. "Jacob, is there any chance you could come all the way in here for a minute?" Burr heard Jacob groan, but his partner walked in, Eve at his heels. Burr spun around in his chair to face the two of them.

"That's much better," he said. "Let's start with the oil men."

* * *

Burr and Zeke followed Maggie's Explorer down the two-track *du jour*. He parked behind her, and stepped into the mud, followed by Zeke, who didn't care about mud. Burr started down a path to the South Branch.

It was a clear, crisp September morning with a deep, blue sky, but it had rained last night, and the two-track was muddy. Sunlight filtered through the trees and lit up the pale green of the aspen, quaking in the breeze. It was fifty degrees, and Burr was glad to have on his Barbour coat. He loved the old-fashioned smell of the waxed cotton.

Burr spotted Maggie and Finn up ahead. Zeke saw them at the same time and ran ahead, spry for an aging lab, but then the dog did have an interest in Finn.

After meeting with the enterprising ornithologist in the jack pines, Burr had called her. "I know you don't like me, but this isn't about me. It's about Lizzie," he'd said. "The canoe paddle started all this. What if there's something more to this?" He had pleaded, cajoled and finally begged. She had given in, but her goodwill didn't extend to riding in the same car.

He caught up with her at the edge of the river.

"Is this where you were looking for the woodcock?"

"Back up the trail, where the aspen start to peter out."

"Is this where Finn brought you the paddle?"

"I think this is where she came out of the river."

"Which way did she come? Upriver or down?"

"She brought the paddle to me back up there." She pointed up the path.

"So you don't know."

"Upstream, I think. But I'm not sure."

Burr kicked a stick into the river. "Zeke, stay."

The stick spun in the current, then started downstream. Zeke studied the stick. Finn waded in after it. She grabbed it and brought it back to Burr. The dog sat in front of Margaret with the stick in her mouth.

"I haven't seen too many setters who like to retrieve."

"She was raised around a lab. My ex had one."

She took the stick from Finn.

"He was a jerk. Not the dog, my husband."

"Of course," Burr said. "Any idea how far she went to fetch the paddle?"

"No, but I don't think she'd have gone too far. Upstream or downstream."

They walked back up the path and drove out of the woods. Burr wasn't sure that any of this had helped very much, but he had spent a little time with Margaret, and he didn't think she hated him anymore.

* * *

"Ex-par-tay. Did I say it correctly, Mr. Lafayette?" Skinner waved a piece of paper at Burr. "That's what this is."

Burr didn't say a word. He wished he was somewhere else, actually anywhere else. Anywhere but here in the chambers of Skinner the Younger.

"You were the one who wanted to meet," Skinner said.

Burr had a death grip on the arms of the chair, his hands red, his knuckles white. He relaxed them ever so slowly. Perhaps he could speak without cursing. Cullen had clearly outsmarted him with his own *ex parte* order, and Skinner had been only too happy to sign. "Your Honor, had I known when the exhumation was going to occur, I would have been there, and I would have had my own expert with me."

Skinner waved the paper at him one more time, then he set it down in front of him.

"Mr. Lafayette, you didn't appeal the Court of Appeals decision. It was sent back to me. You didn't ask for a trial on the merits. Mr. Cullen presented me with the required affidavit for disinterment, which I granted. I'm sure he served you."

Burr squeezed the arms of his chair. "Your Honor, by the time I was served with the order, Cullen had already dug up the remains and conducted another autopsy."

"Sometimes the process servers are a bit slow," Skinner said.

"As long as Mr. Shepherd has been dug up, I'd like my own expert to examine the body."

Skinner twiddled his thumbs. "No can do." Skinner looked at Burr, raising his bent head ever so slightly.

"Your Honor—"

Skinner waved him off. "As you know, Michigan law requires that an order of disinterment be accompanied by an order of re-interment. We don't want poor Quinn's remains out of the ground any longer than necessary."

"Your Honor—"

Skinner waved him off again. "Mr. Shepherd has already been reburied."

Burr reached inside the pocket of his suit jacket and took a sheet of paper folded like a letter. "Your Honor, I have here my own affidavit for disinterment."

"No can do," Skinner said again. "The law does not favor exhumation."

* * *

Burr sat at his favorite table at his favorite restaurant. Like all his favorite tables, this one gave him a view of the door. Sitting with his back to the door always made him nervous. Beggar's Banquet, a dark, smoky and fairly beat-up bar and restaurant in the heart of East Lansing, served up their famous

Sympathy for the Devil, a bowl of chili and a draft, for a dollar, every day. It was a rare day, though, when they cooked up their five-alarm chili.

Jacob burst into the bar.

"This can't be good," Burr said.

"I beg your pardon."

"Never mind." Burr ate a spoonful of the chili. "It's five-alarm. Can I order you a bowl?"

"That will destroy your insides. If the beer doesn't first," Jacob said.

Jacob unfolded a paper napkin, set it neatly on a chair and sat down. "The worst has happened," he said.

As far as Burr was concerned, the worst had already happened at least a dozen times. "Jacob, we are warm and dry. We have a little money for food and drink."

Jacob reached into his jacket pocket, a corduroy jacket, harvest gold, in keeping with the season and the weather. He handed Burr a piece of paper.

At least it isn't the letter from the mortgage company.

Burr put it next to the chili crackers.

"Aren't you going to look at it?"

"After lunch."

"Well then, I'll tell you. The wound on Quinn Shepherd's skull matches the canoe paddle."

Burr, ever trying to live in the moment, finished his beer, and ordered a second.

* * *

Burr and Zeke stopped for the red flashing lights in front of the lodge. They watched Josh climb out of the school bus. He ran up to his mother and hugged her around one leg. The two of them walked into the lodge like they were in a three-legged race.

"Zeke, this is going to be even more unpleasant than I thought," Burr said.

Burr found Lizzie and Josh in the kitchen, Josh up to his elbows dunking a cookie in a glass of milk. "Gingersnaps. Want one?" Josh said.

"I do."

The dark brown cookie, perfectly round, had cracks on the top where it had expanded while baking. Rolled in sugar, it sparkled in the afternoon sun.

"Want to dunk?"

Burr loved gingersnaps, and he loved dunking. He dipped the cookie into Josh's glass.

"How bad is it?" Lizzie said. She folded her arms across each other and covered her chest.

"Pretty bad," Burr said.

"We'll be right back, honey." Lizzie left Josh with the gingersnaps. Burr followed her into the dining room. Josh didn't look up from his dunking.

"The wound matched the paddle," he said.

Lizzie sat down and held onto the edge of table.

Burr sat cross from her. *She's holding on for dear life.*

"The exhumation report says the wound on Quinn's skull matched the blade on the paddle."

"I didn't kill Quinn. I swear I didn't."

"I know you didn't." Burr wasn't so sure, but he didn't see any reason to argue about it right now.

"And the report could be wrong."

"It could," Burr said.

"Someone else could have hit him," she said.

"That's what we have to prove."

"This can't be happening." Lizzie kept her grip on the table and started to rock back and forth, ever so slightly.

Burr looked out the window. He watched one of the orange leaves fall from the maple tree. It landed in the river and drifted downstream.

"When did you notice the paddle was missing?"

"I don't remember." She looked down at her hands.

"Lizzie, this is not helpful."

"I don't know. I told you I never thought about it." She looked at Burr. "A man called," she said. "He wants money."

"I beg your pardon."

"He said he wants money."

"Who is he?"

"I don't know. He said Quinn owed him money."

"For what?"

"He said he'd call back with a place to meet." Lizzie stopped rocking. "What do we do?" she said.

"We have to wait."

* * *

Burr tracked down Jacob at the Small Planet, a vegetarian restaurant across the street from his building. Jacob was eating steamed vegetables drowned in tamari sauce, and sipping carrot juice through a straw.

"How did you find me?" Jacob said.

"It's the only place within fifty miles that serves carrot juice."

As if on cue, Jacob took a drink of the gooey orange liquid.

"Is that good for you?"

"Quite."

"What did you find out about our friends in the oil business?" Burr said.

"Nothing on Hawken or Osterman," Jacob said.

Jacob swabbed a piece of broccoli in the last of the tamari and chewed it slowly. Finally he said, "It seems that Mr. Gleason ran afoul of the authorities, but I don't see how that helps us."

"What did he do?"

"According to the State of Michigan securities agency, he sold one hundred twenty-five percent of an oil well in Manistee County."

"What happened?"

"They found oil," Jacob said.

"What was Gleason's defense?"

"He said he thought it would be a dry hole, so it wouldn't matter if he sold more than a hundred percent. He pled to one count of securities fraud. But that was ten years ago."

"The land man? Malone."

"He pled to one count of selling securities without a license." Jacob waved for the check.

"Allow me," Burr said.

"Thank you, Burr."

"There's just one more thing," Burr said.

"There is always just one more thing."

"We need the same information on Quinn and Lizzie. And you might as well check on Wes while you're at it. Thompson, too."

Burr paid the bill and left.

* * *

"That is a beautiful shotgun," Margaret Winston said.

"It was my grandfather's." Burr held a Parker twenty-eight-gauge side-by-side in the crook of his arm. It was part of a matched set, which also included a twenty-gauge and a twelve-gauge. He had inherited them from his father, all that was left after Colonial Broach failed, and his father drove his Cadillac into a bridge abutment on the Lodge freeway in Detroit.

Burr had spent the evening at The Gray Drake's annual grouse opener party. Black tie, champagne, wine and a five-course meal. Four young women in black dresses had played *The Four Seasons*. Wes held court, and Lizzie cooked, but Burr didn't think either of them had their hearts in it.

Now, at eight the next morning, he and Margaret Winston were standing somewhere east of Hartwick Pines, about fifteen miles north of the lodge. She bent and clipped a bell on Finn's collar. "Follow the bell. When it stops ringing, she's on point. Then walk to the last place you heard the bell."

She put two shells in her over/under. Then she looked at Burr. "I'm sorry I've been rude. It's just that you were so hard on me at the preliminary exam. I felt like you were trying to trick me."

Burr wasn't used to apologies from witnesses. "I'm sorry, but I have a client to defend."

"I know you do. I hope this hunt makes up for it."

She closed the breech of her shotgun and headed off into the woods. "Find a bird, Finn."

* * *

Burr sat by himself in a corner of the dining room at the Doherty Hotel, his back to the wall. Lizzie sat by herself five tables away from his and faced the door to the lobby. The mystery man had called back.

The Doherty Hotel, circa 1924, was a dark brown, brick four-story building, and the tallest building in Clare. The murals on the walls told the story of leprechauns brewing ale. Legend had it that a guest, who couldn't pay his bill, painted them for his room and board. *Something like me and that damned Sage*, he thought.

Burr couldn't understand why this of all places was packed at lunchtime on a weekday. Looking at the salad bar, Burr didn't think it could be the food, but then Burr hated salad bars. If he was going to eat at a restaurant, he wasn't going to make his own salad.

They waited. And waited.

Finally, a blond man with movie-star good looks stood in the doorway. He was lean and moved with the grace of an athlete. *He could have been a quarterback twenty years ago.* He surveyed the room, then walked over to Lizzie and sat down.

Lizzie sat very still and didn't say much. She did her best not to show any emotion, but it looked as if it was all she could do to sit across the table from him. After about twenty minutes, the man who looked like a quarterback got up. He looked around the room, then left.

* * *

Burr found Lizzie right where he expected to find her, in the kitchen of The Gray Drake. She was kneading bread dough.

"What did he want?" Burr said.

She looked up at him. There weren't tears in her eyes, but there could have been.

She kept working the bread dough. "He wants twenty-five thousand dollars that I don't have."

"What did he say?"

"I know I'm always in the kitchen, but I have to do this, and I don't know what else to do."

"It's all right, Lizzie."

"He said he wanted twenty-five thousand dollars," she said again.

"For what?"

"He said that was what was owed."

"What did you tell him?"

"I said I didn't have it. He said get it from Wes or Thompson."

"What's his name?"

"Ben. He said it was Ben."

"Really. I followed him. He went back to Mt. Pleasant. To his office, I think. As far as I can tell, his name isn't Ben. It's Cox. Charles Cox. He's a CPA."

"This keeps getting worse and worse. I don't know who to believe."

Burr didn't know who to believe either. Lizzie flipped the dough over and started kneading again. "Wes doesn't have that kind of money, and I don't see how I could ask Thompson. This whole thing is just too terrible."

"Did you have any idea that Quinn might be dealing drugs?"

"None." Lizzie kneaded the dough, then pounded it with her fist. "I have to do something."

"What if we ignore him?"

"He said if he didn't get the money, something bad would happen to Josh."

CHAPTER SEVEN

Margaret Winston, now Maggie, had asked Burr to dinner.

He turned off a gravel road, onto yet another unmarked two-track, to yet another cabin, on yet another river.

This one was the Chevrolet version of Thompson Shepherd's Cadillac log cabin. It was on the Manistee River, about ten miles west of Grayling.

Maggie opened the door. She had on a hunter-green A-line dress, tucked at the waist, a small black jacket and a pearl necklace. She had her hair in a French braid, her bare legs still tan late in September. Burr thought she was dangerously good-looking.

She slipped a little on the driveway. Burr grabbed her by the elbow.

"Heels and gravel are a tough combination," she said.

He opened the passenger door. "Zeke, back seat," he said. Maggie slid in.

"Would you mind if Finn came?"

"Not if she doesn't mind riding with Zeke."

Maggie went back for Finn. The dog jumped on Maggie's lap. She pushed her into the back seat, which delighted Zeke.

Burr climbed in. *How can this beautiful woman be living in what, by any stretch of the imagination, was a rundown cabin, that, at the very least, needed a coat of paint.*

He reached for the ignition, but she put her hand on his.

"Listen, you can hear the river. I know the cabin needs some work, but I like it the way it is. My grandfather built it in the twenties. The Manistee fishes every bit as well as the Au Sable. And there's no pressure. It's one of the best kept secrets up here."

Along with what happened to Quinn Shepherd.

When they got back to the paved road, Burr stopped. "Which way?" he said.

"Have you ever been to Tapawingo?"

Forty-five minutes later, Burr parked in front of a small gray house, facing a lake and surrounded by flower gardens in bloom, with the colors of fall – burnt orange, crimson, purple and yellow.

The maître d' sat them at a table facing the lake.

"This is my favorite restaurant," she said.

Burr nodded. He had been here many times, all paid for by Fisher and Allen. Tapawingo was the best restaurant Burr had ever been to in the middle of nowhere, and quite possibly the best restaurant he had ever been to. Not to mention the priciest. He had just enough room on the Lafayette and Wertheim credit card to pay for dinner.

Maggie ordered them a bottle of champagne. The waiter uncorked the bottle, poured them each a glass and left the bottle in an ice bucket.

Maggie raised her glass. "To rising fish."

"And tight lines," Burr said, the only fly-fishing toast he knew.

Maggie finished her champagne. Burr poured her another glass.

"Veuve Clicquot is my favorite," she said.

"Mine, too," Burr said, fibbing. He liked champagne well enough, but he had no real taste for it.

She finished her second glass. Burr split what was left in the bottle between them and stuck the dead soldier upside down in the ice bucket. Maggie flagged the waiter down and ordered another bottle.

As much as he liked this somewhat eccentric, altogether beautiful woman, there was something he had to say before things went any further. He thought they'd probably gone too far already.

"Maggie, as you know, Lizzie Shepherd has been charged with murder. I am defending her, and you are a key witness."

"That's how we met." She reached her hand across the table to his.

"Of course. But it's inappropriate for a lawyer to have a personal relationship with a witness."

"What are you talking about?"

"We really shouldn't go out until this is over. It's an ethics violation. Cullen will crucify me if he finds out."

"Just my luck," she said, but she didn't pull her hand back.

"It's only until the trial is over."

"So our date is over?" Maggie said.

"I didn't say that."

"What exactly did you say?"

Burr lost the courage of his convictions. "Let's figure this out after dinner," he said.

"You're still a bit of a wet blanket."

"I'm sorry. Forget I said it."

"How can I do that?"

"I'm sorry I brought it up. Please, let's keep going."

Maggie smiled, but Burr thought he had spoiled everything.

The waiter arrived with the second bottle of Veuve. He poured them each a glass. Maggie asked him to leave the cork and the cap.

She studied the cap and then turned it so Burr could see it. The cap was black and shiny with a picture of a woman's face on it.

"Do you know the story?"

"No," Burr said.

"This is a very old, very famous champagne. The owner, Monsieur Clicquot, died suddenly. His wife refused to sell the winery and decided to run it herself. It was scandalous at the time, but she made a great success of it. So much so that she put her picture on the cap and changed the name from Clicquot to Veuve Clicquot."

At least she's over my speech. He was over it, too.

"Veuve is French for widow."

"Of course," Burr said.

"I wonder if Lizzie was as resourceful as the Widow Clicquot, or cunning enough or maybe mad enough to kill her husband?"

Burr looked over her shoulder at the twilight on the lake, the trees a black band between the silver of the lake and the fading blue of the sky. He looked at Maggie. "I hope the only similarity is that they're both widows."

"I'm sorry, Burr. I was getting carried away."

"You're not the only one who wonders about Lizzie."

Burr poured them each another glass of champagne. "To fair winds and following seas." They clinked their glasses and drank.

"I don't ask men out, but I could see you like dogs, and you understand them."

"That's why you asked me to dinner?"

"I'm fussy, and I don't like most men. I think it's my father. Brilliant, but unapproachable."

"And I'm neither."

"That's not what I meant."

"I didn't think so." Burr didn't quite know how to take her, but he couldn't take his eyes off her.

The waiter arrived. "Do you mind if I order for us?" she said.

"Please do."

She ordered dinner and a bottle of wine to go with it. While they ate, Maggie asked him about duck hunting and sailboats. He quite liked her, and he was sure the champagne and the wine had nothing to do with it.

For her part, Maggie didn't seem as crisp as she had been, but maybe she was just relaxed.

The ever-attentive waiter arrived again. Burr was sure they had rung up at least five hundred dollars' worth, and he needed to stop the bleeding. Just as he was about to ask for the check, Maggie ordered them two Cognacs and a crème brûlée to share.

"We're on the way to six hundred," Burr mumbled.

"What was that?"

"Nothing."

After the Cognacs, Burr finally got the check. It was all of six hundred dollars. He reached for his wallet, but Maggie snatched the check from him. "I'm the one who asked you out."

"Thank you, Maggie. I've had a lovely time."

"My treat." She took the check from him and paid the bill. Burr walked behind her and pulled her chair back. She stood up, then sat back down.

"Is something wrong?"

"I'm afraid I had too much to drink."

Thank God, Burr thought. *There was no way I could keep up*. He pushed her chair back in and ordered two cappuccinos. "These are on me."

They finished their cappuccinos. Maggie pushed her chair back and stood up. "Now I'm wide-awake drunk. Let's try for a walk."

When Burr stood, he knew she wasn't the only one who'd had too much to drink.

"We won't be long." She led him on a brick path around to the lake. The moon had just risen, a crescent-shaped new moon. It cast a silver glow on the lake—flat calm in the late September night. They walked down to the beach. Maggie handed Burr her heels and stepped in. "It's still warm." She took

Burr's hand and they walked along the beach—Burr in the sand, Maggie in the water.

"Maggie, I think we're on someone else's property now."

"I think you're right." She led him another two hundred feet. "Follow me." The beautiful professor stepped onto a dock that stretched out into the lake.

"We're trespassing. This dock belongs to that cottage." Burr pointed behind him.

"I have a very fine lawyer."

Out she went. Burr, an inveterate rule breaker, and decidedly under the influence, didn't know why any of this troubled him. He followed her to the end.

"You sit there," she said pointing to a chair. Maggie walked to the edge of the dock and sat down. She dangled her legs over the side and splashed. "It's colder out here."

Burr eased himself into the chair. He shut his eyes and breathed in the night air off the lake. Wet, sandy and full of leaves.

He felt Maggie standing over him. She bent over and kissed him full on the lips. "You are a handsome man, Burr Lafayette. Maybe a bit old for me." Then she unzipped his slacks and fumbled in his shorts. "There you are." She got down on her knees.

This can't be happening.

As suddenly as she started, she stopped and stood up in front of him.

"I think you're ready." Maggie Winston reached under her dress and stepped out of her panties. "Hold these." She handed Burr a pair of white satin panties with lace on the front.

She thought better of it, took them back and folded them like a handkerchief and stuck them in the breast pocket of Burr's blazer with the lace sticking out.

"What if someone comes?" Burr said.

"I hope we both do." She sat down on him.

Thirty minutes later, they stumbled back to Burr's Jeep. There was no way he could drive her back to her cabin. They made it as far as the closest motel. Burr checked them in. Maggie had slept all the way, snoring softly next to him.

Burr couldn't understand why the desk clerk, mid-sixties, balding and bifocals, kept staring at his chest until he looked down his nose and saw Maggie's panties hanging out of the breast pocket of his jacket. He half carried Maggie to their room, the farthest of six cabins. He was at a loss as to what to do next, but finally got her out of her dress, back into her panties and put her in the single bed closest to the bathroom.

* * *

Two days later, Burr sat in Skinner's chambers, the judge in front of him, Cullen to his right.

He had just now gotten rid of his Tapawingo hangover and had sworn off alcohol forever.

He had spent the night in the motel in the other bed with Zeke. Finn slept with her mistress. The next morning Maggie looked absolutely radiant, but it was clear that she was more hungover than he was. She didn't say a word about what happened on the dock. If she wondered how she got to the No Tell Motel or how her dress had gotten hung up, she didn't let on.

After a shower, they each had steak and eggs with hash browns, rye toast and tomato juice. When he dropped her off, she kissed him on the cheek and said she'd like to see him again. Burr didn't think she remembered anything about his ethical issue. He was clearly in over his head.

"Mr. Lafayette, are you with us?" Skinner said.

Burr snapped to attention. "Of course, Your Honor."

"As I was saying, I think the best thing to do is settle this here and now."

Burr didn't say anything.

"The State would accept a plea." Cullen turned to him.

"Thank you, Mr. Cullen. What would you accept?"

"Second-degree murder."

"My client is innocent," Burr said.

Skinner sighed. "Mr. Lafayette, that's a bad decision, but if you are not going to agree to a plea, we are going to have a trial. And we are going to have it soon."

* * *

Back in East Lansing, Burr made a U-turn on MAC Avenue and parked in the no-parking zone in front of St. John's Catholic Church. He crossed himself, said a Hail Mary and got out of the car, followed by Zeke. A cold wet rain was falling. The two of them dashed up the street to his office.

As soon as he walked in, Eve and Jacob ambushed him. Before either of them could say a word, he squeezed by and sat at his desk, a position he thought he could defend.

They followed him in. Eve handed him an envelope.

This can't be good. He handed it back to her. "What does it say?"

"It's a summons from the Crawford County Probate Court. Thompson Shepherd is suing Lizzie for custody of Josh."

Burr took the envelope back and read the summons. "Will it never end?" He folded the summons and put it back in the envelope. Then he crumpled it into a ball and threw it in his wastebasket.

* * *

Burr waited for yet another judge, this time the Honorable Judge Horace Gilmore of the Crawford County Probate Court. Lizzie sat to his left, Jacob next to her. It was obvious it was all Lizzie could do to hold herself together. Eve and Wes sat behind them. And there in the back, who else but John Cullen. There was no sign of the judge, Thompson Shepherd, or his lawyer, whom Burr knew only too well.

Burr heard the door open behind him and watched none other than Roy Dahlberg glide into the courtroom with his new client, Thompson Shepherd. Roy Dahlberg of Dahlberg and Langley, the Ford family's lawyers. Dahlberg was the patrician's patrician. His black suit made Burr's look like it came from Goodwill. In his prior life Burr had sparred with Dahlberg. Many times. Burr had won more than he'd lost, but he had met his match in Dahlberg.

Dahlberg stopped in the aisle across from Burr and offered his hand. Burr thought it over, stood, and shook hands.

"Good to see you, Lafayette. I'm afraid you're on the wrong side again."

Burr winked at him and sat back down. The same wispy-mustached bailiff entered. "All rise."

He's doing triple duty.

Judge Horace Gilmore shuffled in, a painfully thin man. His robes hung over him like a funeral shroud. Two big ears stuck out from a fringe of white hair, which also grew out of his ears. Wire-rimmed bifocals hung halfway down a long, pointed nose. He had a sour expression on his face. Burr thought it entirely fitting that such an elderly man served as probate judge.

Judge Gilmore sat and caught his breath. He shuffled through the papers in front of him, painfully slowly. His lips moved as he read. He turned the pages back and forth. Back and forth. *The judge could have memorized the pleadings by now.* At last, Judge Gilmore looked at Burr, then at Dahlberg, then he boomed, "I note two strange lawyers in my courtroom." Gilmore had at least one foot in the grave, but he had a voice like a foghorn.

"Let us begin," Gilmore said.

Dahlberg stood.

"Sit down, Mr. Dahlberg. This isn't going to take but a minute." The judge shuffled his papers again, his lips moving again. At last, he looked over to Dahlberg. "Mr. Dahlberg, in your emergency petition, you ask that custody be awarded to your client, Thompson Shepherd, the father of the deceased, Quinn Shepherd, and the paternal grandfather of Joshua Shepherd, the lad in question."

"That's correct, Your Honor."

"Mr. Dahlberg. You allege that the lad's mother, Elizabeth Shepherd, is not fit to be a custodial parent because, among other things, she has been accused of murdering her husband, engages in drug trafficking, and is otherwise an unfit mother. That is quite a laundry list of bad behaviors." Judge Gilmore cleared his throat, which pinned Burr's ears back.

"If even a scintilla of this is true, the lad should be removed from the household immediately. Based on your pleadings, I am going to rule in your favor and award custody to the grandfather, pending the outcome of the trial."

"Thank you, Your Honor," Dahlberg said.

Burr couldn't believe what he just heard. Jacob's jaw dropped. Lizzie started to cry. Burr jumped to his feet. "Your Honor, I object. My client has been wrongly accused of a crime, and she certainly has not been convicted. She hasn't even been tried, yet. Quinn Shepherd's death was an accident. Just because the plaintiff alleges these things does not make them true."

"I do not like to chance with the life of a young lad."

"Your Honor, what is the emergency? Joshua is in a stable living situation. He goes to school. He has two grandfathers."

Dahlberg bounced to his feet. "Your Honor, this most certainly is an emergency. There is to be a trial shortly. What would happen if the defendant's bail were revoked?"

"Yes," the frail judge thundered.

"Your Honor," Burr said, "that is highly unlikely, and if it were to happen, Joshua has two grandfathers close at hand."

Lizzie looked up at Burr.

"It is prudent to make a change now before there is an emergency," Dahlberg said.

Judge Gilmore cleared his throat. "Mr. Lafayette, while I find your argument compelling, I am going to rule in favor of Mr. Dahlberg."

"Your Honor, the law favors the custodial parent, especially the mother. If you believe there may be an issue with Mrs. Shepherd, I ask that you appoint a Friend of the Court to conduct an investigation. We will agree with the Friend of the Court's recommendation."

"A Friend of the Court," the judge said, mostly to himself. "A Friend of the Court," the judge, thundering this time.

"I object, Your Honor," Dahlberg said. "This is a grave situation that you must deal with immediately."

"Your Honor, nothing is lost and everything is gained by appointing a Friend of the Court. I think it's the most prudent thing to do," Burr said.

"Mr. Lafayette, I think you may be on to something," Judge Gilmore said. He looked at Burr, then Dahlberg. "So ordered." He tapped his gavel, a weak tap with all the force of the law.

* * *

Burr had just finished his first Labatt when his cheeseburger arrived.

The Keg O' Nails, a stone's throw from the courthouse, smelled like stale beer and smoked cigarettes. It was built of logs, had a sunken bar and eating area, and the best cheeseburger in Grayling.

Burr took a bite of his cheeseburger.

"How can you possibly eat that?" Jacob said.

"Arguing makes me hungry."

"That will kill you," Jacob said.

Eve looked up from her chicken Caesar. "My guess is that something or someone will get to Burr before a cheeseburger does."

"Are you sure you don't want anything?" the waitress said, a robust woman of fifty, who had managed to smear her lipstick outside the confines of her lips.

"I am quite sure," Jacob said.

Lizzie picked at her Caesar salad but mostly rearranged the romaine without eating any of it. "Burr, thank you, but I'm not sure what just happened."

"We won," Burr said.

"It's not clear to me that we did win," Jacob said.

What was clear to Burr was that Thompson Shepherd wouldn't be paying for Lizzie's defense.

"All you did was get a Friend of the Court appointed. That hardly constitutes a victory."

"Jacob, by the time Gilmore gets a Friend of the Court appointed, and by the time the investigation is done and the findings are reported to the judge, the trial will be over. Lizzie will have had custody of Josh the entire time."

Burr drowned a French fry in ketchup, which then dripped on his tie. Eve, ever at the ready, dipped her napkin in Jacob's water and dabbed the ketchup off Burr's tie, a subdued red paisley with a black and yellow pattern.

"What are you doing?" Jacob said.

"If I get to it quick enough, the Scotchgard keeps it from staining." Eve had long ago figured out that the only way to keep Burr from buying a new tie after every meal was a generous spray of Scotchgard.

"It's still not a victory," Jacob said.

"Delay is often the best victory." Burr took another bite of his cheeseburger.

* * *

Burr sat at his desk, Jacob and Eve in the side chairs. "Why must everyone in this state plan their life around November fifteenth?"

"November fifteenth?" Jacob said.

"Opening day of deer season." Eve looked down her nose at Jacob. "You must know that by now."

"I don't keep track of the days on which otherwise civilized men kill animals with the blessing of the law." Jacob turned to Burr. "What little planning you do revolves around duck season."

"Eve, I need you to find us an expert, who will say this was all a terrible accident. While you do that, I am going to see our drug dealer friend in Mt. Pleasant."

* * *

"Mr. Cox will see you now."

The offices of Cox and Lindeman, Certified Public Accountants, were on the first floor of a brick, two-story office building on the east side of Mission and two blocks from Central Michigan University. Burr wondered if Lindeman had anything to do with drugs or, for that matter, if Cox did.

The receptionist showed Burr into Cox's office, a corner office with a private entrance.

The accountant stepped around his desk to shake hands with Burr. *With a grip like that, he could probably throw a football seventy yards.*

"Charlie Cox," Charlie Cox said. "Please sit down."

Burr started to sit in one of Cox's side chairs.

"Let's sit here." Cox motioned Burr to yet another leather chair in the corner of his office. Cox sat on a matching couch, a coffee table between them.

"Coffee, Mr. Lafayette?"

"With cream."

"Missy," Cox said. The receptionist scurried out.

He does look like a football player.

"Did you ever play football?"

"I beg your pardon?"

"Football."

"Why, yes," Cox said. "Quarterback. How did you know?"

"Lucky guess."

Missy brought the coffee and scurried away again.

"How can I help, Mr. Lafayette?"

"It's a tax matter," Burr said.

"That's what I do," Cox said. "What kind?"

"Income taxes," Burr said.

"Yes."

"Actually, unreported income."

"Can you tell me about it?"

Burr sipped his coffee. *This must have been brewed before Labor Day.* "It's all in cash."

"Cash is king. Although unreported income can be tax evasion," Cox said.

Burr tried his coffee again. It hadn't improved.

"How long has this been going on?" Cox said.

"I'm not exactly sure. Quite a while, I think."

"You could go to jail for income tax evasion. That's how they finally caught up with Al Capone."

"I thought he was a bootlegger."

"He was, but they could never pin that on him. They got him on tax evasion. It was precedent-setting."

"So you are an expert in income-tax evasion?"

"I am." Cox slurped his coffee.

Apparently he enjoys prehistoric coffee.

"Does anyone know about this?"

"Elizabeth Shepherd knows about it. Do you know her?"

"Elizabeth Shepherd. No. No, I don't think so." *Cox might be losing a bit of his helpful attitude.*

"She said she knows you."

"What do I have to do with this?" Cox put his coffee down.

"She said you demanded money for drugs you sold to her husband."

"I have no idea what you're talking about."

Burr took a swallow of the coffee. "This may be the worst coffee I have had in my entire life." He put the cup down. "Income-tax evasion and drug dealing. A modern-day Al Capone." It was Burr's turn to be knowledgeable. "You could go to jail for one or the other. Or both."

"I have no idea what you're talking about," Cox said again.

"I think you do."

"I have no idea what you're talking about," Cox said for the third time.

"Mr. Cox, unless you tell me exactly what was going on with you and Quinn Shepherd, I will see to it that you lose your license and spend a very long time in a very small space with very unpleasant people."

Cox jumped to his feet. "This is outrageous."

"Mr. Cox, you forced Elizabeth Shepherd to meet with you at the Doherty."

"I have no idea who she is."

"I saw you with her there."

"I was never there."

Burr looked down at his coffee, then up at the accountant. "Mr. Cox, I think you were selling Quinn Shepherd drugs. He owed you money. I think you were at The Gray Drake on the night of the auction. You followed him out to the river. And you killed him. You probably would have gotten away with it if you'd left it there. But you got greedy. You wanted your money, didn't you, Mr. Cox. So you threatened Lizzie. Isn't that how it happened?"

"Get out."

"Income-tax evasion and selling drugs. We can add murder. Which is it?" Burr said. "All three?"

"Get out."

Burr leaned back in his chair. Cox glared at Burr. He looked around his office, then at his hands. He stormed out by his private entrance.

Burr sat where he was. "I've been thrown out of courtrooms, offices, and bars, but I've never had anyone leave their own office with me in it. I wish Jacob were here to see this." He stood and left the same way Cox did.

* * *

Burr led Eve and Jacob to Wes's office, their headquarters until the trial was over. There was more to be answered before the trial started, but there was never enough time, and there were never enough answers.

Burr sat at Wes's desk, Eve and Jacob in the chairs in front of him, Zeke napping on the couch. *Just like in East Lansing*, he thought. "Eve, please send Mr. Cox a subpoena for the trial. I want to hear what he has to say under oath."

"Shouldn't we bring in the police now?" Jacob said.

"No. The trial is right around the corner, and I don't want it delayed by an investigation."

"Aren't Lizzie and Josh in danger?" Eve said.

"I don't think so. Especially not after Cox gets a subpoena. If he tried anything he'd be pointing the finger at himself."

Jacob stood up and shivered. "This room is beastly cold."

"I'll light a fire." Eve stood and walked to the fireplace. She got down on her hands and knees, and laid a fire.

"I've seen screens that do a better job of keeping out the wind than these windows," Jacob said.

Eve opened the flue. She reached for a crumpled piece of paper on top of Burr's yellow legal pad. Burr snatched it away from her.

"I need more paper to get this going."

"Not this piece," Burr said.

"It's crumpled," Eve said.

Burr tossed it up in the air and caught it. "This is Cullen's witness list. I was mad at it."

Eve grabbed Burr's yellow pad and ripped out six or seven sheets. She crumpled up the papers, stuck them under the grate and lit them.

Flames from the legal-pad papers licked up against the kindling. *The logs might actually catch fire.*

Eve pulled her side chair up to the fire.

"I suppose there's a reason you were mad at the witness list," she said.

"If I get any colder, I will have frostbite," Jacob said.

"You should have been here last night. The wind was really howling," Burr said.

"The witness list," Eve said.

"It's just what you'd expect. Everyone who testified at the preliminary exam."

Burr felt the heat on his back and turned toward the fire. The logs burned merrily.

"Cullen added two more of the oil men. Hawken and Osterman."

"Why would he do that?" Eve said.

"They are all each other's alibis," Jacob said.

"Anyone else?" Eve said.

"Two more," Burr said. "Heidi Grettenberger and Virginia Walker."

"Who are they?" Eve said.

"I don't know, and it's too late to find out. We'll have to take our chances at the trial."

"This is the most god-awful place I've ever been in." Jacob clutched his coat around him.

"The only reason we're here is because of you. You're the one who loves the Au Sable and The Gray Drake," Burr said.

"It's not cold during the summer."

Eve went back to her chair and reached into her purse. She handed Burr a piece of paper.

"What's this?" Burr said.

"Your expert," Eve said. "And his resume."

Burr read the paper. "This is who you found?"

"Doctors don't like to testify against doctors," Eve said. "And that goes double for doctors who are coroners. He's the only one I could find."

* * *

"Shouldn't you be getting ready for the trial?" Victor Haymarsh said. He took a cigarette from the pack Burr had given him and lit it. He was one of Burr's oldest friends, half Ojibwe, half Pottawatomie, and a chief. Custom required that guests present a chief with a gift of tobacco.

"This is on my way to see our expert."

"Walpole Island isn't on the way to anywhere."

Burr had crossed the St. Clair River by ferry into Canada and had met Victor at five this morning. The two of them, plus Zeke, sat in a stake blind and looked out on Half Moon Pond, waiting for the ducks to fly.

"Have you got it figured out yet?" Victor said.

"No."

"Love or money?" Victor said.

"I beg your pardon."

"Everything in life is about love or money."

* * *

Burr drove off the ferry at 2:30 that afternoon. He and Zeke, along with three mallards and three wood ducks, cleared customs. They drove to 941 Vine, a brick Cape Cod in Dearborn with peeling white trim and a sidewalk full of cracks.

A goliath of a man in a Red Wings baseball cap answered the door. He ducked and came out. Burr backed off the porch onto the sidewalk. There clearly wasn't room for both of them on the porch.

"Dr. Traker?"

The giant nodded.

He's at least six-eight. Burr offered his hand. "Burr Lafayette. I think my assistant spoke with you about being an expert witness."

The giant shook Burr's hand. Burr was sure his hand would be crushed, but he'd had more forceful encounters with a hand towel.

"Robert Traker," he said in a voice barely above a whisper. He had glasses with black frames that covered most of his face, ivory skin and a nose two sizes too small for the rest of him.

"I'd invite you in, but it's a little messy." He took off his hat and swatted at a fly. He was bald as a cue ball. He put his hat back on and took off his glasses. *What happened to his eyebrows?* Not a hair on his head. No eyebrows, and as far as Burr could tell, no trace of any whiskers.

Eve, what have you done?

"I need an expert witness who can cast some doubt on the second autopsy."

Traker arched what would have been his eyebrows.

"I'd like you to testify that Quinn Shepherd wasn't struck by a canoe paddle."

The good doctor put his glasses back on. *That's better. I'll have to tell him not to take off his glasses when he's testifying.*

"Could you testify to that?"

"I might be able to," Tracker said, just above a whisper.

"You'll have to speak up in court, Dr. Traker." Burr wasn't sure how a bald giant who spoke in a whisper would come across to the jury, but Traker was all he had. He kicked at a piece of loose concrete on the sidewalk.

"Take it easy on my sidewalk."

"Can you testify to that?" Burr said.

"How much do you pay your experts?"

*   *   *

It was the eve of the trial. Jacob came into Wes's office and dropped three files in front of Burr. "Clean as a whistle," he said.

"Yes?"

Jacob started pacing in front of Burr's desk. "Lizzie has excellent credit. Quinn has, or had, good credit, too. Selling drugs without getting caught does help get the bills paid." He started pacing again. "Nothing on Thompson, either."

"Please," Burr said.

"Please what?"

"Please stop pacing and sit down."

Jacob stopped in front of Burr and threw down a fourth file. "But, Wes," he said. "Wes, on the other hand, is a disaster. He has terrible credit. The Gray Drake has terrible credit. And he hasn't paid the property taxes here in two years."

"What do you suppose it means?" Eve said.

"It probably means the fishing hasn't been too good," Burr said.

"Burr, please," Eve said.

"I don't know," Burr said. "Maybe he just isn't good with money, or maybe he has more to do with this than I thought. Maybe it doesn't mean anything."

Jacob started pacing again. "The trial starts tomorrow, and we still don't have any suspects."

"I am painfully aware of that," Burr said.

"What are you going to do?" Eve said.

Burr opened one of the files. He made a show of studying it, but he wasn't studying anything. *What am I going to do?*

"Burr, looking at a file is not the solution," Eve said.

Burr closed the file and picked up one of his No. 2 yellow pencils. "As of now, our defense is that Quinn Shepherd drowned."

"Do you think that's what happened?" she said.

"No."

Jacob started pacing again. "My God, man. There is more."

"I know there is, but I don't know what it is."

Jacob kept pacing.

"Jacob, please stop pacing," Eve said. She turned to Burr. "What are you going to do?"

"I'm going to start with an accidental drowning and see what happens." He kept tapping his pencil.

"Would you please stop that tapping?" Eve said.

Burr broke his No. 2 yellow pencil in half.

CHAPTER EIGHT

The courtroom smelled of Spic and Span, Pledge and Windex. The gallery was full. *Skinner can't possibly have summoned this many people for a jury pool.* The rest of them must want to get a firsthand look at the biggest news in Crawford County since the extinction of the grayling.

The bailiff entered. "All rise."

Shoes scuffed the floor. *There goes all the hard work.*

Judge Lawrence G. Skinner entered the courtroom and sat.

"Be seated," the bailiff said.

"Ladies and gentlemen," Skinner said, "we are here today to select the jury in the matter of the State versus Shepherd." He opened a file in front of him and handed it to the bailiff. "Call the first potential juror."

"John Kuchinski," the bailiff said.

Burr watched a beefy man walk up the aisle.

The bailiff swore him in and Cullen approached the witness box. "Mr. Kuchinski, where do you live?"

"Frederick," he said.

"Your address?"

"216 Maple."

"And what do you do for a living?"

Kuchinski put his hands on the railing. "I'm a plumber," he said.

"I have no objection to this juror." Cullen smiled at Burr and sat down.

Burr stood. "I'd like to ask Mr. Kuchinski a few questions, Your Honor."

"He lives in Crawford County and he's a plumber. What more do you possibly need to know?" Skinner said.

"Your Honor, it's customary for both prosecutor and defense to *voir dire.*"

"What?"

"The court rules give the attorneys the right to question potential jurors."

"You mean *voir DIRE*, with a long *I*, like *dire* circumstances."

Burr bit his cheek. "That's right, Your Honor."

"All right, but let's get our jury." Skinner shooed Burr with his right hand.

Burr walked up to Kuchinski.

"Mr. Kuchinski," Burr said, "are you familiar with The Gray Drake?"

"Yes."

"How, may I ask."

"I did some work there."

"What kind of work?"

Kuchinski tapped his fingers on the railing. "I put in a new hot water line to the kitchen."

"Mr. Lafayette, this doesn't seem relevant," Skinner said.

"Just a few more questions, Your Honor." He turned to Kuchinski. "And how did it go?"

"The work went fine, but it took forever to get paid."

"Thank you, Mr. Kuchinski." Burr turned to Skinner. "Your Honor, I move to disqualify this witness because he may be prejudiced against my client."

"On what grounds?"

"Your Honor, Mr. Kuchinski may be prejudiced because he was paid late."

Skinner peered down at Kuchinski. "How long did it take to get paid?"

Kuchinski sat back in his chair. He started counting on the fingers of his left hand. "One, two, three, four, five." His ring finger was missing from the knuckle up. Then he shifted to his right hand. "Six, seven, eight. No, seven." Kuchinski looked up at Skinner. "It took seven months."

"Your Honor, I move that the witness be disqualified."

"Counselor, that is not grounds for excusing a juror."

"Then I use one of my peremptory challenges."

"Mr. Lafayette, you're not going to run this trial," Skinner said.

"Of course not, Your Honor."

Skinner nodded at Burr, then looked down at the would-be juror. "You may be excused, Mr. Kuchinski."

The plumber with the missing finger looked up at Skinner.

"You're not going to be on the jury. Go back to work. Mr. Cullen, call the next juror."

"Herbert Loomis."

Loomis was as thin as Kuchinski was thick. He was wiry, with Popeye forearms, bulging eyes, a pushed-in nose, and a hairline that looked like it was in a hurry to get to the back of his neck. The bailiff swore him in.

"Mr. Loomis," Cullen said, "where do you live?"

"415 High Street," he said. "Grayling."

"What is your occupation?"

"I own North Country Water Sports."

"Thank you, Mr. Loomis," Cullen said. "The prosecution has no objections."

"Your witness, Mr. Lafayette."

Burr jumped up before Skinner could say anything. "What does North Country Water Sports do, Mr. Loomis?"

He cleared his throat. "Canoe livery," he said.

"Canoe livery?" Burr said. "You mean you rent canoes?"

"That's right."

"To tourists?"

"That's right."

"On the Au Sable?"

Loomis nodded.

"Let the record reflect that Mr. Loomis answered in the affirmative," Burr said. "Your Honor, I move that Mr. Loomis be disqualified on the grounds that he may be prejudiced against fly-fishing and, by extension, The Gray Drake and my client."

"Why is that, Mr. Lafayette?" Skinner looked a little peeved.

"Your Honor, it is well known that canoe liveries and fly fishermen do not get along."

Cullen stood up. "Your Honor, everybody knows everybody around here."

"I object to this juror," Burr said.

Skinner rolled his eyes. "You are excused, Mr. Loomis."

"Linda Germany," the bailiff said.

"At least we have a woman," Burr said, mostly to himself.

Linda Germany had short brown hair, glasses, too much makeup and looked like she hadn't missed a meal in quite some time.

The bailiff swore her in.

"Mrs. Germany, where do you live?"

"Just up the road," she said. "952 High Street."

"And your occupation?"

"Housewife," she said.

"Thank you," Cullen said. "The prosecution has no objection to this juror."

Skinner looked at Burr.

"Thank you, Your Honor." Burr stood up and walked to Mrs. Germany.

"Mrs. Germany, are you married?"

"Yes."

"And what does your husband do for a living?"

"He's a bookkeeper."

"Who does he work for?"

"Crawford Oil and Gas."

"Respectfully, Your Honor, I ask that you disqualify this juror."

"Mr. Lafayette, I don't see any connection between this potential juror and your client."

"Your Honor, it is well known that The Gray Drake is opposed to oil and gas development near the Au Sable. This is prejudicial to Mrs. Germany's husband's livelihood."

"That connection is too tenuous. Mrs. Germany, you are impaneled."

"The Shepherds are all wrong about drilling around here," Linda Germany said.

"I beg your pardon," Skinner said.

"There's no oil that's going in their precious river," she said.

Skinner waved his gavel at her and then pointed it down the aisle. "Mrs. Germany, you are excused." The bookkeeper's wife lumbered off.

"Counsel, approach the bench," Skinner said.

Burr stood up.

"You too, Jack."

The two adversaries stood before Judge Skinner. "Just who would you like to see on this jury, Mr. Lafayette?"

Burr wanted an all-women jury, preferable women who had been cheated on. That and jurors who didn't have anything against The Gray Drake. He thought that could be a tall order. "Your Honor, I'd like a fair and impartial jury. Preferably made up of people who have not had business dealings with my client, who do not have philosophical differences and who are fair-minded."

"Mr. Lafayette, fair-minded and impartial is possible. Jurors who haven't had business dealings or philosophical differences with The Gray Drake may be difficult."

By the end of the day, the jury had been impaneled. Seven men and five women. One alternate, also a woman. Two of the women were divorced, one of the men. Burr couldn't ask them if they'd been cheated on.

It was far from perfect, but it was better than he had feared.

* * *

Cullen paced back and forth in front of the jury, then stopped at the side of the jury box closest to the prosecutor's table. "Ladies and gentlemen of the jury, there are few crimes worse than a woman killing her husband. The crime is even worse when the husband and wife have a child, especially a young child." He stopped talking and looked each juror in the eye, one by one. "And that is exactly what this woman has done." He pointed at Lizzie, then turned back to the jury.

"On the night of June 21st, 1989, under the cover of darkness, Elizabeth Shepherd lured her husband off the South Branch, and she murdered him. She struck him with a canoe paddle. Then she wrapped the anchor chain of his boat around his ankle and put him in the river. She tried to make it look like he drowned. But Quinn Shepherd didn't drown." Cullen stopped again. He looked at the gallery, then the jury. They were all on the edge of their seats.

He pointed at Lizzie again. "That woman, Elizabeth Shepherd, Quinn Shepherd's wife, murdered him." Another pause. "She murdered him with a canoe paddle."

Everyone in the courtroom knew exactly what the case was about, but Cullen had played it like a true showman.

"I object, Your Honor." He had no earthly reason to object, but Cullen was doing such a bang-up job, Burr felt he had to put a stop to it.

Judge Skinner looked at him. "On what grounds?"

"Your Honor, the prosecutor's comments are inflammatory."

"Mr. Lafayette, this is an opening statement in a murder trial. Over-ruled."

Burr looked over at the jury. They had calmed down. His job done, Burr sat down. "Yes, Your Honor."

Cullen continued. "As I was saying, the defendant, Elizabeth Shepherd, murdered her husband. She tried to make it look like an accident, but it was not." Cullen glared at Lizzie. "It most certainly was not."

Lizzie looked directly at Cullen, just as Burr had instructed. She sat up straight but without looking defiant. Then she looked down. *Perfect*, Burr thought.

Cullen turned back to the jury. "Not only did the accused murder her husband, she made her son fatherless." Cullen paused. "Fatherless."

Lizzie shook her head. "No," she said softly.

"Ladies and gentlemen," he said with all the gravitas he could muster, "I am going to prove to you beyond a reasonable doubt that Elizabeth Shepherd murdered her husband. In cold blood. I am going to prove that she commit-ted murder in the first degree. Murder in the first degree."

Burr thought Cullen was off to a good start. He started to tap his pencil. Cullen looked over, then walked toward him. He lined himself up between Burr and the jury. Cullen turned his back to Burr and faced the jury so they couldn't see Burr.

I was wondering when you'd figure that out.

"Ladies and gentlemen," Cullen said again, his back squarely to Burr. "First degree murder has three requirements. First, there must be a death. Second, the defendant must have intentionally killed the deceased. And, third, the defendant must have had a plan to kill her husband." Cullen stopped again. He eyed the jurors, one by one. "I will show you that Elizabeth Shep-herd intended to kill her husband. It was no accident." He paused. "Do you know *why* she killed her husband?" Cullen paused again, then paced in front of the jury.

As much as he hated to admit it, Burr thought it was a nice touch.

"I'll tell you why," Cullen continued. "She was jealous. That's right. Elizabeth Shepherd was jealous." Cullen took a deep breath. "Quinn Shep-herd wasn't perfect. Far from it. But is that a reason to kill him?" Another pause. "Of course not. Elizabeth Shepherd saw her husband with another woman that night. First at The Gray Drake. Later that night, in a bar. The sight of her husband with this woman enraged her."

"That's not true," Lizzie said. Burr put his hand on Lizzie's shoulder.

Cullen pointed at Lizzie again, then turned back to the jury. "She was jealous, and she killed her husband. She had a plan. She ambushed him on the river. She lured him to shore, then she struck him with a canoe paddle. She tried to make it look like he drowned. That was her plan." Cullen stood between Burr and the jury again. He turned back to Lizzie and pointed at her again, careful to let the jury see her but not Burr. "I will prove that she murdered her husband." Cullen walked up to the jury box. He smiled at them as if they were his flock. And when I do, I ask that you find the defendant guilty of first-degree murder." Cullen walked back to his table and sat down.

"Mr. Lafayette," Judge Skinner said.

Burr stood. He pulled down the cuffs of his shirt that didn't need pulling down. He straightened the knot on his tie that didn't need straightening. All was as it should be.

Skinner shook his head but didn't say anything.

Burr walked halfway to the jury box. "Ladies and gentlemen, my name is Burr Lafayette, and I represent Lizzie Shepherd." He wouldn't call her the defendant or the accused. He wanted Lizzie to have a personal relationship with the jury.

"Ladies and gentlemen," he said, "a tragedy has occurred. A tragedy." Burr paused. It was his turn to look each juror in the eye, one by one. "A tragedy," he said again. "The tragedy is that Lizzie has lost her husband. And her son has lost his father. That is the tragedy." Burr took another step closer. "But there is another tragedy." He put his hands in the pockets of his slacks.

The jury leaned toward Burr, who looked down at his shoes, then scuffed the faded linoleum with one foot. He looked up again. "The tragedy is that this man . . . " Burr stepped toward Cullen. He pulled his right hand out of his pocket and pointed at Cullen, a foot away from the prosecutor's nose. "This man has taken a tragedy and accused Lizzie Shepherd of murder."

Cullen sat bolt upright. Whatever trace of a smile he may have had disappeared. He pushed Burr's hand away and jumped to his feet. "Your Honor, this is outrageous."

Burr stepped back to the jury. "This was an accident," Burr said. "A terrible accident. Quinn Shepherd drowned. But it was an accident. That's what Clyde Fowler said. Do you know who Clyde Fowler is?" Burr was sure they all did, but he'd tell them anyway. "Clyde Fowler is the Crawford County Medical Examiner. The coroner. He investigated the accident, and he performed the autopsy." Burr looked at his shoes again. He counted to ten, then looked at the jury. "And do you know what he found? He found that Quinn Shepherd drowned. He drowned." Burr poked at the jury with each word. "Quinn Shepherd wasn't murdered. Dr. Fowler said it was an accident. An accident." Burr swept his right arm toward Cullen. "Sometimes in life there are accidents. And this is one of them." Burr turned away from the jury. He took two steps toward Lizzie, then turned back to the jury.

"Ladies and gentlemen," he said, "the Shepherds did not have a perfect marriage. Do any of us?" The jurors shook their heads. Burr had them. *If I could stop right here and now, I would win,* he thought. "Theirs was not a perfect marriage, but it was a good marriage. Quinn did what he loved. He fished for a living. Lizzie did what she loved. She cooked. At the place where she grew up. In the place she loved. And the most important thing was," Burr paused, then, "they had a son together. A beautiful son, Joshua. He's six years old." Burr stepped toward Cullen and pointed at him again. "This man will try to string together one improbability after another. One after another. And when he's done, he'll try to convince you that this thread of improbabilities is murder. Well, it's not!" Burr said, clapping his hands.

Cullen jumped, the jury jumped. Skinner and everyone else jumped.

"Stop it, Lafayette. This is a court of law, not a theater," the judge said.

"Yes, Your Honor."

Actually, Burr did think it was theater.

"This was an accident, not murder." Burr walked back to his table and sat down.

"The State calls Brian Bilkey."

Burr jumped up. "Your Honor, may I approach the bench?"

"Counselor, Mr. Cullen has just called his first witness."

Burr walked around to the front of his table. "Your Honor, at the preliminary examination, Mr. Cullen established that Mr. Bilkey found Mr. Shepherd's body. In the interest of time, the defense is willing to stipulate to that."

Burr had to do everything he could to keep Bilkey from testifying about the leeches and waving his arms. It would be devastating to start the trial with this image in the jury's mind. He had to keep this theater out of the beginning of the trial, which was exactly what Cullen wanted to do.

The prosecutor launched himself out of his chair. "I object, Your Honor. The defense has no right to interfere with my witnesses."

"Your Honor, may I approach the bench?" Burr said.

Burr hurried up to Skinner as quickly as he could and before Cullen could get there. Burr spoke so only Skinner could hear him. "Your Honor, as I said, at the preliminary examination, your father said both Mr. Cullen and I should have stipulated that Mr. Bilkey found Mr. Shepherd's body. He said that would have saved time." Burr lowered his voice. "And drama."

"Drama?"

Burr nodded. Cullen appeared beside him. His face was red and his teeth were clenched.

Thank you for being so furious.

"Your Honor, I have the right to call whomever I want. I am the prosecutor and this is my trial."

"And I'm in charge here," Skinner said. "Mr. Cullen, if Mr. Lafayette is willing to so stipulate, I am going to allow it. In the interest of time."

"Your Honor…"

"Stop it, Mr. Cullen." Then softly, so the jury couldn't hear, "Unless Mr. Bilkey is going to testify that he saw Lizzie hit Quinn with the canoe paddle, we don't need his testimony. Do I make myself clear?"

"Yes, Your Honor." Cullen did his best to compose himself and walked back to his table.

Burr did his best to keep from dancing a jig on the way back to his table.

"Ladies and Gentlemen, the prosecution and the defense have both agreed to the findings at the preliminary examination conducted by Harold F. Skinner, that Brian Bilkey found Mr. Shepherd's body in the South Branch of the Au Sable River on the morning of June 22, 1989. The anchor chain of his boat was wrapped around his ankle." The jury shuddered as one.

Skinner's description was bad enough as it was but far better than it would have been if Bilkey had testified. Burr couldn't believe he had convinced Skinner to skip Bilkey's testimony. It was a clear violation of the court rules. He looked over at Cullen, who was still fuming.

Skinner looked at Cullen. "You may call your next witness."

"The State calls Sheriff Earl Starkweather." Burr watched the jowly sheriff with the droopy eyes lumber up to the witness stand. He had on the same dark brown shirt, tan slacks and shiny badge that he wore at the preliminary exam.

With Starkweather sworn in, Cullen began. "Sheriff, were you the first responder at the crime scene?"

Burr popped up. "Objection, Your Honor, it has not been established that a crime was committed much less that this was a crime scene."

"I'll rephrase the question. Sheriff, were you the first responder to discover Mr. Shepherd's body?" Cullen said.

"I was."

"Sheriff, where did you find the body?"

"In the South Branch, below Chase Bridge, at the end of Dead Man's Hole."

"And where exactly was the body?"

"At the bottom of the river."

"And what did you do?"

"I pulled Mr. Shepherd to the shore. I tried to revive him, but he was dead. It looked like he'd been in the river all night."

"Let me go back a step, sheriff. When did you discover Mr. Shepherd's body?"

"About noon on June 22nd of last year."

"And what do you think happened?"

"It looked to me like he'd been in the river all night, like he had fallen in the river and—"

Cullen cut him off.

"Did you examine the body?"

"I did."

"And what did you find?"

"Mr. Shepherd was bloated and gray from being in the water."

"Were there any wounds?"

"There was a crease on his head. Like he had been struck."

"With what?"

"The edge of a canoe paddle."

"Objection, Your Honor. Calls for speculation," Burr said.

Skinner looked at Burr, then at Cullen, turning his whole body. "Mr. Cullen."

Cullen started in again. "Sheriff, in your opinion, what caused the wound on Mr. Shepherd's head?"

"A canoe paddle."

"Thank you, sheriff," Cullen said. "So, to tie it all together, sheriff, in your opinion what occurred on the night of June 21st?"

"In my opinion," Starkweather said, with the emphasis on opinion, "Mr. Shepherd was struck on the head with a canoe paddle and knocked unconscious. The anchor chain from his boat was wrapped around his ankle, and he was then put in the river where he drowned."

"Do you believe it was an accident?"

"No," the sheriff said. By some medical miracle, his eyelids lost their droop. "In my opinion, he was murdered."

Cullen looked at the jury. "Murdered." He walked back to his table and sat down. "No further questions, Your Honor."

Burr walked up to Starkweather. "Sheriff, was there much current in that stretch of the river?"

"Yes."

"And were you swept downstream when you pulled the body to shore?"

"I suppose I was."

"And then you had to drag Mr. Shepherd to the shore."

"Yes."

"And there were logs and rocks in your way."

"Yes."

"So by the time you reached the bank, both you and the body had a rough time of it."

"We did."

"Sheriff, isn't it also possible that the bruising and trauma on Mr. Shepherd's head was the result of being in the river for an extended period of time?"

"I don't—"

Burr stopped him. "You have no way of knowing when the bruising and trauma occurred, do you?"

"No, but I'm sure I didn't cause it." Starkweather glared at him through his droopy eyes.

Burr pressed the attack. "Sheriff, you testified that you left for the river before the EMS crew arrived."

"That's right."

"Why didn't you wait for them?"

"They're volunteers, and there was no way to know when they'd get there."

"How, may I ask, did you get the body to the morgue?"

"I carried it to my cruiser."

"You carried it?" Burr did his best to look astonished even though he had read the transcript of the inquest. "How far would you say that was?"

"About a quarter of a mile."

"And how much would you say Mr. Shepherd weighed, fully clothed, soaking wet and full of water?"

"At least two hundred pounds."

"You carried him all that way."

"Yes."

"Did you rest along the way?"

"I did." Starkweather said.

"How many times?"

"Three. Maybe four."

"Sheriff, is it possible that you banged up Mr. Shepherd's head when you put him down?"

"No," he said. "Plus, I saw the gash before I carried him."

Damn it all, Burr thought. He pressed on. "Two hundred pounds is a lot to pick up and put down."

"I was careful."

"Of course, you were, but…"

"Objection, Your Honor," Cullen said. "Asked and answered."

"Sustained. Move on, Lafayette," Judge Skinner said.

Burr looked over at the jury. He met their eyes, one by one. He was fairly certain he had hurt Starkweather's testimony. If nothing else, he knew he had succeeded in confusing them. He had already gone from Mr. Lafayette to Lafayette with Skinner. It usually took him three or four days to get this far with a judge.

Burr walked back to his table. Eve handed him a file. "Your Honor, the defense would like to introduce into evidence the Crawford County Sheriff's Office report of the accidental drowning of Mr. Quinn Shepherd on the night of June 21st."

"Objection, Your Honor," Cullen said. "It has not been established that Mr. Shepherd's death was an accident."

"Your Honor, the sheriff himself determined it was an accident."

"Sustained. For now let's just call it a 'death'," Skinner said. "Let this be Defense Exhibit One."

"Thank you, Your Honor. I'll be brief," Burr said. He opened the report. "Sheriff, on page seven, you wrote that Mr. Shepherd's death was accidental. But earlier you testified that you believed Mr. Shepherd was murdered, that he was struck by a canoe paddle and then drowned."

Starkweather didn't say anything.

"Sheriff?"

"Yes."

"Yes, what?"

"Yes, that's what it says."

"That what?" Burr, the ever-theatrical litigator, said.

"Please," Skinner said.

"I'll start over. Sheriff, earlier you testified that you believed that Mr. Shepherd was struck on the head with a canoe paddle. That he was then thrown in the river where he drowned. Is that right?"

"Yes."

"But here, Sheriff, on page seven of your report, you wrote that Mr. Shepherd struck his head on the rail of the boat and was unconscious. He then fell into the river and drowned. Isn't that what you wrote in your report?"

"There was new evidence," Starkweather said.

"In this report you said that Mr. Shepherd slipped and struck his head on the rail of his boat. He was knocked out. He got tangled up in the anchor chain of his boat and fell into the river where he drowned." Burr looked over at the jury, then back at Starkweather. "You concluded that his death was an accident. Is that right?"

"That was before—"

"Is that what the report says?"

"Yes, but—"

"No further questions, Your Honor."

Skinner adjourned them for lunch. Burr and his entourage descended on the Robin's Nest, a diner in a dingy white building on old US 27, north of the courthouse.

Burr had picked the Robin's Nest because Robin served breakfast all day and because she didn't have a liquor license. There was no reason to tempt fate at lunchtime. He ordered the Robin's Nest—two eggs, sausage, hash browns, toast and pancakes, from Robin herself, a thin, fortyish woman with short brown hair, who didn't look like she ate her own cooking.

"How can you possibly eat all that?" Jacob dabbed at his oatmeal.

"Arguing always makes me hungry," Burr said.

"It seemed like it went well this morning," Wes said.

"It was genius to trap Starkweather the way you did," Jacob said.

Wes cut into the steak part of his steak and eggs. Lizzie looked at her poached eggs, but didn't touch them.

After lunch, Cullen called Margaret Winston.

That's exactly what I would do. She had on those glasses with the black frames. He couldn't keep his eyes off her. He'd known that Cullen would call her, but he didn't know his stomach would be in knots when it happened. Maybe it was the sausage.

The bailiff swore her in, and Cullen got right to the point. "Professor Winston, would you please tell us your occupation?"

"I'm a professor of ornithology at the University of Michigan."

"An ornithologist?" Cullen said, his smile restored.

"I study birds."

"Of course. And where were you on the morning of April 27th this year?"

"I was on the east side of the South Branch, downstream from Chase Bridge."

"And what were you doing?"

"I was studying woodcock." She paused. "Their nesting habits."

"Thank you, Professor Winston. And did you find any?"

"I did."

"They are small birds, aren't they, Professor Winston?"

"A little bigger than a robin."

Isn't this just grand. Cullen practiced this with her.

"But with a long proboscis."

"Proboscis?"

"Beak. Woodcock have a long beak."

Burr had had enough. "I object, Your Honor. This is irrelevant."

"Your Honor, I am about to show why this is important."

"Overruled. You may continue, Mr. Cullen," Skinner said.

Burr knew it was relevant. He wanted to stop Cullen's momentum. Or was he jealous?

"I believe woodcock nest on the ground, don't they?" Cullen said. "How could you possibly find their nests?"

"I have a dog. An English setter. She points them."

"I see," Cullen said. "And did she find anything else that day?"

"She did."

"Please tell us what happened."

"We were working our way toward the river. When we got close, Finn, my setter, disappeared for a few minutes. Then she came back with a canoe paddle in her mouth."

Cullen paused, then looked at the jury. He turned back to his witness. "A canoe paddle?"

"Yes."

"And what did you do?"

"I took it from her, and I looked it over."

"Thank you, Professor Winston." Cullen walked to the prosecutor's table. He reached underneath it and picked up something wrapped in brown paper.

"I wonder what that could be," Burr said to himself.

Cullen walked back to his witness. He made a show of unwrapping it.

"Do you recognize this, Professor Winston?" Cullen handed her the paddle.

"It's the canoe paddle I found."

"How do you know?"

"It has a jagged, damaged edge." She held up the paddle and ran her finger along the splintered part of the blade.

"And what does this say?" Cullen pointed at the throat of the paddle.

"Q.S."

"Could that stand for Quinn Shepherd?"

"Yes," she said.

"Objection. Calls for an opinion," Burr said. He didn't object because he had a legitimate objection. He objected because he couldn't think of anything else to do, and he thought he needed to do something to disrupt Cullen.

"Overruled."

"Your Honor, the prosecution would like the court to admit this canoe paddle as State's Exhibit One."

"Bailiff, enter this as State's Exhibit One."

"Thank you, Your Honor," Cullen said. "Professor Winston, what did you do with the paddle after you found it?"

"I took it to the sheriff's department."

Cullen took the paddle back from Maggie. "And what made you think to do that?"

"I read that Quinn Shepherd drowned a year ago. I thought it might be important."

I thought she was on my side, but I suppose she should tell the truth.

"Indeed, it was." Cullen turned to the jury. "This, ladies and gentlemen, is the murder weapon. This is the canoe paddle that the defendant, Elizabeth Shepherd, used to kill her husband, Quinn Shepherd."

Burr jumped up. "Objection, Your Honor. There is no foundation for that statement."

"I withdraw the question," Cullen said, the damage done.

Margaret Winston started to get up.

"Just a few more questions, Professor." She sat back down and crossed her legs. "Professor," Cullen said, "you have a relationship, a personal relationship, with Mr. Lafayette. Isn't that true?" Cullen pointed at Burr.

"I beg your pardon?" Maggie said.

"You're dating. Isn't that right?"

Maggie turned white. "I beg your pardon," she said again.

Burr launched himself from his chair. "Objection, Your Honor. This is not only irrelevant. It is outrageous."

"Your Honor," Cullen said, "it is absolutely relevant. It lends even more credibility to Professor's Winston's testimony." Cullen waved the paddle at Burr. "This canoe paddle is damning evidence. If anything, Professor Winston would want to play down the canoe paddle's importance to protect the defendant and her lawyer." Cullen pointed at Burr. "This man has committed such a breach of ethics. You can't believe anything he says." Cullen turned to the jury and looked at them one-by-one.

"I move for a mistrial," Burr said. "The prosecutor has prejudiced this entire sham of a trial."

"I'm going to allow the testimony," Skinner said. "Anything further, Mr. Cullen?"

"No, Your Honor."

Margaret Winston glared at Skinner, this part of the testimony obviously not part of the script she had practiced.

This is a fine mess. At least Skinner hadn't pushed it. He probably didn't want any more theatrics, but it's too late for this. They hadn't seen each other since he dropped her off, but that didn't matter. Burr had a brand-new pencil, just like all the other ones. He broke it in two, just like all the other ones. He stood up and walked slowly to the witness stand. "Professor," he said, "do you know where your dog found the paddle?" Burr smiled at her, a soft smile that no one else could see.

"Upstream from where I was."

"And why do you say that?"

"That's the way she came from."

"What is the cover like there?"

"It's thick."

"How thick?"

"Very thick."

"Is it possible that your dog could have found the paddle downstream, gone back upstream and then found you?"

"Objection," Cullen said. "It doesn't matter where the dog found the paddle."

"Your Honor, it may well matter," Burr said, but of course it didn't matter. He was just trying to calm things down and confuse the jury.

Skinner shook his head. "You may answer the question."

"I suppose that could have happened, but the only tracks I saw were upstream."

"Thank you, Professor," Burr said. "Does your dog like bones?"

"Bones?"

"Objection."

"You may answer the question, Dr. Winston."

"Yes," she said. "Yes, she does."

"Does she chew them?"

"Yes."

"Does she like to fetch?"

"Yes."

"So she likes sticks?"

"Yes."

"Does she ever chew on them?" Burr said. "Like a bone?"

"Sometimes."

"Professor Winston," Burr said, picking up the paddle. "Is it possible that your dog, while out of your sight, found this paddle and chewed on it?" Burr ran his finger along the jagged edge. "Right here."

"It's possible."

"Objection, Your Honor," Cullen said. "The prosecution will show that the paddle matches the wound on Mr. Shepherd's skull."

Burr looked at Cullen. "Let's save that for another day, shall we?" Burr handed Cullen the paddle. "No further questions," he said.

"You are excused, Professor Winston."

Margaret Winston stood and smoothed her skirt. She walked past Burr without looking at him.

CHAPTER NINE

Burr woke to six inches of heavy, wet snow and no plows out on the roads. He started the Jeep and wrenched the gearshift on the floorboard forward, back, then forward again. The only way he could get to court today was in four-wheel drive, if he could get in gear. The Jeep's gearbox ground, metal on metal. "Finally," he said. He pulled down on the gearshift of the steering column and shifted into drive. "Off we go."

Burr made it to court on time as did Cullen, the jury, and the spectators. A half an hour late, Skinner made his grand entrance. Apparently, he had had his own transportation problems. "Call your first witness, Mr. Cullen."

"The people call Sergeant Boyd Wilcox."

Burr watched Wilcox walk to the witness stand and sit down. He had forgotten how much his glasses looked like they were part of his face.

After Wilcox was sworn in, Cullen led him through his qualifications as a forensic medical examiner. He picked up the paddle, handed it to Wilcox. "Did you examine this canoe paddle?"

"I did," Wilcox said.

"And what did you find?"

Here it comes.

"There was hair tangled on the jagged part of the blade." Wilcox ran his finger along the blade of the paddle. "Here."

"And what did you find?"

"The hair matched the hair of the deceased, Mr. Shepherd."

"Objection, Your Honor," Burr said. "There has been no foundation established to show where Sergeant Wilcox obtained the hair sample from Mr. Shepherd."

"Sergeant, where did you obtain the hair sample?" Skinner said.

"When we examined the body at the exhumation."

"And did you also find that the wound on Mr. Shepherd's head was consistent with being struck by the canoe paddle?"

"Yes."

Cullen took the paddle from Wilcox. He turned to the jury and held it out to them. "Is it your opinion that this is the murder weapon?"

"Yes," Wilcox said. "Yes, in my opinion the canoe paddle was the murder weapon."

"No further questions."

Burr stood. Cullen had used the exhumation to get around Burr's illegal search argument, so that was out. He really didn't have much of anything except what he'd tried at the preliminary examination, but he knew he had to try something. "Sergeant, are you familiar with the autopsy conducted of Quinn Shepherd by Dr. Fowler, the Crawford County Medical Examiner?"

"I am."

"Sergeant, you said you read the report. What was the cause of death?"

Wilcox jammed his glasses even harder onto his face. "I don't remember."

"Sergeant, you did say your read the report." Burr paused. "Didn't you?"

"Yes."

Burr knew exactly what it said, but he wanted Wilcox to say it and contradict what he just said. "Sergeant Wilcox, I'm not sure how you could conduct a forensic examination with such a poor memory, particularly an examination of evidence over a year old." Burr paused. He wanted the jury to think about what he had just said.

"Let me refresh your memory. Dr. Fowler concluded that Mr. Shepherd struck his head on the rail of his boat. Isn't that right?"

"Yes."

"So, the opinion of a medical doctor was that Mr. Shepherd's death was accidental. Is that right?"

"Yes."

"Dr. Fowler said it was an accident."

"Yes."

"An accident."

"Objection, Your Honor. Asked and answered," Cullen said.

"Move on, Lafayette. You're beating this to death," Skinner said.

Exactly. "I have no further questions."

"Call your next witness."

Cullen stood. "The State calls Norwynn Potter."

The bull of a man with the black beard took the witness stand. He raised his baseball-mitt hand, and the bailiff swore him in.

Cullen walked the burly barman through the ins and outs of the Two Track, the backwoods bar with a food-poisoning-waiting-to-happen menu. Cullen got right to the main course.

"Did you see Quinn Shepherd in the Two Track on the night of June 21st?"

Potter scratched at his beard. "Yeah, I seen him there that night." Burr wondered what might be living in Potter's beard. It looked like Potter did, too. He picked something out of it, studied it for a minute or two, then he ground whatever it was between his thumb and forefinger. Cullen pretended not to notice.

"Thank you, Mr. Potter. Would you please tell us what you saw?"

Cullen has some faith in Potter. They must have been practicing.

"Well, Quinn comes in and sits in the corner by hisself. He orders a shot, then another. Then this woman comes in and sits down at his table."

"Mr. Potter, did you see what they were doing?"

"They looked to me like they liked each other." *He's right on script.*

"What made you think that?"

"They were sitting next to each other. She had her hand on his knee, and she was whispering in his ear."

"Did it look like they were romantically involved?"

"Yeah, it did."

"So, Mr. Potter, it looked to you that Mr. Shepherd and this woman were romantically involved. Did anything else happen?"

So Cullen had decided that Potter couldn't be trusted to tell the story without prompts.

"Yeah, then Lizzie came in."

"The defendant, Elizabeth Shepherd?"

"Yeah."

"And what did she do?"

"She sees the two of them in the corner and marches right over. She's madder than hell. Finger pointing. Arms waving." Potter pointed his finger like he was poking out someone's eye, then waved his arms like a windmill. Cullen grimaced. Burr was sure this was an ad-lib.

"Then what happened?"

Potter grinned. "She slapped him."

"Who?"

"Lizzie," Potter said. "Quinn left. The two chicks kind of got into it. So I go over then and throw both of 'em out."

"Did anything further happen?"

Burr thought Cullen knew the story was over and was clearly expecting a "no," but Potter said, "Yeah."

There was nothing Cullen could do but ask, but he surely didn't want to. "What was it?"

Potter gripped the rail in front of him with both hands. "I didn't get paid for any of them drinks."

"Oh," Cullen said, relieved. "No further questions."

Burr approached Potter. "Mr. Potter, did you hear what Mr. Shepherd and this, this mystery woman were talking about?"

"Nope," Potter said.

Just what Cullen told you to say.

"Did you hear what Mr. Shepherd, Mrs. Shepherd and the mystery woman said to each other?"

"Nope." Potter stroked his beard. "I had a band there, so it was loud. Plus, I'm a little hard of hearing." He flashed a yellow-toothed smile through his beard.

Burr thought that if he had teeth like that, he'd grow a beard over them, too. "So, Mr. Potter, you don't know what they were saying?"

"Nope."

"Is it possible Mrs. Shepherd slapped Mr. Shepherd about something completely unrelated to this mystery woman, whoever she might be?"

"Nope."

"And the two women might have been arguing about something that had nothing to do with Mr. Shepherd."

"Nope."

"If you didn't hear what they said, you don't know." Burr paused. "Do you?"

"I know what I saw."

Burr turned to the jury. "Ladies and gentlemen, Mr. Potter is reciting what he believes he saw in a loud, dark bar. Mr. Potter admits that he didn't hear a word that was said at the bar that night." He turned to Skinner. "I have no further questions, Your Honor."

"The State calls Virginia Walker," Cullen said.

Burr looked at the witness list. He leaned behind Lizzie and tapped Jacob on the shoulder. "Who is Virginia Walker?"

"I don't know."

Perfect. She was on Cullen's witness list, but he had no idea who she was. He watched a fortyish woman walk up the aisle. She had on a little too much makeup, and she was well-rounded. The young bailiff couldn't take his eyes off her breasts. She sat down and crossed her legs.

"Who in the world is that?" Burr said.

"That's her," Lizzie said.

"Who?"

"The woman at the Two Track."

"Damn it all," Burr said. He leaned back and to his left again. "Jacob, why didn't you find her?" Jacob shook his head.

"Where do you live, Ms. Walker?" Cullen said.

"I live in Mount Pleasant." She uncrossed her legs.

"I didn't look in Mount Pleasant," Jacob said.

"That's just ducky."

"Counsel," Skinner said, "kindly be quiet while Mr. Cullen is examining the witness."

"And what is your marital status?" Cullen said.

"Single," she said, re-crossing her legs. "Divorced, actually."

"Thank you, Ms. Walker." Cullen did his best not to smile. "Did you meet Mr. Shepherd at the Two Track on the night of June 21st?"

"I did."

"Why did you meet that night?"

"He said he was going to leave his wife. He wanted to talk about it."

Lizzie shook her head. "That's not true."

"Mrs. Shepherd, please no outbursts," Skinner said.

"Perhaps I should take a step back," Cullen said, glowing. "What was the nature of your relationship with Mr. Shepherd?"

"We were lovers."

"Lovers?"

"Yes, for two years."

Burr thought he might well find himself tried for murder after he strangled Jacob.

Cullen glowed. "And did Mrs. Shepherd say anything to you or to Mr. Shepherd that night? Did she make any threats?"

"She said if she ever saw Quinn with me again, she'd kill him. And me, too."

"No further questions."

This is another fine mess. How could we miss this? He walked up to Virginia Walker. Burr thought she was attractive, but not like Lizzie, and she was at least ten years older. What exactly had Quinn been thinking? If any of this was true, he obviously hadn't been thinking. Burr knew he'd have to be careful. "Ms. Walker, had you ever met Mrs. Shepherd before that night?"

"No."

"I see," Burr said. "And the two of you were having a clandestine affair for two years?"

"What?"

"A secret affair."

"I guess so."

"So you were sneaking around?"

"We weren't sneaking." Virginia Walker's lip quivered.

"If this went on for two years, and Mrs. Shepherd didn't know anything about it, wouldn't you call that sneaking?"

"I didn't say she didn't know. I said I hadn't met her." Virginia Walker had regained her composure.

"Did she know?"

"At the end, I guess she must have."

"Thank you, Ms. Walker," Burr said. "You testified that Mrs. Shepherd said that the next time she saw you with her husband, she'd kill him."

"That's right."

"In light of what occurred, is it possible that Mrs. Shepherd might have just lost her temper?"

"It looked to me that she meant it. I was scared." Her lip quivered again.

A nice touch.

"Did you see Mrs. Shepherd follow her husband out of the Two Track?"

"Yes."

"Mr. Potter testified that Mr. Shepherd left, and Mrs. Shepherd stayed in the bar with you."

"Yes."

"So you didn't see Mrs. Shepherd follow Mr. Shepherd out of the bar?"

"I guess not."

"No further questions."

Skinner adjourned them after this little bombshell. The snow had largely melted. Burr put the Jeep back in two-wheel drive and drove himself to the Keg O' Nails and ordered a Labatt. How could he let this happen? Surprised by a witness he knew nothing about. Lizzie said she hadn't ever seen her until that night, and Jacob couldn't find her. How did Cullen find her?

Burr stewed and ordered another Labatt. Then another and another. And what if he had talked to her before the trial? Would it have made a difference? She'd still say what she said. Burr drained his beer and waved at the waitress. "It might as well be a six-pack," he said.

"You got a ride home?"

"I have a Jeep."

"Be careful," she said. "The prosecutor likes to get after drunk drivers. He smiles too much, but he's smart."

* * *

Burr tap-tap-tapped his pencil on the defense table, keeping time with the pounding in his head. Lizzie sat to his left, but Jacob wasn't next to her. Burr had convinced him to try and find something out about the mysterious Virginia Walker. Lizzie swore she had never seen her before, and she was sure Quinn hadn't been having an affair with her. Burr didn't know who to believe, but he hoped Jacob could find something. *Please, Jacob. It's what you're good at.*

The bailiff announced the arrival of Judge Skinner.

Cullen addressed the jury, "Ladies and gentlemen. First, we established that the canoe paddle was the murder weapon. Yesterday we showed the motivation for the murder, that Elizabeth Shepherd was jealous. Today we will show that Elizabeth Shepherd was at the scene of the crime." Cullen paused. "With the murder weapon."

"Damn it all," Burr said under his breath.

Cullen looked out at the gallery. "The State calls Heidi Grettenberger."

This was the other name on the witness list. *Why did Cullen save her for the trial?*

Burr watched a sixty-five-ish woman waddle up to the witness stand. She had a puffy face, glasses that pinched her nose, and short, henna-colored hair. She wore a brown pantsuit about the size of a parachute that clashed with her hair.

After the bailiff swore her in, Cullen said, "Mrs. Grettenberger, would you please tell us where you live?"

"595 Spruce Street, Roscommon." She smiled, displaying a smear of lipstick on her front teeth.

"Thank you, Mrs. Grettenberger. And would you please tell us where you were on the night of June 21st, 1989?"

"I was in Grayling."

"And what were you doing?"

"There was a midsummer's night bingo party at St. Mary's. I won seventy-eight dollars."

"Well done, Mrs. Grettenberger. And can you tell us what route you took on the way home and what you saw?"

"Sure thing."

Cullen waited for an answer. Heidi Grettenberger looked at him, but didn't say anything.

He took a deep breath. "Well then, please tell us."

"Sure thing," she said again. "I was going south on Chase Bridge Road. I was past 72, but I hadn't got to Chase Bridge, yet. I see this car come barreling down the middle of the road right at me. Lickety-split. I thought it was going to crash right into me, so I pulled off on the shoulder, and it zoomed by." She stopped again.

Cullen tapped his foot. "And then what happened?"

"Well, it goes a ways, but not too far. The brakes slam on. The car skids, then cuts into one of the them two-tracks."

"What did you do?"

"I almost peed my pants." Mrs. Grettenberger said this with such force that her glasses slipped down her nose. Someone in the gallery laughed.

Skinner banged his gavel. "Quiet," he said. "Mrs. Grettenberger, while we are certainly interested in what occurred, and how you felt, please skip over the intimate details."

Heidi Grettenberger looked over at Skinner and pushed her glasses up her nose and looked at Skinner again. "Hmm," she said.

"About what time would you say this was, Mrs. Grettenberger?"

"One, maybe two."

"Two in the morning?"

"It was nighttime, don'tcha know?"

Cullen tapped his foot again. Finally, "And then what did you do?"

"I was kinda scared and kinda curious. At the same time. So I took a deep breath and turned around. When I got to the two-track, I stopped and looked down there. I just couldn't see why anyone in their right mind would go down there at that time of night."

"Did you see anyone?"

"Yeah, I did." She stopped again.

Burr didn't think she was following the script.

Cullen was irritated with his witness. Mrs. Grettenberger thought she was doing just fine. More foot tapping. "And?"

"Why do you keep tapping your foot like that?" she said.

Cullen didn't say anything.

"Are you nervous or something?"

Cullen stopped tapping. "Mrs. Grettenberger, please continue."

"Like I said, I was mad as hops. I wanted to see what was going on, so I turn around and park my car by the two-track. I get out and peek down there."

"And what did you see?"

"I seen the door open, and she got out." Heidi Grettenberger pointed a stubby finger at Lizzie.

"Let the record show that Mrs. Grettenberger is pointing at the defendant, Elizabeth Shepherd. And did you see her do anything?"

"She stands there a minute, then she starts walking down the two-track, toward the river."

"And was she carrying anything?"

"She sure was."

"Could it have been a canoe paddle?"

"Yep."

"Could it have been this canoe paddle?" Cullen walked to the evidence table and picked up the infamous paddle and showed it to Grettenberger. "Could it have been this one?"

"Sure, could have . . ."

"Damn it all." Burr said. He jumped to his feet. "Objection, Your Honor. The witness said it could have been a canoe paddle, and now the prosecutor would have us believe that it was this canoe paddle, and that this canoe paddle is the murder weapon. One does not necessarily follow the other."

"Your Honor, I asked her if it could have been this canoe paddle. Not if it was."

"Overruled."

"Thank you, Your Honor," Cullen said. "Your witness."

Burr turned to Lizzie. "What else haven't you told me?"

"There's nothing else."

"How can I possibly defend you if you won't tell me what really happened."

"There's nothing else. I swear there isn't."

"Counsel, if you would prefer to interrogate your client rather than the witness, I will excuse her."

Burr walked up to the large woman. "Mrs. Grettenberger, on the night in question, you were playing bingo in Grayling. Is that right?"

"That's what I said."

"Yes, that is what you said." Burr paused, then, "But you live in Roscommon."

"That's right."

"And the quickest way for you to get here would be on I-75. Isn't that right?"

"I like to take the back roads."

"And why is that?"

"I like the scenery better."

"Isn't it a bit difficult to see the sights in the dark?"

The witness took a deep breath and her ample bosom rose and then fell.

"Mrs. Grettenberger, were you drinking at bingo night?"

"Pink lemonade." She sneered at Burr.

"Pink lemonade," Burr said. "Pink lemonade," he said again. "By pink lemonade, do you mean white zinfandel?"

Another up and down of her massive bosom.

"Mrs. Grettenberger?"

"I might."

"You might mean that pink lemonade means white zinfandel, and that is what you were drinking?"

"I suppose so." Heidi Grettenberger glared at Burr. He was relieved that looks couldn't kill.

"Mrs. Grettenberger, isn't the real reason you took Chase Bridge Road home because you had been drinking white zinfandel and didn't want to risk getting stopped by the police on I-75?"

"I can hold my liquor."

"I'm sure you can, but isn't it possible that you ran over the centerline of Chase Bridge Road and the oncoming car had to swerve to avoid you?"

"No."

"Are you sure?"

"No. I mean yes."

"And it was dark. Isn't that right?"

"For mercy's sake, it was nighttime. Of course, it was dark."

"If it was dark, how could you possibly see anything?"

"There was a moon."

"Of course, there was a moon, Mrs. Grettenberger, but that area is heavily wooded. I don't see how you could possibly see anything in the dark."

"I saw what I saw." More huffing and puffing.

"You had been drinking wine. You took the back roads home to avoid the police. You ran off the road, and saw Mrs. Shepherd in the dark with a canoe paddle." Burr looked her in the eye. "Is that right?"

"Yes."

"Could the canoe paddle have been a stick?"

"Nope."

"Is it possible that Mrs. Shepherd wasn't holding anything at all?"

"I saw what I saw."

Burr turned to the jury. "Ladies and gentlemen, I have grave doubts that Mrs. Grettenberger saw Mrs. Shepherd holding anything at all. In fact, I have grave doubts that Mrs. Grettenberger even saw Mrs. Shepherd." He paused and put his hands in his pockets, then turned back to the witness.

"Mrs. Grettenberger, how long did you practice with Mr. Cullen to get your story straight?"

"About a day and a…."

"Objection, Your Honor."

Burr turned to Skinner. "I withdraw the question, Your Honor." Then to Mrs. Grettenberger, "If I were you, I'd be careful out there. I understand that Mr. Cullen is very tough about drinking and driving."

Cullen ignored Burr and called Joe Gleason. The oil man stepped up to the witness stand. He sat and swept his unfashionably long brown hair back over his ears. His gold Rolex flashed, but his tortoise-shell glasses were nowhere in sight.

He's preening for us. I suppose I do that. Every now and then.

"Mr. Gleason," Cullen said, "you were a guest at The Gray Drake on the night of June 21st, the night Mr. Shepherd was murdered."

Burr stood to object.

"Killed," Cullen said.

"I object," Burr said.

"Died," Cullen said.

Burr sat down.

Cullen started over. "Mr. Gleason, were you a guest at The Gray Drake on June 21st, the night Mr. Shepherd died?"

"I was."

"And you were at the auction earlier in the evening?"

"Yes."

"Thank you, Mr. Gleason," Cullen said. "Would you please tell us what you did after the auction?"

"I listened to the string quartet, had a nightcap, and then I went to bed."

"What happened after you went to bed?"

"I didn't make it through the night." Gleason looked a little sheepish.

This is just like the preliminary exam. Cullen rehearses all of his witnesses. I don't like him. I don't like his smile, but he is a good lawyer.

"So I had to get up," he said. "As usual."

"And what time was that?"

"About three. It could have been four."

"In the morning?"

"Yes."

"How do you know?"

"I looked at my watch." Gleason flashed his watch.

"You don't take it off when you go to bed?"

"No."

"And what happened when you got up?"

"The bathrooms are down the hall at The Gray Drake, so after that I walked to the end of the hall and looked out the window."

"Did you see anything?"

"I saw Mrs. Shepherd come up the path from the parking lot off to the north."

"Really? That's late, isn't it?"

"I thought so."

"And did you notice anything else?"

"She was hurrying."

Cullen turned to the jury. "Ladies and gentlemen, the auction ended at about ten p.m. Mrs. Shepherd had her altercation with Virginia Walker at the Two-Track at about eleven. Mrs. Grettenberger said that she saw Mrs. Walker around one or two a.m. And now Mr. Gleason says he saw Mrs. Shepherd come back to The Gray Drake between three and four in the morning."

Cullen took a step toward the jury. "So, if all Mrs. Shepherd did was help her husband launch his boat and drop off a car, then she would have been back at the lodge by midnight. One at the latest." Another step. "The reason she got back so late was that she ambushed her husband on the river and killed him."

Before Burr could object, Cullen walked back to his table.

"No further questions," he said.

Burr walked up to Gleason. He put his hands in his pockets. "Mr. Gleason, do you wear glasses?"

Gleason looked down at his shoes.

"Mr. Gleason, this would seem to be a fairly simple question. Either you do or you don't."

"I wear reading glasses."

"Mr. Gleason, are you nearsighted?"

"Nearsighted?"

"Mr. Gleason, before you perjure yourself, you testified at the preliminary exam that you wore glasses because you're nearsighted. Do you remember that?"

"Not really."

"Mr. Gleason, may I see your glasses?"

"Objection, Your Honor," Cullen said. "Mr. Gleason is not on trial."

"Your Honor, Mr. Gleason's vision is on trial."

"Is this necessary, Mr. Lafayette?" Skinner said.

"Your Honor, my client has been charged with murder. All Mr. Gleason has to do is reach in his pocket."

Skinner bent his bent neck toward Gleason.

"Mr. Gleason, I think it would be much easier if you simply got your glasses out of your pocket," Skinner said.

Gleason frowned, but he reached in the breast pocket of his jacket and took out his glasses.

"Please put them on," Burr said.

Gleason looked at Skinner, who nodded at him.

Gleason put the glasses on.

Burr leaned in. "Mr. Gleason, your reading glasses seem to be bifocals. Is that right?"

"I don't hardly need them."

"But you do have a prescription for nearsightedness."

"Not much of one."

"Mr. Gleason, did you have your glasses on the night you claimed to have seen Mrs. Shepherd through the window?"

"Yes."

"Mr. Gleason, at the preliminary exam, you testified you didn't have them on. Are you lying now?"

"No."

"Were you lying then?"

"I don't remember," Gleason said.

Burr had to hurry. "Mr. Gleason, you sell oil and gas interests. Is that right? And you're a convicted felon. Is that right?"

"No."

"No?" Burr said. "Mr. Gleason, let me show you something."

"Objection, Your Honor. This is not relevant," Cullen said.

"Your Honor, the witness's tendency to lie is most certainly relevant."

"I'll allow it," Skinner said.

"Thank you, Your Honor," Burr said. "Mr. Gleason, if I'm not mistaken, you pleaded guilty to securities fraud. Isn't that right?"

"I didn't do it, but I pleaded guilty to avoid a trial," Gleason said.

"I have no further questions, Your Honor." Burr sat back down.

Eve leaned over the railing. "I don't think Joe Gleason will be sending you a Christmas card."

Cullen stood up, "Your Honor, the State calls Noah Osterman."

Burr groaned. "Another member of the liar's club."

The Prussian raised his hand to be sworn in. *Fifty years ago, Osterman would have been a Nazi.*

"Mr. Osterman, were you staying at The Gray Drake on the night of June 21st?"

"Yes." Osterman rubbed his salt-and-pepper Van Dyke.

"And you were at the auction?"

"Yes." He nodded.

"And did you see Mrs. Shepherd that night? Late that night?"

Osterman cleared his throat. "I woke up in the middle of the night and couldn't get back to sleep. Finally, I decided to go downstairs for a glass of milk. When I got there, I saw Mrs. Shepherd in the kitchen."

"What time was that?"

"About four, I'd say."

"And what was she doing?"

"She was at the sink."

"What was she doing?"

"I think she was trying to get some blood out of her jacket."

"Did she see you?"

Osterman leaned forward. "No."

"And what did you do?"

"I watched her for a while. Then I went back to my room."

"Thank you, Mr. Osterman." Once again, Cullen turned to the jury. "Ladies and gentlemen, we now have Mrs. Shepherd placed in the kitchen of The Gray Drake. Mr. Gleason saw her come up the driveway. Mr. Osterman saw her scrubbing blood, her husband's blood, off her jacket. Need I say more?" Cullen sat down.

Burr couldn't believe what he just heard. He could object, but he had other plans for the Prussian. Burr walked up to the witness. "Mr. Osterman, are you sure it was blood?"

"Yes."

"And you're aware that Mrs. Shepherd is the chef at The Gray Drake?"

"Yes."

"And chefs often spill when they cook?"

"I don't know."

"Mr. Osterman, could Mrs. Shepherd have been trying to get red wine off her clothes, or perhaps, beets? Or how about ketchup?" It was Osterman's turn to scowl at Burr. "Mr. Osterman, what you saw on Mrs. Shepherd's jacket was red?"

"Yes."

"How can you be certain it was blood?"

"It was blood."

"I see . . . And you have proof?"

"No."

"Mr. Osterman, you represent Mr. Gleason. Is that right?"

Osterman didn't say a word.

"Objection, Your Honor," Cullen said.

"I read the pleadings of Mr. Gleason's trial, Mr. Osterman. You represent a liar, is that right? What does that make you?" Burr turned on his heel and started back to his table, but stopped in front of Cullen. "I suppose Hawken is next. Is he going to testify that he saw Lizzie hit Quinn with the canoe paddle?"

Skinner adjourned them for lunch. Burr followed Lizzie out of the courtroom and into the hall. He took her by the arm and led her into an empty conference room. "Why didn't you tell me you went down to the river? Why didn't you tell me? If I'd known, maybe I could have done something about it."

She pulled her arm away from Burr. Then she brushed her hair out of her eyes. Burr thought she looked scared. "I didn't think anyone saw me."

"You didn't think anyone saw you? And that's why you didn't tell me?"

"I didn't kill Quinn. I swear I didn't."

"But you went down to the river and ambushed him."

"I didn't ambush him." She looked away from Burr.

"But you hit him with the canoe paddle."

"No. I didn't. I swear I didn't.

Burr thought Lizzie was begging him to believe her.

"But you hit him."

"I slapped him. That's all I did."

"What did you talk about?"

"We didn't talk."

"Come on, Lizzie. You went all the way down to the river, and you didn't talk?"

"He said we'd talk later. He got back in the boat and that was the last time I ever saw him." Now she was pleading.

"If the jury believes Grettenberger, you are going to be convicted of murder." Burr turned on his heel and walked out, got in his Jeep and drove off by himself. "Why do they always lie?" He slammed his fist on the dashboard. "Why?"

Burr drove for an hour and got back to the courtroom just before Skinner entered.

The bailiff called them to order.

"Mr. Cullen, do you have more witnesses?" Skinner said.

"No, Your Honor."

"You may proceed with your closing argument."

"Yes, Your Honor."

Cullen paced back and forth in front of the jury. He stopped at the corner of the jury box closest to the witness stand where he could see the jury and Lizzie. "Ladies and gentlemen, the State has broken its case into three pieces, all of which connect, and each of which requires you to convict Elizabeth Shepherd of first-degree murder in the death of her husband.

"First, we showed you the murder weapon, the canoe paddle, that Mrs. Shepherd used to kill her husband. The forensic examiner from the state police corroborated that the canoe paddle dealt the fatal blow to Mr. Shepherd. Second, we showed why Mrs. Shepherd killed her husband. She was jealous. And finally, three different witnesses put her at the scene of the crime or put her whereabouts in a place where she could only have been if she had killed her husband."

Cullen walked to the other end of the jury box. "Ladies and gentlemen, there are three elements to the crime of first-degree murder. First, the means. In this case, the canoe paddle. Second, the motive. In this case, jealousy.

And third, the opportunity. Mrs. Shepherd was at the river with her husband. These three elements, the means, the motive and the opportunity require you to convict Mrs. Shepherd of first-degree murder." Cullen stopped pacing, looked at the jury one by one, then, "It is a terrible thing to have to judge someone, but that is your duty. Your duty is to convict." With that, Cullen walked back to his table. "Your Honor, the prosecution rests."

Skinner made a big show of looking at his watch. It was only three o'clock, but he adjourned them for the day.

* * *

Burr met Jacob outside the courthouse.

Despite his client, who he thought might well have murdered her husband, Burr wasn't about to give up. *She has never told me the whole truth. Is she lying, or is she so terrified she only answered in bits and pieces? Or was she lying?* The evidence pointed to her, but Burr thought there was more. On top of that, he hated losing, and he had no intention of losing to Cullen, even if Lizzie was guilty.

Jacob had on a belted camel overcoat that looked like it was very warm, but he had his hands in his pockets, and he was shivering.

"Where is Virginia Walker?"

"I have no idea. I waited outside her house all day, but she was nowhere to be found."

"Why aren't you still there?"

"I am not a private detective." He stomped his feet. "And I got cold."

Apparently. "Jacob, go back to Mount Pleasant and find her."

Jacob took his hands out of his pockets and wrapped his arms around his chest. "You go."

"Jacob, please go back to Mt. Pleasant and find Virginia Walker."

Jacob sulked, then turned to go.

"Just one more thing," Burr said. "If I wanted to find out who bought and sold real estate in Crawford County, what would I do?"

"Go to the Register of Deeds office and check the grantor-grantee file."

"How about the plat book?"

"The plat book is for amateurs."

"There has always been something going on with these oil men. I just don't know what."

Burr gave Jacob a blanket from his car and sent him on his way. He got into his Jeep and drove to the Register of Deeds office, just up the road from the courthouse. By the time he got to the county offices, it was 4:30. A very pretty young woman with sparkling green eyes, who looked more suited for the runway than a rundown county office, wasn't any too happy to see him.

He gave her his most helpless look. "Could you please show me the grantor-grantee file?"

"Which one?"

"Is there more than one?"

"There's a room full of them."

This made Burr nervous. He hated research of all shapes and sizes. "I'm looking for anything concerning the name Shepherd."

"You and everyone else."

"Really?"

"Really."

"Who?"

"I can't say."

"Ms. . . ."

"Fletcher," she said. "Come this way." She led him to a room full of bookshelves overflowing with brown-leather books. Big books. Each one the size of the Rand-McNally atlas. Each one looked like the other.

Burr shuddered. "How about a plat book?"

"The plat book is for amateurs." She started back to the front desk. Burr followed her. Back at the counter, the comely clerk reached down and came up with an 8-by-11 spiral-bound book with a paper cover. She set it down in front of him. "The Crawford County plat book," she said. "That'll be twenty-five dollars. If you need anything else, I'll be here tomorrow at nine."

Burr paid her. "Thank you, Ms. Fletcher. If you were me, where would you start?"

"I would start at page one." She put a *CLOSED* sign on the counter and left.

Burr climbed back in the Jeep with his brand-new Crawford County plat book. He headed west on M-72. A dozen miles later, he pulled into Dingman's Tavern, a one-story brown building that had started out as a log cabin but had lost its charm with the construction of at least three additions that matched the color of the original log cabin, but not its style.

After his first beer, he felt brave enough to open the plat book. It wasn't that he didn't know what a plat book was, or that he had never seen one, it was just that he hated research. He was always afraid he was going to miss something, which he almost always did. "Where is Jacob when I need him?" he said out loud. Burr knew full well where Jacob was, but he sorely wished it was Jacob looking at this damned plat book.

His second beer arrived. Emboldened, he flipped through the pages. Page after page. Township after township. Each page was a map that showed the parcels and the owners. Most of Crawford County belonged to either the federal or state government, neither of which paid taxes. "No wonder the county doesn't have any money." By the time he made it to page ten, he had lost interest and rifled through the rest of it. He finished his second beer and ordered a third, determined to make it last. "Damn it all," he said, "I suppose I might as well start at page one. Just like she said." He turned back to the beginning of the book. And there it was. An index. He hated indexes, but here was an index by owner. He ran his finger down the columns until he came to *S* listings. Santini, Saxman, Seeley, Selfridge. "Shepherd," he said. "Shepherd, Thompson." Then Shepherd, Quinn. *Quinn and Lizzie's house.* Burr turned the pages. "That's it?"

He slammed the book shut. What a colossal waste of time. He downed the rest of the beer, thought long and hard about one more, but called for the check.

Burr flipped through the pages one more time. Nothing. He turned back to the index. What's this? Just after Shepherd, Quinn. The Alexander Thompson Shepherd Trust. There were five-page references. "Good God, what's this?" He rifled through the book until he found the first one. A section northeast of Grayling. Three hundred acres just north of the lodge. Six more parcels, all big acreage. Burr left a twenty on the table and ran out to the Jeep.

* * *

Back at the lodge, Zeke was the only one who was glad to see him. The dog led him to Lizzie, who was in the kitchen doing something with a Cuisinart that looked like it could be dangerous.

Burr set the plat book down on the butcher-block island.

"That's a very good place for that plat book to get ruined," she said. He didn't think she was particularly glad to see him.

"Since I'm still your lawyer, we have some work to do." He opened the plat book. "Lizzie," he said, "who is Alexander Thompson Shepherd?"

She dropped a whole carrot in the blender and looked at him suspiciously. "Quinn's grandfather." Lizzie turned on the blender. It made a grinding noise and destroyed the carrot. She turned off the blender. "Alexander Thompson Shepherd started the bank."

"In Hamtramck?"

"Yes."

"And what about the trust?"

"Grandpa Thompson made a lot of money, and he bought a lot of land."

"What kind of land?"

"Wild land," she said. "The trust is supposed to keep it that way."

She poured carrot juice into a glass. "Would you like to try it?"

"That can't possibly be good for you."

"It's for Jacob."

Sometimes she's distant. Sometimes I think she's about to cry. I just can't quite figure her out.

An hour later, Jacob made it back to The Gray Drake. He took his carrot juice to their temporary headquarters.

"How can you possibly drink that?" Burr said.

"It is as close to a miracle drink as there is."

Burr looked out the leaded windows, not that there was much to see in November, especially in the dark. "For my money, I'd nominate a very dry, very dirty martini with Bombay Sapphire."

Jacob drank his carrot juice, quite obviously pleased with himself.

"Did you find her?"

Jacob set his carrot juice down. "I did."

"You did?"

"I did."

"You found her, and all you can do is sit there and drink that wretched-looking orange goop?"

"She finally showed up at her house, which, by the way, is very nice. It's a brick colonial." He picked up his carrot juice and swirled it like a glass of wine. "She finally came home. She left an hour later, and I followed her."

"Where did she go?"

"She has a nice car, too. An Audi. An A-8. Top of the line." Jacob, not to be rushed, drank a little more of his carrot juice. "She seems to have some money."

"Where did she go?" Burr said again.

"My dear Burr, the question is not where did she go? The question is who did she go with?"

"I give up."

"You'll never guess."

"Who?"

"Our drug dealer."

"Charlie Cox?"

"The one and only. He picked her up in his BMW."

"Maybe he's her accountant," Burr said.

"Only if he kisses all his clients and takes them home for the night."

Burr dashed back to the kitchen.

"Lizzie, are you sure you never saw Quinn with Virginia Walker? Other than that night?"

"No, but there were rumors."

"Tell me again what you said to her?"

"You think I murdered Quinn."

"I don't. I really don't. But I need to know what happened."

"I told her to stay away from Quinn."

"And what did she say?"

"She said it wasn't any of my business."

"Did she say she was having an affair with Quinn?"

Lizzie bit her lip.

"What if Quinn wasn't having an affair with her?" Burr said.

"That won't bring him back."

"No, but what if she was the go-between between Charlie Cox and your husband?"

"That still won't bring Quinn back."

"No, but maybe, just maybe, we have a suspect."

CHAPTER TEN

Burr woke up early. In the dark, actually. He could hardly wait for his day in court. "Zeke, it's finally our turn."

Back in the courtroom of the Honorable Lawrence G. Skinner, the bailiff called them to order, then Skinner said, "Mr. Lafayette, you may proceed with your defense."

"Thank you, Your Honor." Burr stood and made his way to the jury box. "Ladies and gentlemen," he said, "perhaps the only thing Mr. Cullen and I agree on is that it is, in fact, a terrible thing to have to judge someone." He started pacing. "And, as I'm sure you know, the law requires a very high standard to convict a person of murder. Do you know what that standard is?" He stopped pacing. "To convict Elizabeth Shepherd of murder, you must be convinced beyond a reasonable doubt." He paused. "Beyond a reasonable doubt," he said again. "And do you know what reasonable doubt means? It means almost positive. There is no way you can be almost positive that Mrs. Shepherd killed her husband.

"But there is doubt. There is great doubt. First, there is doubt about the canoe paddle. Reasonable men, experts, may differ, and they do. I will present two of them who will tell you that Quinn Shepherd was not killed with a canoe paddle. Second, and most importantly, no one saw Mrs. Shepherd kill her husband. No one saw her strike him with a canoe paddle. No one even saw her at the river that night. Not a soul."

Burr gripped the rail, and like Cullen, made eye contact with each juror.

"But, you ask, what happened? After all, Quinn Shepherd is dead." Burr paused again. "Quinn Shepherd is dead, and Mrs. Shepherd is his widow, and she must raise their son, Josh, by herself." Burr stood up straight and thrust his hands into the pockets of his slacks.

"But what did happen that night? I'll tell you what happened. Mr. Shepherd was fishing by himself. At night. He slipped and struck his head on the rail of his boat. His leg got tangled in the anchor chain of his boat, and he fell in the river." One more pause. "And he drowned. Mr. Shepherd drowned. It was a terrible accident. But it was an accident. It was not a murder. And that is what I am about to show you."

He knew his opening statement had gone well. If he could prove what he just said to the jury. But that was the problem. He looked down at his shoes, and then at the gallery.

"The defense calls Clyde Fowler."

The Crawford County Medical Examiner took the witness stand. He was a small man with a big head. His ears, nose and mouth looked like they were stuck on his face. Burr thought he looked like Mr. Potato Head.

After the bailiff swore in Fowler, Burr ran through the medical examiner's credentials, which, if not world-class, were certainly good enough for Crawford County. Plus, Fowler had been the coroner for the past twenty-three years. He was sure that most of the jury knew who Fowler was.

"Dr. Fowler," Burr said, "you examined Mr. Shepherd's body. Is that right?"

"Yes."

"And when did you perform your examination?"

"On June 23rd, 1989."

"The day after Mr. Shepherd's body was found?"

"That's right."

Burr walked to the evidence table and picked up Fowler's autopsy report and walked back to the witness stand. "Dr. Fowler, I have in my hand Defense Exhibit One, which is your autopsy report." Burr handed the file to the medical examiner. "Dr. Fowler, is this, in fact, the report of your findings concerning the death of Mr. Shepherd?"

Fowler thumbed through the report, made a show of studying a few of the pages. "It is," he said.

Just like we practiced. Very good. Very good indeed. "Dr. Fowler, what did you conclude to be the cause of death?"

"Death by drowning."

"Drowning," Burr said.

"Yes, Mr. Shepherd drowned."

Perfect again. "Dr. Fowler, how did this occur?"

"Mr. Shepherd slipped and fell. He hit his head on the rail of his boat and

166

was rendered unconscious. His leg became wrapped in his anchor chain. He then fell in the river and drowned."

Cullen jumped up. "Objection, Your Honor. That is not what Sergeant Wilcox testified."

"Your Honor," Burr said, "this is not about Sergeant Wilcox. This is the written report of Dr. Fowler, the Crawford County Medical Examiner, who performed the autopsy the day after Mr. Shepherd died."

Skinner twisted his bent neck back and forth until it cracked.

Ouch.

Finally, Skinner said, "Mr. Cullen, I agree with Mr. Lafayette. Whether or not Clyde is right is not the issue. The issue is what was in his report."

"Thank you, Your Honor." Burr continued, "Dr. Fowler, please repeat what your autopsy said about the wound on Mr. Shepherd's head?"

"I concluded that Mr. Shepherd struck his head on the rail of the boat."

Very good again. "Dr. Fowler, did you examine Mr. Shepherd's boat? Specifically, the rail?"

"I did."

"And what did you find?"

"I didn't find any marks on the rail."

"Did this surprise you?"

"No."

"And why not?"

"The rail was made of white oak. It's a very hard wood. I would have been surprised if there had been any damage to the rail."

"Could the rail have caused the wound?"

"Oh, yes." Fowler took off his glasses. "The edge was sharp."

"Was there any blood or hair on the rail?"

"No."

"And did this surprise you?"

"No. The boat had been in the river for at least twelve hours. With the current, there would have been water splashing on the boat."

Burr looked back at Cullen, who was seething behind his smile.

"Dr. Fowler, Mr. Shepherd was in the river all night. And there was rough treatment of the body when Mr. Bilkey tried to get his Woolly Bugger back. We also heard that Sheriff Starkweather dragged the body out of the river and carried it all the way up to the EMS truck. Could either of these actions have caused the wound?"

"Yes, and Mr. Shepherd was at the bottom of the river. No doubt he was bouncing on whatever was at the bottom. There were other bruises and contusions on his head."

"So, Dr. Fowler, you had no reason to believe that Mr. Shepherd was struck by a canoe paddle, much less murdered."

"No, I thought it was an accident."

"Thank you, Dr. Fowler. One more question. We all know that Mr. Shepherd spent his life on the river. He was an excellent guide and extremely competent around boats. Having said that, did you measure Mr. Shepherd's blood-alcohol content?"

"I did."

"And what was it?"

".16."

".16," Burr said. "And what is considered drunken driving in Michigan?"

".08."

".08," Burr said. "So Mr. Shepherd was drunk."

"Quite."

"And do you think this contributed to his death?"

"I concluded that Mr. Shepherd was drunk. He slipped and struck his head and knocked himself out. He became tangled in the anchor chain of his boat. He fell in the river and drowned."

"And your autopsy concluded that Mr. Shepherd's death was an accident?"

"Yes."

"An accident."

"Yes."

Burr was about to say *accident* one more time, but Skinner stopped him before Cullen could object. "You made your point, Mr. Lafayette. Do you have anything further?"

"No, Your Honor." He hoped he had made his point because he knew what was coming next.

Cullen marched up to the witness stand. "Dr. Fowler, did you have the canoe paddle in your possession when you did the autopsy?"

"No."

"I see." Cullen walked to the evidence table and picked up the paddle. He walked back to the witness stand. "Dr. Fowler, you are familiar with this?"

"Yes."

"Could a blow from this canoe paddle have caused the wound on Mr. Shepherd's skull?"

"I suppose so."

"You suppose so?"

Burr jumped up. "Objection, Your Honor. Asked and answered."

"Overruled."

"Dr. Fowler, does 'I suppose' mean yes?"

"Yes."

"Dr. Fowler, if you had this canoe paddle in your possession at the time of your autopsy, might you have come to a different conclusion?"

Burr jumped up again. "Objection, Your Honor. Calls for speculation."

"Answer the question," Skinner said.

"I might have."

"You might have come to a different conclusion?"

"Yes."

He's giving it all back.

Cullen walked back to the evidence table. He laid the paddle down and picked up the exhumation report. "I have in my hand People's Exhibit Two, the exhumation report." Back in front of Fowler, Cullen handed it to the witness.

"Dr. Fowler, have you read this report?"

"I have."

"And what does this report conclude?"

Fowler squirmed in his chair. "It concludes that the canoe paddle caused the wound on Mr. Shepherd's head."

"Objection, Your Honor," Burr said. "The prosecutor is making it sound like Dr. Fowler wrote that report, and he did no such thing."

"I was making sure Dr. Fowler had read the report," Cullen said.

Turnabout is fair play.

"Overruled," Skinner said.

Here it comes.

"Dr. Fowler, in your opinion, and in light of the canoe paddle, could the wound on Mr. Shepherd's head have been caused by the canoe paddle?"

Fowler slumped in his chair. "Yes," he said.

"No further questions," Cullen said.

Burr really wanted to skip Robert Traker, but the retired medical examiner was the only expert witness Burr could find. He hoped Cullen hadn't found any of the warts that Burr had found when he had done a background check on Traker. This could turn out to be a disaster, but he stuck with his plan.

Burr shuffled through his papers, then stood. "The defense calls Dr. Robert Traker."

Burr turned to the gallery. The retired Wayne County Medical Examiner made his way to the witness stand. No one could take their eyes off the bald giant.

"Dr. Traker, you are a pathologist. A Ph.D., is that right?"

"Yes," Traker squeaked. He looked like a defensive tackle, but he had a voice like a chipmunk. "Would you please talk a little louder?"

"Yes." Now he sounded like a goose with a sinus infection.

"You were a medical examiner in Wayne County. Isn't that right?"

"Yes."

"For how long?"

"Thirty years."

Burr continued with the good doctor's qualifications, then started in. "Dr. Traker, did you review Dr. Fowler's autopsy?"

"I did."

"And the exhumation report of Sergeant Wilcox?"

"I did."

"Dr. Traker, what, in your opinion, was the cause of death?"

"Mr. Shepherd drowned."

"Thank you, Dr. Traker." Burr looked at the jury. He hadn't lost them yet, but Traker's voice wasn't helping. He'd try to keep Traker's answers short. Burr walked to the evidence table and picked up the canoe paddle. *I hate this thing. If only Finn hadn't found it.*

Back at the witness stand, Burr showed the paddle to the good doctor. "Dr. Traker, are you familiar with this canoe paddle?"

"I am."

"In your opinion, was Mr. Shepherd struck with this paddle?"

"Possibly."

"Possibly?" Burr said. "What does that mean?"

"The hair samples match and the wound could have been caused by the canoe paddle, but there are any number of other explanations."

"Such as?"

Traker took off his glasses. He had tiny black eyes behind them. Burr took a step back then, stepped in between Traker and the jury. "Put your glasses back on," Burr mouthed.

"What's that?"

"Your glasses."

"Speak up, Mr. Lafayette," Skinner said.

Traker cleaned his glasses with his tie. Satisfied they were clean, he put them back on.

"Dr. Traker, what else might have caused the wound?"

"Mr. Shepherd may have hit his head on the rail of the boat. Or he might have hit his head on a rock. And as far as that goes, he may have hit the back of his head first and then fallen forward. The wound on his head may have happened second, not first."

"Can you tell us about the wound on the back of Mr. Shepherd's head?"

"It was a contusion, a bruise. In layman's terms there was a large bump on the back of Mr. Shepherd's head."

"Can you say what caused it?"

"Not definitely. But I think he probably fell on something very hard. Like a rock."

"A rock."

"That's right."

"So, Dr. Traker, do you agree with Sergeant Wilcox's findings?"

"His findings are a possibility." Traker stopped. "But just one of many possibilities."

"Thank you, Dr. Traker." Burr walked back to the defense table. Other than the glasses, Traker's testimony had gone better than Burr had hoped. If Cullen didn't ruin things, Burr thought he had refuted Wilcox's testimony, and he still had Charlie Cox.

Cullen walked up to the witness.

"Dr. Traker, can you tell us the definition of necrophilia?"

"Necrophilia?" Traker's cue ball complexion turned from white to cherry tomato.

Here it comes again. "Objection, Your Honor. Irrelevant."

"I will show the relevance, Your Honor."

"Continue Mr. Cullen."

"Dr. Traker, please tell us the definition of necrophilia."

"I don't know what it is."

"Dr. Traker, you spent your entire working life around dead people. Corpses. And you say you don't know what necrophilia is?" Cullen looked over at the jury. "I find that hard to believe." He turned back to Traker. "What is necrophilia?"

Burr jumped up. "Asked and answered. He said he doesn't know."

Cullen turned back to the jury. "I'll tell you then. Necrophilia is the act of having sex with a corpse."

There was a deathly silence in the courtroom.

Cullen turned back to Traker. "You were accused of necrophilia, Dr. Traker. Isn't that right?"

"It wasn't true."

"Isn't it true that you were suspended for six months because you were suspected of necrophilia?"

"Objection, Your Honor. This is not only irrelevant, it is an outrage. There was no conviction. Not even a trial."

Skinner thought this over. He bent toward the jury. "Ladies and gentlemen, you will disregard Mr. Cullen's questions regarding necrophilia." Skinner turned to Cullen. "Mr. Cullen, you may continue."

"I have no further questions, Your Honor." Cullen walked back to the prosecutor's table and sat down.

Skinner adjourned them for lunch. Twenty minutes later, Burr and company had their heads buried in their menus. Not that there was much to choose from at Spike's. Burr was grateful that no one had anything to say.

Jacob looked up from his menu. "Did you know about Traker and his kink?"

"Yes."

"And you called him anyway?"

"There were no charges brought, nothing on Traker's record. All he had to do was deny it. We practiced it."

"It certainly didn't help us."

"Cullen's questions were out of bounds. They were inadmissible," Burr said. "Skinner should never have allowed them."

"As far as Skinner goes, you probably should have anticipated he would do something he shouldn't do," Jacob said.

Burr slammed his menu on the table. They all jumped. "It is difficult to anticipate stupidity. At least the jury has a lunch recess to forget about it. The real show is this afternoon."

* * *

Charlie Cox sat in the witness chair looking every inch like an accountant. He had on a three-piece navy suit, with a white shirt and a striped tie. His wire-rimmed glasses couldn't quite mask his NFL quarterback good looks. He didn't look a bit like a drug dealer.

Burr knew he had his work cut out for him, but he didn't think Cox knew that Jacob had discovered his paramour.

"Mr. Cox, what do you do for a living?"

"I'm an accountant. A CPA actually."

Burr nodded. "And where do you live?"

"Mount Pleasant."

"Thank you, Mr. Cox. And did you know the deceased, Quinn Shepherd?"

"No."

"You didn't know Mr. Shepherd?"

"No."

"I see." Burr looked back at Lizzie. "Do you know Mr. Shepherd's widow, Elizabeth Shepherd?"

"No."

"Mr. Cox, lying under oath is a serious offense. It can result in five years in prison."

Cullen popped up. "Objection, Your Honor, the defendant says he doesn't know either Mr. Shepherd or Mrs. Shepherd."

"Your Honor, I happen to know that Mr. Cox does indeed know both Mr. and Mrs. Shepherd."

Skinner glared at Burr. "If you would like to so testify, I suggest you become a witness."

"Mr. Cox, do you know Virginia Walker?"

Cox cleared his throat. "Who?"

"Virginia Walker."

"I don't think so."

"Mr. Cox, isn't it true that two nights ago you picked up Virginia Walker and took her to your home where the two of you spent the night?"

"I don't remember."

Cullen popped up again. "I object, Your Honor. This is totally irrelevant."

"Your Honor, I am about to show the relevance."

"You are on a very short leash, Mr. Lafayette."

"Yes, Your Honor." Burr turned to the jury. "Ladies and gentlemen, you may recall that Mr. Cullen called Virginia Walker as a witness. She testified that Mrs. Shepherd threatened both her and Mr. Shepherd." Burr paused. "Because Mrs. Shepherd thought Virginia Walker was having an affair with her husband." They nodded. "Ladies and gentlemen, let me tell you what really happened that night. Virginia Walker met Quinn Shepherd at the Two Track not because they were having an affair. She demanded money from Mr. Shepherd. After Mr. Shepherd died, Mr. Cox met with Mrs. Shepherd at the Dougherty Hotel in Clare and demanded money."

This time Cullen jumped to his feet. "Objection, Your Honor, this is pure speculation."

"Mr. Cox, you were selling Mr. Shepherd drugs, weren't you?"

Cox stared at Burr but didn't say a word.

"And when he didn't pay Virginia Walker at the Two Track, you followed him to the river and killed him. Isn't that right?"

"No."

"No, you didn't sell Mr. Shepherd drugs or no, you didn't kill him?"

Cox let his breath out slowly. "I didn't kill him."

"But you did sell him drugs?"

"No."

"Perjury is a serious offense, Mr. Cox." Burr looked back at the jury. "And so is murder."

"I swear I didn't."

"No further questions." Burr stopped at Cullen's table on the way back to the defense table. Before he sat down, he smiled at Cullen. "Now we have a suspect."

Cullen didn't seem too worried. He approached the accountant. "Mr. Cox, you testified that you are an accountant, is that right?"

"That's right."

"And are you familiar with The Gray Drake?"

"I am."

"How, may I ask?"

"Everybody knows The Gray Drake."

"Of course. We all know The Gray Drake. Have you ever been there?" Cullen said.

"I have."

"Were you there the night of June 21st, the night Quinn Shepherd was murdered?"

"I was."

"And did you stay there that night?"

"No."

"Where did you stay that night?"

"At my home."

"And did you spend the night with anyone?"

"Yes."

"Who, may I ask?"

"Virginia Walker."

"And did you go out to the river that night?"

"No."

"Mr. Cox, do you have any business dealings with The Gray Drake?"

"No."

"Mr. Cox, do you know why Virginia Walker met with Mr. Shepherd at the Two Track that night?"

"No."

"Thank you, Mr. Cox. No further questions."

Burr stood. "Redirect, Your Honor." Burr was damned if he'd let Cox get away with this.

"You had your turn, Mr. Lafayette."

"Your Honor, there are a number of inconsistencies in Mr. Cox's testimony."

Skinner shook his head but waved Burr forward.

"Mr. Cox, earlier you testified that you didn't know either Quinn Shepherd or Elizabeth Shepherd. Yet you just testified that you knew both of them."

"I'm sorry," he said. "I was a bit flustered, and I forgot."

"You forgot?" Burr pointed at Cox. "You didn't forget. You lied."

"Objection, Your Honor."

"Mr. Lafayette, if this is your idea of a redirect, stop right here."

Burr kept going. "Mr. Cox, you also testified that you didn't know Virginia Walker, your live-in lover. Did you forget that, too?"

"Objection."

"Mr. Cox, did you also forget that you were selling Mr. Shepherd drugs? And when he didn't pay, you killed him?"

Skinner glared at Burr. "That is quite enough, Mr. Lafayette. You may not make this type of accusation."

"Your Honor—"

Skinner raised his hand and cut Burr off. "Do you have anything further?"

"No, Your Honor."

Skinner turned to Cox. "As for you, Mr. Cox, while I will prevent you from being abused, your testimony is, at best, inconsistent. What say you to that?"

"I'm sorry, Your Honor. I was flustered."

Burr didn't think Cox had a flustered bone in his body.

"Do you have anything further, Mr. Cullen?"

"No, Your Honor."

"Very well. We are adjourned for the day."

After Skinner adjourned them, Burr met Maggie in the courthouse parking lot. This was the first time he had been alone with her since their date. He knew he shouldn't be with her, but he was getting desperate and needed her help.

They took I-75 north. Maggie had the plat book open. She told him to get off the freeway at County Road 612.

The sun had melted the snow from the side of the road, but there were still white patches in the woods. Burr headed east for two miles, and then

Maggie had him turn north on a dirt road. About two miles later, she told him to turn on a two-track.

Here we go again.

"Let me know when we've gone a mile and a half," Maggie said. She flipped through the pages of the plat book. Back three pages, forward one. They climbed up a hill, a clear cut on the right. Aspen on the left. Then more old growth hardwoods.

"This is a mile and a half," Burr said.

"The first property should start right about here," she said. "On the right."

Burr pulled off to the side of the road next to a stand of aspen.

"This is too old to hold grouse. There's not enough stem density," Maggie said.

Burr wasn't here for the finer points of the grouse woods.

"Why exactly are we here?" Maggie said.

"We're here because I can't think of anything else to do. Every time I think I've got this figured out, something happens, and I'm right back where I started." Burr put his hands on the steering wheel. "Which way to the next piece?"

Two hours later, they pulled up at the last piece of the trust property. Another woods, this one mixed hardwoods. "Woods, woods, and more woods," Burr said. "We've been all around Robin Hood's Barn."

"The last person I heard say that was my grandfather."

"This has been a colossal waste of time." Burr stopped the Jeep. "Let's get out and stretch our legs."

Burr let himself out and opened Maggie's door for her. They headed up the two-track, dodging puddles from the melting snow.

"This was a wild goose chase," Burr said. He kicked at a stone. "The trust owns acres and acres of woods. So what?"

"It might matter," Maggie said.

"Really?"

"Listen," she said. "Hear that? That humming?"

"What is it?"

"It's a diesel. From an oil rig. We're in the middle of the oil patch."

"I beg your pardon."

"There are oil wells all around us."

* * *

Burr dropped Maggie off at the courthouse, then drove back to The Gray Drake. He followed his nose to the sweet, smoky smell drifting out from under the door to Jacob's room.

He knocked twice.

"Go away, Burr. I'm busy."

Burr walked in. "How did you know it was me?"

"Everyone else respects my privacy."

Burr stood in a cloud of smoke. He thought he might get a buzz just standing here. "Jacob, you're going to burn this place down." He coughed. "I'm surprised the smoke alarms haven't gone off."

Jacob exhaled. "Smoke alarms haven't made an appearance here, yet."

"Jacob, I need you to do something while I'm in court tomorrow."

"What is it this time?"

Burr was shocked Jacob agreed so quickly. *It must be the marijuana.* "There's something going on with the property the trust owns. I need you to find out what it is."

"And how am I supposed to do that?"

"I'd start with the plat book." Burr left before Jacob could answer.

CHAPTER ELEVEN

The next morning, the bailiff swore in Harley Hawken.

Burr had no real plan for Hawken. He was buying time, hoping that Jacob came up with something. Burr knew he was grasping at straws, but there was something more than fly-fishing going on with Hawken, and he was sure there was something going on with Charlie Cox. But what?

Burr walked up to the witness.

"Mr. Hawken, you were at The Gray Drake the night of June 21st. Is that right?"

"Yes." Hawken's lips barely moved when he spoke.

"And why were you there?"

"I was there for the charity auction."

"And did you bid on anything?"

"Yes," he said.

"And did you buy anything?"

"Yes."

"Mr. Hawken, in your own words, please tell us what you bought."

Hawken pursed his lips. He looked annoyed he'd actually have to string a few words together. "I was the winning bidder of Quinn Shepherd's guided Hex float trip."

"Thank you, Mr. Hawken. That wasn't so bad, was it?" Burr smiled at Hawken, who didn't smile back. "And how much did you pay?"

"Twelve thousand dollars."

"Twelve thousand dollars. That's a lot of money," Burr said.

"It was for charity."

"Of course, it was," Burr said. "What happened with the trip?"

"How could I take it?"

Burr thought he was getting under Hawken's skin, which was the point. "And what about your check?"

Hawken didn't say a word.

"I assume you let the Friends of the Au Sable keep the check," Burr said.

A stony silence.

"Mr. Hawken?"

"Yes?"

"Your check."

"I stopped payment on the check."

"That was generous of you."

"Objection, Your Honor. There is no point to any of this," Cullen said.

"I will show the point, Your Honor."

"Do it in a hurry, Mr. Lafayette," Skinner said.

"Mr. Hawken, you paid twelve thousand dollars for a fishing trip, for charity. Then you stopped payment on the check. Is that right?"

"Yes."

"Why would you do that?"

"Because I couldn't take the trip." Hawken looked at him, his face blank.

"Mr. Hawken, is it possible that there was more going on with your bid than just a fishing trip?"

The blank stare continued.

"Were you paying off Mr. Shepherd for something—drugs for instance— and when he was killed there was no reason to continue with the charade?"

Still nothing.

"Or perhaps you killed him, and then there was no reason to let the Friends of the Au Sable keep the money."

"Objection, Your Honor," Cullen said. "These are wild accusations. Pure speculation. These are the rantings of a desperate man."

"Sustained."

Good point. I am nothing if not desperate. "Mr. Hawken, what did you do after the auction?"

"I went to the bar with Mr. Osterman and Mr. Gleason. I had a scotch, and then I went to bed."

"And did you leave The Gray Drake that night?"

"No."

Burr turned on his heel and walked back to his table. "That was a complete and total failure," he said mostly to himself. "Your witness."

"Mr. Cullen?"

"No questions, Your Honor."

Burr called Kathryn Kennedy, the cellist from the string quartet. Burr didn't think she'd have much to say either, but as long as he was still grasping at straws, he thought he might as well keep grasping and keep stalling in the hope that Jacob could come up with something at the Register of Deeds Office.

Kathryn Kennedy had doe eyes, creamy skin and full lips, an altogether comely young woman.

"Ms. Kennedy, you performed at the auction on the night of June 21st? Is that right?"

"Yes."

"What instrument do you play?"

"I play the cello."

"A lovely instrument. And where did you stay that night?"

"At The Gray Drake."

"Really? May I ask where?"

"I stayed on the third floor."

"The third floor. I didn't know the lodge had rooms on the third floor."

"It's an attic really. But there are a few rooms up there. It's stuffy, but it was free."

"Ms. Kennedy, did you happen to see any of the guests that night, coming or going?"

"Yes."

"Really?" Burr said. Maybe this wasn't going to be a wild goose chase. "Ms. Kennedy, did you happen to see Mr. Gleason?"

Burr pointed at Gleason, about halfway back in the gallery.

"No, I don't think so."

"How about him?" Burr pointed at Osterman.

"I saw him."

"Let the record show that the witness is pointing at Noah Osterman." Burr turned back to the witness. "How do you know it was him?"

"I saw him through my window."

"Do you remember what time you saw him?"

"About two, I think."

"And what was he doing?"

"He looked like he was in a hurry, but then he stood by his car and smoked a cigarette."

"Thank you, Ms. Kennedy. And how about him?" Burr pointed at Harley Hawken.

"Yes, I saw him go outside a few minutes later. They both got in Mr. Osterman's car and drove off."

"Ms. Kennedy, are you aware that both Mr. Osterman and Mr. Hawken testified that they never left the lodge that night?"

"I saw them both leave."

Burr knew this didn't prove anything, but it didn't hurt. "Ms. Kennedy, did you happen to see that man?" Burr pointed at Charlie Cox, sitting by himself at the back of the gallery.

Kathryn Kennedy looked down at her feet, then put her hands in her lap.

"Ms. Kennedy?"

"I did."

"Let the record show that Ms. Kennedy has identified Charles Cox." Burr turned back to his doe-eyed witness.

"And where did you see him?"

"He was at the auction and then I saw him in the kitchen. With Wes."

"Wes Godspeed?" Burr said. *What the devil is going on here?*

"It was hot in the attic, so I came downstairs. I saw the two of them in the kitchen."

"What were they doing?"

"They were arguing."

"What did they say?"

"I'm not sure. I saw Wes hand an envelope to him, and then the man left."

I knew Cox was involved. But Wes? Burr thought. "Ms. Kennedy, did you see anyone else?"

"No."

"Did any of these men see you?"

"No," she said. "No, I don't think so."

"And then what did you do?"

"I went back to bed."

"Thank you, Ms. Kennedy." Burr looked up at Skinner. "No further questions, Your Honor." Burr walked back to the defense table. *What just happened? Someone is lying. There's probably more than one liar.* Burr shook his head. *I'm sure they're all lying.*

Cullen approached the witness. "Ms. Kennedy, why were you awake at that time of night?"

"It was hot up in the attic."

"I see. What time did you say it was?"

"About two in the morning."

"So it was dark?"

"Yes."

"How do you know who you saw?"

"There was a moon that night."

"Could it have been someone else?"

"Who?"

"Someone other than Mr. Osterman?"

"I don't think so," she said. "Maybe."

"Maybe it wasn't Mr. Osterman," Cullen said. "So you're not sure?"

"I'm pretty sure."

"You're pretty sure," Cullen said. "Well, then how about Mr. Hawken. Are you sure you saw Mr. Hawken?"

"Yes," she said.

"You're sure?"

"Asked and answered," Burr said.

"Your Honor, it's not clear that Ms. Kennedy knows who she saw."

"That's for the jury to decide," Burr said.

"Please be quiet, Mr. Lafayette," Skinner said. "Anything further, Mr. Cullen?"

"No, Your Honor."

"We will recess for lunch," Skinner said. He banged his gavel, then glided out like a hunchback in a black robe.

Burr herded Lizzie, Wes and Eve to Wes's office at The Gray Drake. Jacob was still missing. Burr looked out at the river. It was up a little thanks to the melting snow.

Lizzie walked in with a tray of sandwiches and a pitcher of milk. *She's worn out, but she's still making lunch.*

"How can you keep doing this, day after day?"

"Doing what?" She offered him a sandwich.

"Breakfast, lunch, dinner. Cooking. For God's sake, you're on trial for murder, and you act like it's a parking ticket."

"What, exactly, am I supposed to do?" Lizzie pushed the tray toward him.

Burr was starving, but lunch was going to have to wait.

"I think it helps keep her mind off things," Wes said.

Burr had had enough. "While you're dealing drugs under her nose."

Wes sat bolt upright and looked at Burr, stunned.

"Don't give me that look. While your daughter is running this place, you're running drugs."

"I don't know what you're talking about," Wes said.

Lizzie held the tray, frozen like a statue.

Burr looked at Lizzie. "Quinn wasn't having an affair. And he wasn't selling drugs. It was your father."

Wes' eyes darted around the room. "It's not true."

"Charlie Cox was selling you drugs, and you were selling them to the sports. You couldn't pay him. So he sent his girlfriend to get money from Quinn. That's what it was about. When Quinn threatened to tell Lizzie, you followed him to the river and killed him."

"That's not what happened. It wasn't like that."

"Wasn't like what?" Lizzie said.

Wes rushed over to her and tried to put his arm around her. She pushed him away. The tray crashed to the floor. The pitcher shattered. Milk splashed everywhere. The sandwiches scattered across the room.

"I didn't kill Quinn," Wes said.

"But you let me think Quinn was having an affair and selling drugs?"

"I didn't want you involved."

"What kind of father are you?" she said, standing in the middle of the spoiled lunch.

Burr walked up to the two of them. "Charlie Cox wasn't on the guest list, but he was at the auction. What was in the envelope you gave Cox? The cash you stole from the auction?"

"That's not what happened." His eyes darted around the room again.

Burr glared at him. "I think you killed Quinn and tried to make it look like an accident."

"I didn't kill Quinn." Wes started for the door. Burr grabbed him by the arm.

"You're one of the few people who could pull it off and make it look like an accident. And it would have worked. Except for the canoe paddle."

"Dad, how could you do that?" Lizzie started to tear up.

Wes' eyes fixed on Lizzie. "I didn't. I swear I didn't."

"You thought your daughter would have a better chance of getting off than you would?"

"I wasn't at the river. I was here. With Charlie."

"Dad was watching Josh that night. He couldn't have gone to the river."

"He could have left Josh by himself," Burr said.

Lizzie looked down at the floor, broken dishes, spilled milk, sandwiches everywhere. She got down on her hands and knees and started cleaning up. Then she stopped, stood, and walked over to her father. "It's all been about The Gray Drake. It always has been. Your precious fishing lodge on your precious river. That's all you ever cared about." She looked down at the floor, then back at her father. "Clean up your own mess."

* * *

After lunch, Jacob was waiting for Burr and Eve on the courthouse steps. "You were right about the trust property. There are mineral leases with Reef Oil and Gas."

"Mineral leases?" Eve said.

"Oil and gas exploration," Jacob said. "On three separate parcels."

"Does the trust have the authority to enter into mineral leases?" Burr said.

"I have no idea. We'd have to look at the trust agreement," Jacob said.

"Where is it?"

"It's not on file," Jacob said.

"What is on file?"

"Just the trust certificate. It lists the trustees."

"Who are they?"

"Thompson Shepherd." Jacob paused for effect. "And Quinn Shepherd."

"Jacob, look again. We have to have a copy of the trust." Jacob rolled his eyes and walked back to his car.

They filed back into the courtroom. The bailiff called them to order. Skinner entered, then he sat and poured over the witness list. He ran his finger up and down the paper, counting to himself. He looked down at Burr. "I see that you have called all of your witnesses. If you have nothing further to say, we'll move to closing statements. Mr. Cullen, you may begin."

"Your Honor, the defense has discovered new evidence."

"Mr. Lafayette, we've gone through all this, and we're still not done?"

"Not quite, Your Honor."

"What is it?"

"Your Honor, the defense believes that certain land transactions concerning Reef Oil and Gas and the Alexander Thompson Shepherd Trust may have a bearing on the case."

"How can that have anything to do with the murder of Quinn Shepherd?"

"Your Honor, the defense asks that you require the trust document to be produced."

"What could a trust document possibly have to do with a murder?"

"It's about oil and gas, Your Honor. Men have been killed for less."

Skinner drummed his fingers. "Mr. Lafayette, I am not going to order the Alexander Thompson Shepherd Trust to be produced. We have come too far, and I don't see the relevance. I will allow you to call additional witnesses or redirect."

This was better than nothing. But not much.

"Thank you, Your Honor." Burr turned to the gallery. "The defense calls Noah Osterman."

Noah Osterman looked none too pleased to be back on the witness stand. "I remind you that you are still under oath, Mr. Osterman," Burr said.

"I am aware of that."

"Mr. Osterman, you are the attorney for Reef Oil and Gas. Is that right?"

"Yes."

"And did you draft oil and gas leases for your client to enter into with the Alexander Thompson Shepherd Trust?"

"No."

Burr walked back to his table and picked up a folder. Back at the witness stand he opened it up and handed Osterman a document. "Mr. Osterman, what are you holding in your hand?"

"I don't know."

"Mr. Osterman, what are the first four words on this page?"

"I can't read them without my glasses."

"You are wearing glasses."

"They're not my reading glasses."

What is it with these guys and their glasses? He grabbed the document from Osterman. "Your Honor, the defense would like to introduce into evidence three oil and gas leases by and between Reef Oil and Gas and the Alexander Thompson Shepherd Trust."

Cullen jumped up. "I object, Your Honor. These leases have no bearing on the matter at hand."

"Your Honor, these leases are connected to the death of Quinn Shepherd."

Skinner waved his gavel at Burr. "I'll allow it."

"Thank you, Your Honor. Please admit these leases as Defense Exhibits Three, Four and Five." Burr looked at Osterman. He flipped to the last page of each lease. "Mr. Osterman, I know you can't read these leases without your glasses, so I'll do it for you." He smiled wickedly at Osterman. "It says here you drafted every one of these leases. And they were each signed by Harley Hawken and Thompson Shepherd. They were then recorded in the Crawford County Register of Deeds office. Does that ring a bell?"

"I don't remember."

"Of course, you don't. Just how long has Wes Godspeed been selling you drugs?"

Osterman sat back in his chair.

"Answer the question, Mr. Osterman," Skinner said.

"I have never bought any drugs from Wesley Goodspeed."

"Where did you go with Mr. Hawken after the auction ended?"

"I never left the lodge." Osterman set his lips and his lower lip stuck out like a pouting child.

"That's not what Kathryn Kennedy said."

"She was mistaken."

"I have no further questions, Your Honor."

"Mr. Cullen?"

"No questions, Your Honor."

"Gentlemen, we will have closing arguments tomorrow. Is that clear?"

"Yes, Your Honor," Cullen said.

Burr nodded.

"Mr. Lafayette, I will take your silence as an assent. We are adjourned."
Down came the gavel. Out went Skinner.

Burr walked out of the courthouse. He thought his defense had gone
well so far, but probably not well enough to get Lizzie acquitted. And, he
was running out of time.

Jacob was waiting for him on the courthouse steps.

"Did you find the trust?"

"No. And I looked everywhere. Twice."

Burr ground his teeth. "I need you to do a little more research."

Jacob gave him a peeved look. "I can't find the trust. I just told you that."

"There is something going on with the money," Burr said.

"What about the trust?"

"We'll get back to that later," Burr said.

"Now what?" Jacob said.

"We didn't look into People's State Bank."

"It's a bank. I'm sure it's full of money."

"Just this once."

Jacob put his hands on his hips. "With you, it's never just this once. And
besides, it's too late."

"There is enough time if you start now."

Jacob gave Burr a disgusted look, but off he went.

Burr needed to find something out at the river while there was still
daylight, and he needed Maggie's help. They took the Jeep down the
two-track, the infamous two-track where Heidi Grettenberger said she had
seen Lizzie with the canoe paddle and the same two-track that led to Dead
Man's Hole where Brian Bilkey had found Quinn.

About two hundred yards in, the two-track turned into two ruts. Burr put
the Jeep in four-wheel drive. In another three hundred yards, the ruts turned
into a path. Burr parked the Jeep. Zeke ran ahead of them.

They walked the path another two hundred yards to the river. It was
about a hundred feet wide and ran a little over its banks. Burr smelled the
wet of the snow and mud on the riverbank and the fishy smell of the river.
Zeke waded in the river up to his chest.

Maggie stood beside Burr. "What are we looking for?"

He pointed above a run out, a flat spot near the middle of the river. "See that. That's Dead Man's Hole. That's where Bilkey saw Quinn's boat, and just below that is where Bilkey found Quinn."

Maggie shuddered. "Why do I have to see this?"

Burr pointed downriver. "Just down there, around that bend, is the two-track where Finn found the paddle. Come with me." Burr took her hand and led her closer to the river. Their boots sunk in the mud.

"If I take another step, I'll be in over my boots."

Burr let go of her hand and took another three steps. The mud ended, and he stood in the sand on the river bank.

"Now, what do you see?"

"I see the river. I see that you're standing in the sand, and I'm standing in the mud."

"Do you see any rocks?"

"Rocks?"

"Yes, rocks."

"No."

Burr walked back to Maggie. "Come with me." He took her by the hand, and they walked back to the Jeep.

Burr turned the Jeep around. They crossed the river at Chase Bridge and drove along the other side of the river.

"Tell me where to turn. The two-track where you found the paddle."

"You just passed it."

Burr turned around.

"Here," she said. "Turn here."

"How do you know?"

"There's a white pine on one side and a red pine on the other."

There's no way I'd ever have found this. He turned in, drove down the two-track. They stopped short of the river again. He got out and opened Maggie's door for her. He took her by the hand and led her to the river.

"What's different about this?"

"It's on the other side of the river," she said.

"What else?"

Maggie looked around. "I don't know. It's not as muddy."

"What else?"

She took a step to the river and slipped. Burr caught her. "It's slippery here."

"Why is that?"

Maggie looked at her boots. "There are rocks here."

"Exactly."

"What difference does that make?"

"It was something Traker said." Burr crouched down and ran his hand over a basketball-sized rock. "He said Quinn's injury, the wound on the back of his head could have been from falling on a rock." Burr stood back up. "But there are no rocks on the other side of the river. Where Bilkey found Quinn."

"He could have hit his head on the boat."

"Or he could have been killed here and then dragged back upstream in his boat."

"Why would anyone do that?"

"And that's why Finn found the paddle here."

"The paddle could have just floated down here."

"Or it could have been lost here."

They climbed back in the Jeep. Burr drove back to the courthouse.

"Is it going to the jury tomorrow?" she said.

"I think so."

"Was it an accident?"

"No."

"Do you know who killed Quinn?"

"I think so, but I can't prove it." Burr turned the engine off.

"What are you going to do?"

"I'm going to have to get the jury to believe it was an accident unless Jacob can find what I need."

"Who did it?"

"I really can't tell you."

Maggie didn't look too happy, but she nodded at him. She got out of the Jeep and drove off in her Explorer.

Burr drove back to the lodge. He found Lizzie in the kitchen.

"Did you find the trust document?" he said.

"No, and I looked everywhere. Thompson must have it."

"Of course, he has it, but he won't produce it, and Skinner won't make him."

"Why is that so important?"

"I'm not sure it is, but I'd like to know that it isn't."

"This is all so terrible," she said.

"We're not done, yet." Burr followed his nose again and found Jacob smoking in his room.

"What did you find?"

Jacob sucked on a joint and held his breath.

"This is no time to hold your breath."

Jacob exhaled, in a hiss, like a snake. "People's State Bank is in financial trouble."

"Bless you, Jacob. There's just one more thing."

"No."

"Please...back to the trust. I need a copy of the trust."

"I haven't been able to find the trust."

"I need you to look again. Maybe it was misfiled."

"I doubt it."

"Give it one more try."

Burr went to Wes's office and rifled through all of the books and drawers. Nothing. "There must be a copy somewhere." He went outside and around to the fly shop. He found Billy standing over a vise.

"Billy, do you have any idea where I could find a copy of the trust?"

"Don't talk to me. This is an Adam's Parachute. It ain't that hard to tie, but I have to concentrate."

"I have to find a copy of the trust."

"The Shepherd Trust?"

"Do you know anything about it?"

"Quinn thought it was important." Billy picked up a feather and set it on the fly. Then he wrapped thread around the quill and the body of the fly.

"Why?"

"He was fighting over it. With the oil men." The old guide picked up a tube of glue and dabbed a drop on the fly.

"What did they want?"

Billy looked up. "They wanted him to sign something, but he said *no*."

"What did they want him to sign?"

"Hell, if I know." Billy looked down at the fly in the vise. "The glue just set, and now it's ruined."

"Do you know where I could find a copy of the trust?"

The old guide studied the fly in the vise. "It just ain't that hard to tie an Adam's Parachute."

"Did Quinn have a place here where he kept his valuables? Rods, reels, important papers?"

"Back there." Billy pointed to a row of lockers at the back of the workshop. There was a locker with Quinn's name on it. Burr opened the door. Empty. The locker was empty.

* * *

The courtroom was packed. They were here for the last day of the trial and the verdict. They waited and waited. And waited. At last Skinner made his entrance. Chairs scraped the floor, clothes rustled, throats cleared. Still no Jacob.

The bailiff called them to order.

"Mr. Cullen, you may begin your closing argument," the judge said.

Burr stood quickly. "Your Honor, the defense has one more witness," then softly, "perhaps two."

"I thought you finished yesterday."

"Your Honor, this is most urgent."

Burr desperately needed a copy of the trust, but Jacob was nowhere to be found. He'd have to stall for time and hope Jacob showed up with something, anything.

"Mr. Lafayette, it was most urgent yesterday." The judge wagged his finger at Burr. "You may call two witnesses."

"Thank you, Your Honor. The defense calls Thompson Shepherd."

Thompson Shepherd walked slowly to the witness box, a picture of the upper crust. The bailiff swore in Shepherd the Elder, and he sat down in the witness box.

Burr looked behind him at the door to the courtroom. Still no Jacob. He walked ever so slowly to Shepherd.

"Mr. Shepherd, are you a trustee of the Alexander Thompson Shepherd Trust?"

"I am," he said with an air of authority and superiority.

"And what is the purpose of the trust?"

"To hold certain real estate here in Crawford County."

"And what are you, the trust, to do with the real estate?"

"We are to own it."

"Mr. Shepherd, I thought the purpose of the trust was to preserve the Au Sable watershed's woods, meadows and swamps in their natural condition."

"In part."

Without a copy of the trust, Burr knew he was on thin ice. He couldn't force Shepherd to admit to anything.

"Yet you signed oil and gas leases with Reef Energy that will despoil the very land you are required by the trust to protect."

"Oil and gas exploration is within the purview of the trust." Shepherd looked down his nose at Burr.

He's got me and he knows it.

"Mr. Shepherd, how many trustees are there?"

Shepherd stopped smiling. "Two," he said. "There were two of us."

"And they are. . ."

"Myself and my son."

"And what provision does the trust make in the case of the death of a trustee?"

Shepherd bit his lip. "The matters of the trust are confidential."

"I asked you a question."

"Objection, Your Honor. This has nothing to do with the murder of Quinn Shepherd," Cullen said.

"Your Honor, this has everything to do with the murder of Quinn Shepherd."

"You need not answer the question, Mr. Shepherd," Skinner said.

Shepherd smiled at Skinner, the way a master might smile at his servant.

"Mr. Shepherd, you are chairman of Peoples State Bank. Is that right?" Burr said.

"I am."

"And your bank is having financial difficulties. Is that right?"

"I beg your pardon?"

"Objection, Your Honor," Cullen said.

"Mr. Lafayette, neither the Shepherd Trust nor Peoples State Bank is on trial here. I suggest you move on," Skinner said.

"Your Honor," Burr said in his most pleading voice.

"All I wanted was a simple murder trial. And I have this." Skinner sighed. "I said, move on."

Burr walked back to his table. He broke his last pencil. *Now what do I do?* Then the door in the back of the courtroom opened. Jacob rushed in with a file under his arm.

"Your Honor, may I have ten minutes with my co-counsel?" Burr said.

"You may have two minutes."

Jacob hurried up the aisle to Burr, coat on, out of breath. "Did you find it?"

"No," Jacob said.

"No, what?"

"I couldn't find it. The trust instrument is not on file anywhere in Crawford County. All the law requires is the filing of the trust certificate."

"What's in that file?"

"The trust certificate."

Burr looked at the file. "There's more in that file than a trust certificate."

Jacob passed him the file. The trust certificate was on top. Burr flipped the certificate aside. Underneath, a thirty-page document titled "The Life Cycle of *Hexagenia limbata.*"

"This will do." Burr started back toward Shepherd.

"You're mad," Jacob said.

"Quite," Burr said.

Back in front of Shepherd, Burr dropped the trust certificate on the floor and made sure Shepherd could see it. He put it back in the folder, on top of the treatise on the Hex.

"Mr. Shepherd, I now have a copy of the trust. I can introduce this into evidence, and the entire world will learn all there is to know about the trust." Burr flipped through the pages of Jacob's file. "Or . . . you can answer a few questions, and we'll be done with it."

"Where did you get that?"

"The Crawford County Register of Deeds."

"It's not supposed to be there."

"An overzealous lawyer, no doubt," Burr said. "Mr. Shepherd, how many trustees does it take to enter into an oil-and-gas lease?"

Thompson Shepherd looked at Burr, but this time without the disdain.

"Mr. Shepherd?"

"Two."

"How many trustee signatures were on the oil-and-gas leases with Reef Oil and Gas?"

"I don't know."

Burr walked to the evidence table and picked up the leases with Reef Exploration he had introduced yesterday. He returned to the witness. "Mr. Shepherd, I have the oil- and-gas leases the Alexander Thompson Shepherd Trust entered into with Reef Oil and Gas. Do you recognize them?"

"No."

"Let me refresh your memory." Burr turned to the signature page of the first lease. He showed it to Shepherd. "Mr. Shepherd, is this your signature?" He pointed to the signature line.

Shepherd looked at the signature page, but didn't say anything.

"Mr. Shepherd, is this your signature?"

Shepherd still didn't answer.

"Your Honor, please compel the witness to answer the question."

Shepherd looked at Skinner. This time the servant was the master. "Answer the question, Mr. Shepherd."

"Yes."

"Yes, what?" Burr said.

"Yes, that is my signature."

"Thank you, Mr. Shepherd." Burr pointed at the second lease. "Is this your signature?"

"Yes."

"Yes, what?" Burr said.

"Yes, that is my signature."

"Thank you, Mr. Shepherd." Burr pointed at the third lease. "Is this your signature?"

"Yes."

"Mr. Shepherd, are there any other signatures on behalf of the trust, besides yours, on any of the leases?"

"I have full authority to sign by myself."

"That was not my question. Let me repeat the question. Are there any other signatures on behalf of the trust, other than yours, on the leases?"

"No."

"Thank you, Mr. Shepherd. That will be all." Burr walked back to his table. "Your witness."

Cullen looked like he was in the wrong courtroom. *This is a first.* The prosecutor rose slowly behind his table. "Mr. Shepherd, did you believe you had the authority to enter into the leases with Reef Oil and Gas?"

"Yes," Shepherd said. "I most certainly did."

"Thank you, Mr. Shepherd."

"Now, we'll begin the arguments," Skinner said.

"If it please the court," Burr said, "the defense has one more witness."

"No, it does not please the court." Skinner drummed his fingers.

"Thank you, Your Honor. The defense calls Harley Hawken."

Cullen jumped up. "Objection, Your Honor. The defense already examined Mr. Hawken."

"Sit down, Jack. Let's get this over with."

Hawken was not happy to be back on the witness stand, especially after Burr had produced what Hawken thought was the trust document.

"Mr. Hawken, I remind you that you are still under oath." The oil man nodded. *Now if I can just keep "The Life Cycle of the Hexagenia limbata" out of evidence.*

"Mr. Hawken, did you sign the oil-and-gas leases on behalf of your company, Reef Oil and Gas?"

"Yes."

"And you were aware that the trust required two signatures."

"No."

"Mr. Hawken, surely your attorney, Mr. Osterman, reviewed the trust document."

Hawken squirmed.

That's a first.

"I assume he did."

"And he told you that two signatures were required."

"I don't remember."

"Mr. Hawken, I think you know full well that those leases required two signatures. Thompson Shepherd desperately needed money for his failing bank. He signed those leases. Quinn never signed the leases. You tried to persuade him to sign the leases, but he refused. Isn't that right?"

"I don't remember."

"When Quinn found out what happened, he told you the leases weren't valid and the trust wouldn't honor them."

"That's not what happened."

"That's why you bid twelve thousand dollars for a three-hundred-dollar trip. So you could buy off Quinn. Isn't that right? But Quinn said *no*. And then you and Osterman paid Quinn a visit on the river. That's why Kathryn Kennedy saw you in the parking lot. Those leases were worth a fortune to you. Was it you who struck Quinn with the paddle?"

Hawken had finally lost his composure. "No," he said. "No, it wasn't me."

Skinner had no idea what was going on. Cullen still looked like he was in the wrong courtroom. Burr put the file back on the defense table, out of harm's way. Then he walked back to Hawken.

"What did happen that night?"

Hawken rubbed his beard, his composure restored. "I don't remember."

"You are about to be indicted for murder, Mr. Hawken."

Hawken looked at Burr like this was the first time he had ever seen him, then he looked out to the gallery. "After the auction, Mr. Osterman and I drove out to Thompson Shepherd's home on the river."

"What time was it?"

"About two in the morning."

"Why would you go to Mr. Shepherd's house at two in the morning?"

"We wanted to start drilling, and we needed to make sure the leases were valid with one signature."

"And what happened?"

"When we got there, he wasn't home."

"What did you do?"

"We waited."

"Mr. Hawken, how long did you wait?"

"About two hours."

"Then what happened?

"We saw Mr. Shepherd coming down the river."

"Thompson Shepherd?"

"Yes," Hawken said.

"You saw Thompson Shepherd coming down the river?" Burr said.

"Yes."

"From Dead Man's Hole?"

"Yes." Hawken squirmed in his chair.

"Was he in an Au Sable riverboat?"

"Yes."

There wasn't a sound in the courtroom. Cullen looked down at the files on his table. Then he straightened them and stacked them, one on top of the other. His smile faded, and his lips formed a circle as if he was blowing smoke rings. Skinner looked at Cullen, then he turned to the gallery. His trunk turned, his neck still bent. His eyes locked on Shepherd.

Shepherd sat, stone-faced. Then he buried his head in his hands.

Lizzie started to cry.

CHAPTER TWELVE

Burr bent and opened the oven door. He peered in and touched the roasting pan. "Damn it all," he said. He sucked on his finger.

Lizzie handed him a potholder. "Let me do that."

"Just this one time, your place is not in the kitchen." Burr took the potholder and pulled the oven rack toward him. Ever so carefully, he slid the aluminum foil off one of the ducks, the skin crispy and the color of an acorn. "Almost done." He stood up and drank from his glass of cabernet.

Half an hour later, he had Lizzie, Jacob and Eve seated in the dining room. Zeke and Cassie were under the table. Josh had had dinner earlier and was in bed. Wes was nowhere to be found, which was just as well. Lizzie had said she didn't want to have anything to do with her father, at least for now.

The jury had deliberated for an hour and found Lizzie not guilty. Burr had insisted on making the farewell dinner. Roast duck stuffed with canned peaches, the syrup poured over the skin. Wild rice with mushrooms. Squash with ginger and plenty of butter. A spinach salad. Mincemeat pie and as much wine as they could drink.

"Burr, this is actually quite good," Jacob said. He fiddled with the napkin he had tucked into his collar.

"The peaches take out the gaminess," Burr said.

"How did you figure it out?" Eve said. "Not that I ever doubted you."

"It started with Cassie. When she barked at Thompson. I didn't think anything of it. Because she barked at me, too. But later, I wondered about it. I was a stranger to her, but Thompson wasn't." Burr reached under the table and scratched Cassie behind the ear. "She knew all along." He swirled the wine in his glass. "But it was the money that got me going, and then the oil-and-gas leases. Charlie Cox was a dead end. Except for Wes."

"But how did you figure it out?" Eve said.

"It was Peoples State Bank. When I found out about Thompson's money

problems, that's what got me thinking. Then, when there was only one signature on the lease but two on the trust certificate, I took a chance."

"I still don't understand," Eve said.

"The oil-and-gas leases needed two signatures from the trust to be valid.
Quinn refused to sign, so they were no good. When he found out what his
father was trying to do, he put his foot down.

"But Thompson was desperate for money." Burr sliced a piece of duck
from the breast and stabbed it with his fork. He put it in his mouth and
chewed it slowly. "After the auction, Thompson trailered his boat down the
two-track, where Finn found the paddle. He hid his boat and took the trailer
back to the cottage. Then he walked back upriver to his boat and waited for
Quinn. When Thompson saw Quinn on the river, he waved him over. He
had to have Quinn's signature. Quinn refused, and they fought. Thompson
hit him with the canoe paddle. Quinn fell and hit his head on a rock. I'm not
sure he meant to kill him.

"But it was what Traker said about the rock. I thought all the other
bumps and bruises occurred when Quinn was at the bottom of the river, but
that's not what happened. There were no rocks on the shore at Dead Man's
Hole. If someone hit Quinn with the canoe paddle, and Quinn fell and hit his
head on a rock, it wasn't at Dead Man's Hole. But there were rocks where
Thompson hit Quinn.

"But here is the genius. When Thompson saw what he had done, he put
Quinn back in *Traveler* and pulled the boat with Quinn's body in it upstream.
Upstream to Dead Man's Hole. No one would ever think the murder occurred
downstream from where Quinn was found. Thompson wrapped the anchor
chain around Quinn's leg and dropped him over the side. Then he waded
back to his boat and floated home. The canoe paddle must have drifted away
after Thompson hit Quinn with it."

"What about Osterman and Hawken showing up at Thompson's house?"
Jacob said.

"I think that was an unhappy coincidence. Bad luck for Thompson."

"I can't believe you bluffed your way without the actual trust document," Jacob said.

"I took a chance that the trust would require two signatures. Why else
have two trustees."

"What's going to happen to Thompson?" Eve said.

"It's one thing to get an acquittal. We had plenty of reasonable doubt. It's another thing to prove Thompson did it."

"And the custody fight?" Eve said.

"Thompson was getting worried. He wanted to make Lizzie look guilty. Now that Lizzie's been acquitted, the custody suit will be dismissed."

"Thompson would never kill Quinn. It had to be an accident," Lizzie said.

"I'm sorry we thought Quinn might be somehow involved," Jacob said.

Lizzie looked down at her lap, then at Burr. "This is all so terrible. I'll never see Quinn again, and now this. With Thompson."

"I'm sorry, Lizzie," Burr said.

"I know we're supposed to be celebrating, but it doesn't feel much like a celebration."

"What about Wes, Cox, the oil men and the drugs? And Cox's threats?" Eve said.

"Those would be very difficult to prove. Lizzie, you would have to press charges against Cox. And that would bring Wes in."

"They're crimes," Eve said.

"Some crimes go unpunished."

"Josh and I need to get on with life without Quinn, and I need to find some peace with my father. I don't see how we can ever see Thompson again." She got up and started for the kitchen.

This isn't a celebration. He caught up with her halfway to the kitchen.

"I'm so sorry." He put his arms around her and hugged her.

* * *

Burr was wrapped up in a sleeping bag, but he was still shivering. He had lit *Spindrift*'s charcoal fireplace an hour ago, but it gave off about as much heat as a toaster. Even Zeke was cold, curled in a ball at Burr's feet.

He had missed most of summer on a boat he couldn't afford, but he was determined to take one last sail. As soon as it stopped snowing.

He pulled the sleeping bag up around his neck. Then he heard a tap-tap-tap on the hull. "Saints preserve us, Zeke."

The dog looked up, barked once, and curled back up in a ball.

More tapping.

"Jacob, go away. I am blissfully freezing to death."

More tapping.

"Damn it all." He got to his feet, still wrapped up in the sleeping bag. He climbed the companionway, slid back the hatch cover and peered over the side.

There in the dinghy, Maggie and Finn. She smiled at him. Finn wagged her tail.

THE END

Acknowledgements

Thanks to my wife, Christi, for her encouragement, support, tolerance, patience, and most of all, her love.

To Ellen Jones for her copyediting, research, sage advice, and for her infuriating attention to detail.

To Laurie Supinski, Mark Lewison, Emmy Homan, Teresa Crumpton, Julie Spencer, and Steve Spencer for their help in editing the manuscript.

To Matt Supinski and Bob Linsenman for their technical help with the fly-fishing aspects of the book.

To Matt Supinski again for his friendship, encouragement, promotion and unflagging enthusiasm for the project.

To John Wickham for the cover design.

To Kathryn McLravy for managing my Facebook page.

To Allison Clemons for redesigning my website.

To Spencer McCormack for producing the trailer.

Thanks to Mission Point Press: C.D. Dahlquist for her careful editing, Bob Deck for the book's interior design, and Doug Weaver, who kept it all on schedule.

About the Author

Mr. Cutter is a recovering attorney. He lives with his wife, two dogs and four cats in East Lansing. He has a leaky sailboat in Harbor Springs and a leakier duck boat on Saginaw Bay.

Also by Charles Cutter

Praise for *The Pink Pony*

"Cutter's debut legal thriller tells the story of a litigator in Mackinac Island, Michigan, who defends a man accused of murder. Attorney Burr Lafayette is called to a bar called The Pink Pony by police chief Art Brandstatter, who suspects that Burr stole a pink hobbyhorse that normally hangs above the bar's door. But inside the bar is a scene of a far more serious crime: Jimmy Lyons lies dead by strangulation. The novel spotlights a lawyer, Burr Lafayette, who shines at trial. His snide, often mumbled commentary becomes fitting when he's facing a judge who clearly doesn't like him and who's more interested in wrapping things up quickly. The story's legal banter is snappy, vibrant, and not without humor; one of the prosecutor's objections against Burr, for example, is that 'Counsel is flirting with the witness.' Burr's investigation does eventually get a breakthrough, and there's an effective plot twist near the end. His rapid-fire questioning of defendants on the stand, though, is nothing short of exhilarating. A mystery with a protagonist who's truly in his element inside the courtroom."

– Kirkus Review

"Mackinac Island and the legendary bar, The Pink Pony, doesn't get any more exciting than at the finish of the Port Huron-Mackinac sailboat race, but author Charles Cutter cranks the excitement up a notch in *The Pink Pony*, a first-rate murder mystery where nothing is as it seems. At The Pink Pony on Mackinac Island, you can belly up to the bar, tell a few lies and end up dead in Charles Cutter's original, fast-paced mystery where Islander Burr Lafayette finds himself defending a likely suspect in a totally unique whodunnit. Mackinac Island never shined brighter than in Charles Cutter's original mystery which will keep you guessing to the very end and that's no manure. Charles Cutter mixes a lethal brew in his new mystery, *The Pink Pony*, complete with Mackinac Island lore and licentiousness. When a celebration at the end of the Port Huron-Mackinac sailboat race ends in murder at The Pink Pony, the favorite bar of locals, attorney Burr Lafayette must sink or swim to keep his head above water in a unique and totally enjoyable mystery."

– Bill Castanier, literary writer at *Lansing City Pulse*

"*The Pink Pony* captures all the magic and mystery of Mackinac Island in this delightful page-turner of a whodunnit. Reminiscent of Robert Traver's *Anatomy of a Murder*, author Charles Cutter brings to life colorful northern Michigan and UP characters and customs, while weaving a well-crafted courtroom drama that will keep you guessing to the end. An excellent read."

– Dennis O. Cawthorne, author of
Mackinac Island: Inside, Up Close, and Personal

Made in the
USA
Monee, IL